"You can't go in there! She's on the phone!"

The door burst open and two people shot into the room. Two small people. Children. They lurched to a halt a few feet beyond the door and stared at her. Carrie, standing in the doorway behind them, raised her shoulders apologetically.

Tess pressed down the hold button. Her gaze shifted from the tall boy with the thick chestnut hair to the little girl clinging to his leg. There was something familiar about her. The large, vibrant green eyes and the raven tousle of hair. The same oval-shaped face and a smaller version of a delicate nose. Her nose.

She released the hold button, keeping her eyes fixed on them. Alec Malone was still talking. "Anyway, the reason I'm calling is that they left behind two kids who've just—"

Tess jabbed the hold button again. "Who are you?" she asked them. "What do you want?" But she knew what the boy was going to say even before he spoke.

"I think—well, uh—that you're our sister."

Dear Reader,

Some of you who have read my other Superromance novels will note a recurring theme of family, combined with mystery and suspense. This is no coincidence—I have always been a "family" kind of person. My favorite childhood memories are of sitting at our kitchen table on Saturday mornings over coffee (milk for us kids!) and doughnuts listening to my uncle and my parents tell stories from their pasts. Now my favorite family thing is to reminisce with my own grown children.

Although most of us have family traditions of some kind, there are those who have never experienced the joys of family. Tess Wheaton is such a person. Raised by a loving guardian, Tess has always considered family as something other people had. What she knows about family has been shaped by books, movies and friends. Still, she has succeeded in establishing a promising career as a business executive and considers her longtime guardian, Mavis, her surrogate family. Until the day two youngsters turn up on her doorstep, claiming to be her half siblings. Suddenly Tess is thrust into the tumultuous center of a family shattered by tragedy. Is she up to the challenge? Or more to the point, does she really want to accept the challenge?

With a little help from three people who refuse to give up on her—social worker Alec Malone and half siblings Nick and Molly—Tess learns not only what family is all about, but that she can no longer go on without belonging to one.

Enjoy your families!

Janice Carter

The Second Family

Janice Carter

HARLEQUIN®

TORONTO • NEW YORK • LONDON
AMSTERDAM • PARIS • SYDNEY • HAMBURG
STOCKHOLM • ATHENS • TOKYO • MILAN • MADRID
PRAGUE • WARSAW • BUDAPEST • AUCKLAND

ISBN 0-373-71144-1

THE SECOND FAMILY

This edition published by arrangement with Harlequin Books S.A.

® and TM are trademarks of the publisher. Trademarks indicated with
® are registered in the United States Patent and Trademark Office, the
Canadian Trade Marks Office and in other countries.

Visit us at www.eHarlequin.com

Printed in U.S.A.

For my mother, Lois Gene Carter, with much love.

CHAPTER ONE

HE WAS DEAD.

The thick vellum paper Tess was holding shook and the scrawl of black, fine-tipped pen blurred. Her eyes, hooded in disbelief, flicked across the paper—top to bottom, left to right and back again. Her brain, sluggish with doubt, refused to register more than a fragment of writing at a time.

Regret to inform you…fatal car crash…March 28…as your father's lawyer…please contact…

Tess skimmed the letter once more and this time, the pieces slotted together in perfect, horrifying sequence. She crumpled the paper into a tight ball and tossed it into the wastebasket in the corner of her office. A slam dunk, though she couldn't have cared less. Powered by shock, Tess grabbed her briefcase, slung her handbag over her shoulder, plucked her trench coat from the hook behind the door and strode out the door of her new executive office.

"Tess! Are you leaving for the day?" Carrie called from her receptionist desk in the small antechamber.

But Tess didn't dare stop. Stopping would mean explaining, and Tess didn't trust herself to do that. Instead, she half turned and snapped, "Something's come up, Carrie. Cancel all appointments. Take messages. See you tomorrow." She didn't slow down until the elevator doors closed behind her. Alone, she sagged against the rear wall and took several deep breaths.

Her mind, fired by adrenaline, whizzed through its mental Rolodex of options, strategies and last resorts to come up with a name. Mavis McNaught—her guardian angel. Tess dug into her purse for her cell phone and punched in Mavis's number. The elevator reached the ground floor just as Mavis picked up on the other end.

Tess made herself take another slow breath before speaking. Mavis would never understand what Tess was saying if her voice came out as thin and wobbly. Besides, it wouldn't do for Balfour International's new Vice President of Marketing to be seen having a meltdown in the company lobby. She ducked into a corner behind a potted hibiscus tree.

"Mavis?" she said after the third hello. "It's me—Tess. No, no, something's wrong with the phone. Listen. I…uh just got this strange letter from some lawyer in Colorado and I need to see you. Yes, yes. I know it's only three o'clock. You're not busy, are you? Good. I'm coming right over and I'll explain everything as soon as I get there." She closed her eyes. Inhaled again. The filmy landscape of the lobby cleared, but the ceramic tiled floor seemed, suddenly, to shift beneath her.

Tess clicked off her phone, patted her flyaway curly hair into place and headed out to the street. A sea of faces, some familiar and others simply curious, swam up to her on the way, their disembodied voices fading in and out of Tess's auditory range as she stood on the pavement, flailing her arms for a taxi. A yellow cab zigzagged from across the street. Tess yanked open the door and flung herself inside.

"25 Fairview. On the west side," she said as the cab pulled away from the curb.

Only then did Tess allow herself a moment to take it all in, slumping against the seat, briefcase sprawled beside her. The content of the letter spun through her mind over and over until she finally accepted its awful truth.

The father who'd walked out of her life twenty-five years before was dead.

"MORE?" asked Mavis, reaching for the teapot. Her ample frame bumped against the edge of the table as she sat down across from Tess. She brushed a wisp of gray hair off her cheek and poured herself another cup.

Tess shook her head. What she really wanted was a scotch and soda, neither of which was available at Mavis McNaught's.

"So where's this letter, then?" asked Mavis, her broad forehead wrinkling in a frown.

"I threw it in the trash can on my way out."

"You'll need that letter," Mavis pointed out.

"I got the gist of it anyway. Some lawyer in Boulder, Colorado, informing me that Richard Wheaton was killed in a car accident on March 28." She looked across the table at Mavis and added, "He also wrote he was surprised to learn that Richard had a daughter in Chicago and would I please call him right away."

"And that shouldn't surprise you, given the circumstances," Mavis said gently. "Now what?" she asked, fixing her serenely impassive gaze on Tess.

Tess shrugged, averting her face from Mavis's penetrating, pale-blue eyes. Her one-time guardian could read her like a book. "Nothing, I guess. What's there to do? He died a month ago. The funeral's long past." She paused. "Not that I'd have gone anyway."

"Perhaps you've inherited something and that's why this lawyer wants you to contact him."

Tess snorted. "What could my father possibly have left me? He never gave me a thing after he left Mom and me. He probably died a penniless drifter."

"Don't be speaking ill of the dead," Mavis clucked.

Tess rolled her eyes. "Then I'll have to shut up for I can't think of anything good to say about him."

"Have we gone back in time? Is this the eighties all over? Are you a teenager once more?"

A trace of a smile belied the reprimand in Mavis's voice, but Tess flushed anyway. No one else on earth could pull in the reins on Tess Wheaton quite like Mavis McNaught. The woman had been her foster parent since she was ten years old and knew her better than any person alive. She had been the only family Tess had known after her father's disappearance and her mother's death a few years later.

"If you've made no plans—at least, not for the immediate future—I'll pop a casserole out of the freezer for dinner." Mavis set her palms on the kitchen table to raise herself from the chair.

Tess saw her wince as she took a first step. "Did you take your pills today?"

"Of course, love. Twice a day every day. It's the damp."

But Tess noticed her smile was more strained now. "Go back to the doctor and tell him they're not working. If you like, I can get my own doctor to refer you to another specialist."

Mavis hobbled to the refrigerator and opened the freezer door. "The doctor's fine. There's just little else they can do. Osteoarthritis and old age go together." She pulled a foil-wrapped casserole dish out and set it on the counter next to the stove. "And losing forty pounds or so would help, if I can bring myself to stay away from the goodies."

Tess ducked her head so Mavis couldn't see her smile. They both knew her love of sweets wasn't going to change after all these years. "Why don't you come with me sometime to my club? For a swim?"

Mavis wagged an index finger at her. "Now don't you be teasing an old woman. Come and preheat the oven for me. My glasses are in the TV room and I can't make out the numbers."

Tess pushed her chair back and walked over to where Mavis was standing. "Why don't you use the microwave I gave you?"

"I do use it, love, but it doesn't get the topping all crusty brown, the way you and I like it."

Tess laughed. "True enough." She set the oven temperature, then turned to Mavis. "Still, you ought to be using it as something more than a bread box."

"It makes a dandy bread box. And once in a while, when I'm following my diet, I use it for microwave popcorn."

"I bet that's once or twice a year," cracked Tess. She caught Mavis's eye and laughed with her. Impulsively, she bent down and flung her arms around the older woman. Coming here had been the perfect move, Tess thought. Mavis McNaught's kitchen. Her refuge.

When they drew apart, Mavis said, "Why don't you go upstairs and have a wee lie down? If you like, you can stay the night. I know there's at least one of your nighties still in the drawer in your room."

And because Mavis had been watching out for her since she was ten years old and always knew best, Tess headed upstairs to her old bedroom. It was just the way she'd left it after graduating from university and its familiarity was as comforting as Mavis's embrace. On this day of all days she craved the mindless solace of routine, so Tess kicked off her heels and lay down on the worn patchwork quilt covering the narrow bed. She shifted, adjusting from habit to the mattress lumps, and closed her eyes. But sleep didn't come.

What came instead was a flood of memory. *Her first night in this room.* She was ten and her mother, Hannah, had been taken to a hospital psychiatric ward after being picked up wandering Chicago streets in her nightgown. The incident had been the first breakdown, but not the last. When child care workers and police asked Tess if there was anyone she could stay with, the person who'd come immediately to mind had been Mavis McNaught.

Mavis's parents had been neighbors of Tess's family and Mavis had befriended Hannah and Tess over the course of her weekly visits. After Richard Wheaton left home, Mavis had kept in touch, in spite of living in another part of the city. She was the only person, other than her mother, whom Tess had really known as family after her father walked out. The middle-aged spinster hadn't blinked an eye at the officer's request. She marched out to the police cruiser, wrapped her arms around Tess and led her into the home where she stayed for the next eleven years.

Hannah came to live in Mavis's house in the beginning, too. But her erratic use of medication and frequent breakdowns took their toll on the makeshift family. In the end, Tess figured, her mother didn't so much die from pneumonia as from depression. Tess was fourteen when Mavis became her legal guardian, providing the first stable home she'd known in years.

Replaying the past, Tess came to the conclusion she always reached. Her mother's downward spiral began little more than a year after Richard Wheaton left. That day was still etched in her memory.

They'd been arguing again. Nothing unusual about that, but this time felt different to eight-year-old Tess. She crouched behind her father's favorite chair and watched her mother pace back and forth, puffing on one cigarette after another. Tess hated to see her mother smoke and so did her father. That was one of the things they often quarreled about. The other was money.

Today Tess didn't have to cover her ears. There wasn't any shouting. Instead, their occasionally raised voices fell into low mumbles. They even sat, her mother perched on the couch. Her father, hunched forward in his chair, as if about to spring from it. Tess could have reached out to touch him if she'd dared.

After a silence Tess thought would never end, she heard her mother say the words that would haunt her in the years ahead, "Then leave."

And when Richard rose from the chair, his answer booming around the small living room, "I will," Tess had run out from behind his chair. Flinging her arms around his legs, she'd cried, "Don't go, Daddy. Don't leave."

Hands—she didn't know whose—pulled her away. She threw herself on the carpet, sobbing. Her mother slipped upstairs. It seemed like hours later when Tess heard footsteps in the hall. She sat up and saw her father standing hesitantly at the front door. As if he didn't know what to do next, she thought.

A canvas duffel bag hung from his shoulder. He was holding his wooden box of paints in one hand and a large paper-wrapped frame in the other. One of his paintings.

"Daddy—?"

He stared at her a long time before saying in a husky voice, "Don't forget me, Tess. I won't forget you." He opened the door and walked out.

Tess jumped up and ran to the open door. Her father was climbing into a taxi.

"Daddy!" she called again.

He turned around and paused, a look of indecision in his face.

Tess's heart raced. He was changing his mind. He was coming back.

But then he stiffened, waved a last goodbye and got into the taxi. Behind Tess, Hannah Wheaton snarled, "Let him go, Tess. He doesn't want us anymore...and we don't want him."

She closed the door as the taxi pulled away from the curb.

Over the next few years Tess often wondered what might have happened if her mother hadn't suddenly appeared behind her that day. Would her father have come back inside and tried to patch things up, as he'd done so many times before? Or would he have swept Tess up into his arms and taken her with him?

That was the fantasy that carried her through into adolescence, until she reached the painful conclusion that her mother had been right after all. Richard Wheaton hadn't wanted them anymore.

Tess rolled over onto her side and sighed. She hadn't relived that scene for many years. It had lost much of its power over her now, no longer producing the flow of tears it once could.

So. Her father was dead. She knew she ought to be able to summon even a tiny bit of grief, but could not. Her memory of him was now relegated to that last day. Her love for him disappeared sometime in the years after his leaving. She was glad she'd impulsively thrown away the lawyer's letter. The sooner she got over this latest memory surge, the better. She closed her eyes and let her mind drift through the years until sleep, at last, came.

"COFFEE?"

"Great," said Tess, "but let me make it. Yours is always too weak." She pushed her chair back from the kitchen table and went to the counter.

Mavis shook her head. "I don't know how you can get to sleep at night after drinking that stuff."

"I usually go to bed so late nothing can keep me awake."

"You're working too hard, love. That's why you fell asleep. An hour's nap has done you some good, but it doesn't make up for a real break. Tell me about this holiday cruise you've booked."

Tess finished measuring out the coffee, poured water into the machine and turned it on before responding. She'd known Mavis would get around to asking about the cruise eventually, but wished the question hadn't arisen that night.

"It's kind of up in the air right now," she said.

Mavis raised an eyebrow. "Does that mean you're flying instead?"

Tess laughed. "Good one, Mavis."

"Seriously, don't tell me you're not taking that holiday. You've been talking about it for months."

Tess turned away. *But not in the last few weeks I haven't.* She took her time, getting milk from the fridge, mugs from the cupboard. Anything to postpone the inevitable. She didn't look Mavis in the eye until she sat down in her chair again. When she did, the expression in her guardian's face told her she wasn't going to be able to hide the truth any longer.

"I'm having second thoughts," Tess began.

"About the cruise?"

Tess got up and poured the coffee, then carefully sat down again. She wondered if an evasive strategy would work with Mavis. "There's so much work at the office right now. A big merger coming up. It's all hush-hush so I can't give you any details but…"

"Tess, love, I'm not going to be calling up my stockbroker in the morning. So get on with it."

Her blue eyes zoomed in on Tess. *Scratch the evasive strategy.* Tess laughed. "I can't keep anything from you, Mavis."

"And why would you want to?" Mavis's voice assumed a tone of mock hurt. Then, reading Tess's mind, she added, "I know you want me to stop pestering you—and I will— but I'm curious. I thought you and Douglas had made all the arrangements."

"We had," Tess said, her voice low. She stared down into her coffee.

"And?"

There was no putting her off, Tess thought. She sighed and set her coffee mug down on the table. "I haven't seen him for almost two weeks."

The eyebrow arched again, but Mavis said nothing.

"The last time I saw him we had an argument and I'm afraid…well, I guess I said some pretty blunt things."

Mavis nodded thoughtfully. "Then what happened?"

Did the woman ever give up? "Nothing. He hasn't called."

"So the cruise—?"

"I canceled my half." Tess picked some fluff off her skirt, avoiding Mavis's face. When she glanced up, Mavis was staring at her as if she'd lost her mind. "I had cancellation insurance," Tess murmured. "I got back most of my money."

"That's not the point, dear. You need a holiday. You've been working ten- and twelve-hour days, six days a week, I'm sure, for the last six months."

"Comes with the promotion, Mavis. I explained that when they made me Vice President of Marketing."

"But Douglas? The lad dotes on you."

Tess glanced down again, this time to hide a grin. Douglas Reed—the company's wheeling and dealing head lawyer—was no lad. Probably never had been, Tess thought, even when he was a kid. And the doting part certainly had applied a year ago, but not recently.

How could she explain to Mavis what had happened when Tess scarcely knew herself? Douglas Reed's aggressive, confident courting style had been exhilarating and flattering in the beginning. But over the past few months, Tess had suspected his feelings for her had more to do with image than true love. She knew from comments he'd made that dating an executive from Balfour International was important to his own career plans. His hints about a future together envisioned a team on a meteoric ascent—a couple who would earn a fortune between them and who'd devote their lives solely to one another. And, of course, their careers.

Not that Tess didn't want to have a great career. She'd worked hard, putting herself through university and then going on to acquire an MBA. Success was crucial for her. She just didn't want someone else planning her future for her.

And of course, there was the other thing. The part she couldn't reveal to Mavis. When Douglas took her into his arms, she felt little more than a moment's warmth. Worse still, after the first two or three times, their lovemaking had become an exercise of habit. There was no buzz, no sparkle, no whisper of magic—all the ingredients of a truly romantic relationship. Deep down inside, Tess craved the fantasy she'd imagined since she was a teenager—that someone, somewhere, was going to whisk her away.

She sighed. It hadn't happened yet. Probably never would. And, Tess was sure, it definitely would not happen with Douglas Reed.

"Tess? Are you still with me, girl?" Mavis was leaning forward in her chair. "And what's that sigh all about?"

Tess felt her face heat up. "Nothing. It's just that things haven't been great between us for a while and...well, I thought we should give each other some space."

"In my day we'd call that breaking up," Mavis commented. "Well, so be it. You know best what kind of man you want to settle down with."

Tess bit down on her lower lip. She knew the remark stemmed from love for her, but Mavis simply couldn't accept that Tess's aim in life was not merely to marry and produce a family. Some day, perhaps. But not anytime soon.

After a long moment, Mavis asked, "Are you sure you don't want to talk about your father?"

Tess stared down into her coffee mug. When she finally raised her head to Mavis, her reply was brisk. "No. There's not much to say, anyway. I'll dig that lawyer's letter out of the wastebasket tomorrow or wait for him to call me back."

Mavis heaved a loud sigh, suggesting she knew when to give up. "I have a feeling you want to change the subject."

Tess didn't answer. She drank the last of her coffee and

stood up. "I should go home tonight, Mavis. I've got to be at work early for a meeting and if I stay here—"

Mavis nodded. "I know, love. The distance adds more time to your day. Anyway, tomorrow's my Friday to visit Sophie and I plan to leave first thing in the morning."

"How is she doing?" Tess asked.

Mavis shrugged. "Well as can be expected, I guess. She likes the food there, anyway." Mavis visited her sister once a month, spending the weekend at the retirement home outside Chicago where Sophie had been living for the past year. "I'm sorry to hear about the cruise. I hope you'll still go ahead and take the holiday time, though." Her eyes fixed on Tess. "Think about it. You need it more than you realize, believe me."

Tess mumbled a reply, though she thought this time Mavis didn't know best.

TESS LEFT the conference room and made a sharp right turn when she spotted Douglas exiting an office farther down the hall. They seldom bumped into one another in the eight floors of skyscraper space that the company rented in the John Hancock Center. Since their acrimonious parting two weeks before, Tess had made a point of avoiding the floor where his office was located.

Today was not a good time for a first encounter, she decided. Not after yesterday's stunning news. A face-to-face meeting when she was feeling vulnerable might end up with her agreeing to go on the cruise with him after all.

An elevator opened as she approached the company reception area and she jumped into it, breathing a sigh of relief as the door closed. How long, she asked herself, are you going to keep hiding from him? Ashamed of her own cowardice, she vowed to face up to him the next time. *That's what comes of breaking your own rule, Tess my girl, about dating a colleague.*

As she entered her office, Carrie waved a handful of

phone message slips. "Some lawyer's been calling you ever since late yesterday afternoon, Tess."

"Lawyer? What about, do you know?"

"No, but he's calling from Colorado so—"

"Oh, God!" Tess expelled a mouthful of air.

"Not bad news, I hope?"

"I'm not sure," was all she said, grabbing the messages and retreating into her office. She plunked down into her swivel chair, set her elbows on the desk and lowered her chin into her cupped hands. She needed to calm down. Perhaps Mavis was right after all. A vacation might be the best thing for her now. Except that she'd canceled the cruise and had no place to go.

Tess leafed through the phone messages. They were all from her father's lawyer, Jed Walker, in Boulder. *Jed.* A picture came to mind of a rugged man in a big white cowboy hat puffing on a fat cigar, booted feet propped up on a desk. Or would that be a Texan? She frowned. Whatever, the guy's persistence was annoying.

She set the messages aside and skimmed through her notes from the executive meeting. The merger was proceeding well now and her part wouldn't really happen until all the paperwork was finished, which could take another couple of months. Then she'd have to come up with some flashy ideas to promote the newly formed company, glossing over the reality that jobs would be lost as a result of the merger. The prospect worried her, though when she hesitantly raised the question at the meeting her boss advised her not to dwell on the negatives.

"Other jobs will open up with new manufacturing," he'd reassured her before going on to the next item on the agenda.

Tess had let the matter drop, thinking at the same time how someone like Mavis, underpaid and undervalued in the workforce up to her retirement, would have reacted to such nonchalance. Thoughts of Mavis took her back to the discarded phone messages on her desk.

She had advised her to contact the lawyer, for curiosity's sake if nothing else. Tess picked up one of the slips of paper and stared at it. Could she seriously call someone named Jed without cracking a cowboy joke? More to the point, did she really *want* to pursue the matter of her father?

Except for a birthday card months after he left, she'd had no word from him. Mavis had tried in vain to change Hannah Wheaton's mind about accepting child support and trying to locate Richard. Hannah's standard response had been, "He knows where we are if he wants to find us."

But he doesn't, Tess had wanted to argue. Once they'd moved in with Mavis, all ties to the old neighborhood had been cut. When her mother died years later, Tess hadn't bothered searching through their few boxes of belongings to find an address for her father. She'd finally managed to wipe out his memory.

Her curiosity got the better of her. Tess clamped down on the receiver, about to pick it up, when the phone rang. She waited for Carrie to pick up and a second later, her voice came through on the intercom.

"Tess? Call for you from Colorado—"

"I'll take it," Tess interrupted. *The lawyer.* "Mr. Walker?" she said, after Carrie transferred the call. "I'm sorry I haven't had a chance to get back to you—"

"Mr. Walker? *Jed Walker?* Hell, I'm no Jed Walker. I can tell you that much. That son of a—sorry, just don't get me started on Jed Walker. I'd as soon—well, never mind that, either. Look, I've been trying to find you for about a week now and things have just gone from bad to worse here."

"Wait! Please. I don't have the faintest idea who you are and what you're talking about. I'm sorry if I mistook you for Jed Walker and obviously you're acquainted, though not exactly bosom buddies, but—"

A deep resonant chuckle sounded from the other end. "Well put, Miss Wheaton. Sorry about all the blathering there. The name's Alec Malone and I'm—"

"Mr. Malone, what can I do for you?" Tess snapped impatiently.

"I'm a social worker here in Boulder. I guess Walker's already contacted you about your father. That right?"

Tess closed her eyes. Here it was. "Yes, I got a letter from him yesterday."

"A *letter? And just yesterday?* He's known about you for more than a week."

"Look Mr. Malone—"

"Alec. We don't stand on formality down here."

"Whatever. Alec, then. My father left my mother years ago and I haven't seen or heard from him since. So if his estate owes anyone any money, you can forget—"

"Money's definitely part of it but that's not why I'm calling. Your father and his wife well, I suppose she'd be his second wife—"

Wife! Tess took a deep breath. Her past was snowballing toward her and she had no place to leap.

"She was killed in the car crash, too, with your father. Maybe you didn't know that."

The snowball doubled in size. Tess tried to speak, but couldn't. A commotion from beyond her closed office door distracted her. She heard Carrie's voice pitch indignantly.

"You can't go in there! She's on the—"

The door burst in and two people shot into the room. Two small people. Children. They lurched to a halt a few feet beyond the door and stared at her. Carrie, standing in the doorway behind them, raised her shoulders apologetically.

Tess pressed down the hold button. Her gaze shifted from the taller boy with thick chestnut hair that edged the collar of his jacket to the little girl clinging to his leg. There was something familiar about her. The large, vibrant green eyes and the raven tousle of hair. The same heart-shaped face and a smaller version of a delicate nose. Tess could have been looking at a mirror image of herself at the same age.

She released the hold, keeping her eyes fixed on them. Alec Malone was still talking. "Anyway, the reason I'm calling is that they left behind two kids who've just—"

Tess jabbed the hold button again. "Who are you?" she asked them. "What do you want?" But she knew what the boy was going to say even before he spoke.

"I think—well, uh—that you're our sister."

CHAPTER TWO

"TESS?" Carrie asked.

Their sister? Me? Dazed, Tess looked from the two youngsters to Carrie, standing behind them. Her secretary's eyes were wide with surprise.

"I'll take any calls," Carrie said at once, backing out of the room and closing the door behind her.

The office was dead quiet. Tess's labored breathing competed with the drumming at her temples. The little girl, clad in denim overalls and a nylon windbreaker, looked anxiously up at her brother, whose brown-eyed gaze never wavered from Tess's face. He was a handsome boy on the verge of adolescence, his lanky frame awkwardly thin for the baggy jeans and jacket he wore. Without thinking, Tess released the hold button in time to hear Alec Malone drawling, "Somethin' wrong at that end, Miss Wheaton?"

Tess moistened her dry lips and cleared her throat to ask, "Would those two kids be a teenaged boy and a little girl?"

A whistle of relief sounded from the other end. "They there?" His voice was low and urgent.

"They just walked into my office." Tess caught the sharp glance sent from boy to girl. A reassuring signal, she wondered, or a warning?

"Thank God," he said. "I've got foster parents on standby here, chomping at the bit to call the police. Those two put together one heck of a runaway plan and managed to bamboozle everyone."

"I think you've got some explaining to do, Mr. Malone," she said.

"Right you are. I'm getting to that. I don't know if you've got to the introduction stage yet, but their names are Nick and Molly. He's thirteen and she's six. I've had their case file since they were placed in foster care right after the accident and—"

"Why was that?" Tess interrupted.

"No next of kin and no one close to the family able to take them. We didn't know about you until several days ago."

Before Tess could respond, an exchange of hissed whispers interceded.

"Excuse me," the boy said, "but is there a washroom here? And a water fountain?"

Tess frowned, clamping her palm across the receiver. "Are you thirsty?"

He nodded. "And hungry, too. We only had some apples and crackers early this morning."

"One minute, Mr. Malone," she snapped into the phone, then put him on hold while pressing the intercom button. "Carrie? Could you come back in here for a sec?"

"She'll take you to get some lunch...or dinner...or whatever it is for you," Tess explained to the children. The door flew open as she was speaking. "Carrie, would you mind taking these two down to the concourse for a bite to eat? Hit the washrooms up here first—that may be the more urgent need." She eyed the girl, hopping from one foot to the other.

"I'd love to take them. C'mon, kids. So, I'm Carrie and you are..."

"Nick," the boy said. "She's Molly." A pause, then, "We're Wheatons, too. *Her* brother and sister," he added huskily, his voice trembling slightly.

In case Carrie missed that bit of information the first time around, Tess was thinking. As soon as they left the office, she released the hold button.

"Okay, Mr. Malone, how soon can you get here to pick up these kids and what am I supposed to do with them in the meantime?"

There was a slight pause, punctuated by a heavy sigh. "I was afraid you might say that."

Tess felt the stirrings of a migraine. She closed her eyes, massaging her temples. "I don't know what you mean by that, Mr. Malone, but obviously if people there are looking for the children, they have to be returned as soon as possible. You're their social worker, surely you must have a plan. *So what is it?*"

She thought she heard a low chuckle before he said, "Maybe we're not as busy down here, ma'am, as you seem to be up there. Guess I was half hoping you'd offer to come back with them or, at best, keep them till someone can get to Chicago."

"What am *I* supposed to do with them? I'm at work right now and my day doesn't usually end until eight at night. I don't know much about kids, but I suspect that's too long a day for them. Besides, I only have a one-bedroom condo here and—"

"I get the picture, Miss Wheaton," he interjected. There was another sigh, followed by a low mumbling that Tess suspected was swearing. "Look, someone—most likely it'll be me—will be there as soon as possible but it may not happen until tomorrow. You think you can handle those two youngsters till then?"

Tess grit her teeth. Nothing ambiguous about the sarcasm in his voice. "I don't think it's fair to get short with me, Mr. Malone. It's hardly my fault the children ran away."

"*Short?* Would that be like short as in *snotty?* If so, then I apologize but I gotta admit, those kids took a helluva gamble to make that trip to Chicago on their own looking for a sister they just discovered they had. Kids who've never been outside Boulder, Colorado. I don't have all the details yet, but I do know they got the whole thing together without any adult help and actually made it there in one piece. So if I sound a bit *short* as you put it, well yes, dammit all, that's precisely what I *am* feeling.''

It wasn't often that Tess found herself speechless. A hundred questions swarmed her mind about how the children learned her identity and why they came looking for her. Tess sensed that firing off a slew of defensive inquiries would fuel an already heated conversation with the presumptuous social worker. Her business experience had taught her that obvious anger only made your argument weaker.

''Still there?'' he ventured after a pause.

''Unfortunately,'' she said.

''Sorry if I seem a bit tetchy but I'm real worried about these kids. You haven't had a chance to get to know them yet—''

''No,'' she put in as icily as she could. ''And I'm not likely to, either. Richard Wheaton—my father—walked out on my mother and me when I was eight years old, Mr. Malone, and I haven't heard a word from him or about him since yesterday. So if I appear a tad cool to the notion of family and siblings, please forgive me. I'm not a callous person. If these children need a place to stay until tomorrow, I will provide them with one.'' She hesitated, alarmed at the promise she'd just made. Too late now, she thought. *But there's always Mavis.* Beyond her office door, she heard muted voices. They were back. ''I'll give you my home address and phone number. When might I expect you?''

There was a resigned exhalation from the other end. ''I don't imagine you've dealt much with government bureaucracies, Miss Wheaton—or maybe you have—'' he quickly added ''—but nothing in this office moves faster than a slug on a cabbage leaf. And when it comes to applying for air travel, I should've requested this trip months ago. So…''

Tess was beginning to think *he* didn't move very fast either. *"So?"* she repeated, wanting him to get to the point. If he ever could.

"There's a flight arriving in Chicago after noon."

"Nothing sooner?"

"That's the best I can do."

Tess closed her eyes. "All right, Mr. Malone, I'll be waiting to hear from you."

"There's one more thing," he said. "The kids are real upset about being split up. The accident has pretty much traumatized them, as you can imagine. I'd appreciate it if you avoided making any statements to them about their future."

"How could I do that when I've no idea what future plans exist for them?"

His sigh suggested he was trying to be as patient as possible. "That's exactly the kind of thing I'm talking about. If they bring up the subject about what's going to happen to them, be as vague or evasive as possible. Please."

"Of course I will, but why belabor your point, Mr. Malone? Obviously I *don't* have any idea what the future holds for them."

"You're not getting it yet, are you Miss Wheaton? The kids headed to Chicago because you're the only family they've got."

Family. She'd never felt she had one. There was Mavis, who tried her best over the years to compensate for the real family Tess lacked. Tess tried to come up with a response but words failed her.

"Miss Wheaton? Sorry if all of this is overwhelming but that's the situation. I'll call you as soon as I get into town." And he hung up before she had a chance to say anything more.

Tess replaced the receiver and sat, oblivious to the

hushed chatter outside her office. *Her office.* How odd that at that very moment, nothing in the room was familiar. It suddenly seemed to belong to someone else. She peered down at her tailored, olive-green skirt with its matching, long-sleeved silk blouse. The delicate gold chain around her neck was a graduation present from Mavis and the titanium and gold watch, a gift to herself on her promotion. But the whole outfit might as well be trappings owned by a complete stranger. Tess sighed. The double whammy she'd just received—father dead and two half siblings on her doorstep—had instantly diminished all the rewards of her success.

So she instinctively turned to the one person who'd been her saving grace over the years and punched in Mavis's phone number. After the tenth unanswered ring, Tess remembered that Mavis would be with her sister all weekend. She hung up, propped her elbows on the desk and lowered her head onto her hands. She didn't have the faintest idea what to do—which was, for her, an almost frightening state of mind.

"Tess?"

She raised her head enough to glare at the intercom, wanting desperately to simply tell everyone to go away and leave her alone. "Yes?"

There was a slight hesitation before Carrie continued by, saying, "The kids have had a bite to eat and gone to the washroom, but they're tired. Do you know when you'll be taking them home?"

Taking them home? Tess checked the time. Four o'clock. Leaving early two days in a row would raise more than a few eyebrows.

"Did you hear me?"

Tess swallowed. Taking them home. *To a one-bedroom condo?* "Uh, Carrie, can you come in here for a sec?"

The intercom fell silent and Carrie popped her head

around the door an instant later. "Don't ask," Carrie fore-warned.

"Ask?" Tess ran her tongue along her lips, trying to kick some life into the smile she was squeezing out.

"It's all over your face so let me spare you the humiliation of a no. I've got big plans this weekend." Carrie closed the door behind her.

"This is what comes of having a too familiar relationship with your staff," Tess muttered to herself. She groaned and gently massaged her temples.

"I guess we've caused you a lot of trouble."

Tess jerked her head up. She hadn't heard anyone come in. The boy—Nick—stood in the open doorway. His face was pale, drawn with worry. Something in his expression tugged at her.

"Not a lot," she began. "But—well, there are other issues here."

He nodded. "Something to do with my father."

He was quick, she thought. "Something like that." It wasn't the time or place to get into a lecture on parental responsibility. Besides, what Richard Wheaton had done was hardly his fault.

Nick's sigh echoed in the silence of Tess's office. "I thought there might be a problem. Otherwise Dad would have...well, we'd have known about you."

She waited to see if his trail of logic would lead him where she hoped he'd go.

"At first it was weird thinking someone as old as you could be our sister. Then I started thinking maybe it was kinda good luck. But I knew when Molly and me decided to come here, it might turn out that...you know...you wouldn't be able to take us."

Tess forced her thoughts away from the *old* reference, focusing instead on how he'd said *able* instead of *want*. A face-saving gesture for them, she wondered, or giving her an out? Either way, she figured he'd gotten the message.

"I live in a one-bedroom condo...." she began, her voice falling off as she realized how lame that sounded. "Mr. Malone said he could be here tomorrow to...well, take you back to Boulder." As soon as she uttered the words, Tess had a surge of guilt. She'd promised the social worker to be vague about their return to Boulder.

Nick's face twisted in a grimace. "Yeah," he said huskily, turning his back on Tess to head for the door.

"Where are you going?"

He stopped, but didn't turn around. "To break the news to Molly. I don't want her to freak out." He pulled on the door and walked out of the office.

Tess was quick on his heels, anxious to hear exactly how he was going to tell his little sister. The last thing she needed was a hysterical child. She watched as Nick crouched down to whisper in Molly's ear. The little girl stared at Tess the whole while, her eyes wide and unblinking in her pale face. When Nick finished and stood protectively behind his sister, he said, "Will it be all right if we stayed with you tonight? I've spent all our money."

Carrie shot Tess a look that would have shriveled anyone else.

"Of course," Tess quickly said, casting a *so there* glance at her secretary. "It'll be like camping," she added, catching the incredulous expression on Carrie's face. "We'll get videos and order in pizza," she said, trying for a note of enthusiasm.

"Whoopee!" Carrie muttered as she brushed past Tess to get to her desk.

"Well then," Tess said, "I guess I'll be leaving for the day." She saw Carrie raise an eyebrow, as if silently echoing the *I guess*. For the first time, Tess noticed a backpack and plastic shopping bag on the floor next to Carrie's desk.

"I'll get my coat," she murmured and went back into her office, moving as if in a trance, trying to avoid the question she knew she'd be asking herself the instant they left the office. *What now?*

She grabbed her briefcase, stuffing inside it the files she knew she ought to be working on that very moment, and returned to the small reception area. "Let's go," she announced to no one in particular, thinking she might convince Carrie this unexpected turn of events was no big deal.

"Have fun," Carrie said, adding to the children, "maybe you can persuade your sister to treat you to something more exciting than videos and pizza."

Your sister? For a second Tess wondered who Carrie was talking about. Then it hit her all over again. She felt the air whoosh out of her, but covered up by asking, "What's wrong with videos and pizza?"

Carrie shrugged, winking at the other two. "If you weren't such a workaholic, you'd know. Anyway, I'll take your messages. See you on Monday—maybe," she said, giving the postscript a significant tone.

No one spoke all the way down to the ground floor. When they reached it, Molly said, "Carrie showed us the water fountain under the ground."

Tess had to think for a second. "Oh? When she took you to get something to eat?" She led them through the lobby onto the sidewalk.

Catching up, Molly said breathlessly, "I had french fries, too."

"Uh-huh," Tess murmured, scanning the street for a taxi.

"With ketchup."

"Molly, no one cares what you ate, okay?" Nick said.

"I'm just *telling* her," she protested. There was a hint of a whine in her voice.

Tess glanced sharply at Nick. "What's going on?" she asked, just clueing in to the tone of their voices.

He scowled. "We're just arguing, that's all. Don't you know *anything* about kids?"

"No, frankly, I don't. Anyway, what does arguing solve?"

"Jeez," he muttered.

Tess frowned. He looked tired, too, she thought. Maybe that's what the arguing was about. "Look, I know you two have been through a lot so we'll just hop in a taxi and get to my place as soon as possible. Then you can shower and have a nap or something."

"I'm six now. I don't have naps," Molly piped up.

Tess blew a strand of hair away from her mouth. "Whatever," she mumbled and waved briskly to a taxi about to pull away from the curb. "Damn," she muttered as the taxi kept on going. "Okay, want to take the subway?"

"What's that?"

"A train, stupid. Underground."

"Don't call me stupid, Nick!"

Tess grit her teeth. *Twenty-four hours of this?* "Your case worker will be here tomorrow, hopefully right after lunch. So can we all agree to do our best to get along with each other until he arrives and…" she paused, noticing Molly's stricken face, "well…you know."

Two pairs of solemn eyes stared up at her. Tess noticed for the first time the cowlick poking up from the crown of Nick's head. He was just about shoulder level with her and his slender frame, weighed down by his backpack, made him appear frail and vulnerable. They were *both* just kids, she thought. *Though not just any kids.* The reminder was sobering.

"Okay, so follow me and no more arguing. In fact, no more talking until we get home and you can tell me how you managed to get all the way from Boulder, Colorado, to Chicago without attracting any attention." Tess turned sharply and led the way to the underground.

No one uttered a word until the train was halfway to Tess's stop in Lincoln Park. Then Molly, her dark eyes wide with wonder, exclaimed, "I've never been on a train before,'' and clamped a hand over her mouth when she realized she'd just broken the silence edict. Tess impulsively smiled but saw that Nick's glower couldn't be shifted. He sat half-turned toward the window and stared through it the whole way. Every once in a while, Tess caught his reflection in the glass and once, their eyes met. He lowered his first, but not before a hint of a sneer twisted his upper lip.

Inexplicably, that bothered Tess. Wasn't it enough that she was giving up most of a weekend to look after two children who, in spite of biology, were basically strangers? Miffed, she averted her own face to stare out the other window and was soon so lost in thought she almost missed her stop. She realized at the last instant, jumping to her feet and hustling the kids from the car seconds before the doors closed. On the platform, Tess laughingly cried, "That was close!" and Molly laughed, too.

Nick trudged toward the exit. As Tess was about to follow, Molly reached for her hand, slipping it casually into Tess's. When they reached the upper level, Nick was slouched against a wall waiting for them, looking as if he were the most bored kid on earth. Still, Tess noted how his eyes flickered with interest from left to right as they exited the station and walked along the street.

As usual, the neighborhood was bustling on a Friday afternoon. Rush hour had already begun and Tess knew the expressways would be packed. She'd decided long ago to save herself the expense of a car in the city, especially since most of her waking hours were devoted to work.

They walked north along the lake and the outer edge of Lincoln Park. Tess glanced down at Molly, still clutching her hand, and saw her eyes grow bigger and bigger at each new sight. The park and zoo might be an option for tomorrow morning, she thought. Unless they slept in, though from what Tess had gathered about kids from the parents in her department, that wasn't a likely occurrence.

The appearance of the six-story building where Tess lived elicited another gasp from Molly and, though Nick remained silent, Tess saw that his eyes widened, too. It had been renovated by a well-known architect when the area was undergoing a transformation from its more humble origins.

"You live *here?*"

Tess almost smiled at the wobble in Nick's voice. She guessed what he was thinking. "Yes, but don't worry. It's not really a factory—just looks a bit like one from the outside."

She unlocked the exterior door and led them into a foyer festooned with thick, multicolored tubular pipes that ran back and forth along the ceiling.

"I feel like I'm in Legoland," Molly gasped.

"Yeah, right," Nick scoffed. Still, his eyes gleamed as they scanned the foyer.

"Neat, isn't it?" Tess remarked.

"Neat?"

There was a hint of disdain in his voice. "Well, whatever kids say these days," she said.

"Yeah, whatever," he mumbled.

When they were on the elevator going up to Tess's sixth-floor loft, Molly unexpectedly asked, "Do you have any other brothers or sisters?"

"God," muttered Nick. "She didn't even know she had *us.*"

"That's not her fault," Molly put in. "Anyway, we didn't know about her either, until after the…"

Her unspoken word—*accident*—boomed in the silence. Tess struggled to find something to say, but was saved by the elevator reaching her floor. She stepped out first, noticing that now both kids were pale-faced and red-eyed. If Mavis were here, she thought, she'd feed them and send them to bed.

They didn't utter a word when she unlocked her door,

but Nick's jaw dropped slightly and Molly gasped. The ten-foot ceiling-to-floor windows facing east afforded an impressive view of Lake Michigan. Since Tess spent most of her time at the office, she'd devoted little effort to furnishings. The sparseness of the condo added to the effect of space and light created by the unadorned windows.

The children stood in the doorway until Tess herded them inside. "The kitchen's at the end of this main room and the bathroom's off that hall there," she said, pointing to her right, "just before the bedroom."

"Is there a door on the bathroom?" Molly asked.

Tess smiled. "For sure. And on my bedroom, too."

"Where will we sleep?"

"We'll work that out. Just put your stuff anywhere. Are you two hungry? I know you just ate something but I can order pizza."

"We just had french fries," Molly said. "But by the time the pizza comes, I know I'll be ready for it."

Tess smiled. "What about you, Nick? Pizza?"

He shrugged. "Sure."

Tess hesitated. Did he want her to persuade him some more? Or was he really so indifferent?

"I only like pepperoni on mine," said Molly, advancing farther into the living room.

"Oh?" Tess paused. She hadn't given a thought to preferences. "And what about you, Nick?"

"Same," he mumbled, letting his pack fall to the floor.

"Okay," Tess murmured, mentally bidding goodbye to her usual feta, spinach and roasted red peppers. She headed for the galley kitchen at the opposite end of the room and used the telephone on the counter there to order. When she finished, she opened the refrigerator and took out the half bottle of Chardonnay she'd been sipping on that week. She'd just finished pouring a glass when she glanced up to see Molly watching her from the other side of the counter. "Uh, thirsty?"

Molly nodded. "But I don't drink wine," she said.

"I've got some cranberry juice and mineral water."

Molly's face screwed up in thought. "No milk?"

"Sorry. I drink my coffee black."

"Apple juice?"

"Only cranberry. But if you want, I can call the pizza place back and get them to bring some pop with the order."

The face brightened. "Okay! Coke, please."

Tess reached for the phone. "Nick?" she asked.

He was standing in front of one of the windows, staring out. There was something about the slump of his shoulders. Maybe he wasn't as tough as he was trying to be. "Sure," he finally said.

"What kind?" Tess asked, impatience edging her voice.

Molly whispered, "He likes Coke, too."

That settled it as far as Tess was concerned and she quickly made the phone call before there could be any more changes. Once the pizza arrived and had been devoured in what Tess considered an alarmingly short time, the two kids were sagging into the pillows on the sofa, mesmerized by a television show Tess had never seen before in her life. She glanced across the room at the clock in the kitchen nook. Not quite seven o'clock. Normally she wouldn't be home for another hour. Perhaps she could do some work after they went to bed. The problem was, where was bed going to be?

"Does this couch pull out?" Nick asked some time later. "Molly's fallen asleep."

Tess glanced up from the newspaper she was reading. Molly was slumped over in a corner of the sofa. "No, it doesn't pull out, but one of you can sleep there."

"Then it'll have to be me," he said, "so Molly can sleep with you."

Tess wasn't sure whether to marvel at the way he took charge of the situation or his omission at seeking her approval of the plan. Without waiting for a reply, Nick shook

Molly awake. Tess headed for the bedroom, followed by Nick dragging Molly behind him. As soon as Tess drew back the bedcover, Molly flopped onto the bed.

"She can sleep in her underwear," Nick said. "You take off her clothes while I set up the couch."

Tess watched him leave the room. Obviously, he'd had plenty of experience at looking after Molly. In spite of his constant bickering with her on the way home, Nick really cared for his sister. Tess figured that, except for providing a place to stay and paying for dinner, the two didn't really need her at all.

Which was good, she thought, considering that after tomorrow they'd be gone and she could get on with her life. Encouraged by that, she tucked Molly under the covers and headed for the linen closet to get some bedding for Nick.

He'd changed into a T-shirt and sweatpants and was watching a baseball game on television. He hurriedly flicked off the set when she entered the room.

"Go ahead and watch it if you want. I've some work to do anyway. I can set up my laptop on the kitchen counter," she said, setting a comforter and pillow on the sofa next to him.

He mumbled something inaudible, but turned the set back on as he sank farther into the cushions. His hair was spiked up from pulling the T-shirt over his head and, against the bulky frame of the couch, he appeared much younger than his thirteen years. Tess suddenly recalled what Alec Malone had said about the kids reaching Chicago all on their own, despite never having been outside Boulder.

"How did you manage to get all the way to Chicago?"

His answer was nonchalant, as if he'd made the journey many times. "Bus to Denver and airplane here. We took a taxi from the airport to your office 'cause I couldn't figure out the transit map."

Welcome to the club, she was thinking. "And how did you pay for the tickets?"

The look he gave her was a blend of embarrassment and pride. He hesitated for a moment, then admitted, "I used my dad's credit card for the airfare. I was at our house getting some things with Alec. There was a stack of mail and Alec asked me to go through it to separate out the junk. One of the envelopes was my dad's new credit card and when Alec wasn't looking, I...well, I kinda kept it in case I might need it."

"Some airline clerk let you use a credit card?"

"I bought the tickets over the Internet. It wasn't hard."

Tess let that register a moment. "So when you took the credit card, you obviously were *planning* to run away."

His head turned sharply away from her gaze.

"Weren't you?"

The face that swung back to her was red, contorted with anger. "They were gonna separate us, put us in different foster homes. And then Molly'd probably be adopted because she's little and cute and I'm a teenager. No one wants teenagers." Nick swiped a hand across his eyes. "And I'd lose my sister."

Tess tried to think of something to say but found she couldn't speak at all. When she finally managed to, she knew she had blundered the instant the words came out. "Well, I'm sure you'll still be able to see one another."

She didn't know when she'd last felt so intimidated by a look. He flicked off the television, tossed the remote aside, got up from the couch and headed for the bathroom. She noted the square set of his adolescent shoulders, somehow more adultlike from behind, and oddly familiar.

Tess closed her eyes, forcing herself to stay calm when the bathroom door slammed shut. She began cleaning up plates, glasses and leftover pizza crusts and was just setting up her laptop on the diner-style eating counter at the kitchen end of the room when Nick returned. Without a word, he placed some of the couch cushions onto the coffee table, turned off the lamp next to it and lay down, his back to Tess.

She watched him for a bit, then slipped her disk into the computer and logged into her file. After a long silence, she said, "I'm sorry, Nick, I didn't mean to sound so unfeeling. But really...this Alec Malone sounds like he has your best interests at heart. I'm sure he'd see that you and Molly would keep in touch." Her voice trailed off into the room.

Nick didn't say a word. He was either asleep, she decided, or pretending to be. She turned her attention back to her work but after ten minutes, gave it up. On her way into her bedroom, she pulled the comforter over him and quietly said good-night.

Molly was sprawled in the middle of the bed. Tess stared down at her small face, flushed with sleep, then gently rolled her over until there was enough room for herself. She took her nightwear—designer T-shirt and boxer shorts—out of a drawer and went to the bathroom to change. The silent and shapeless lump that was Nick didn't move as Tess walked back and forth to the bathroom and the kitchen for her nightly glass of water.

By the time Tess got back to the bedroom, Molly had reclaimed the bed's center. She repeated the rollover, climbed in and automatically reached for her bedside reading, the latest literary prize winner. But after several attempts at the first paragraph of a new chapter, Tess set the book aside, extinguished the light and sat, propped against her pillows to think. Snippets of unrelated and varied events whose only connecting strand was her father overwhelmed her.

English Leather aftershave and the patch of toilet paper on his cheek or neck. *Battle wounds,* he'd tease. *You'll have them someday, but on your legs.* Tess never understood what he'd meant until she was a teenager and by then, she'd made herself stop thinking about her father anyway. She recalled how he'd swing her up into the air or let her climb onto his back while he rode her around their tiny living room. And last of all, the way he'd marched down the sidewalk that day, his shoulders ramrod straight.

Like Nick's, Tess thought. She expelled a mouthful of the day's emotion, held in check the way she'd taught herself so many years ago, and sank under the covers. Eventually, she fell asleep until cries in the night shook her awake.

"I want my mommy," wailed Molly, over and over.

Tess turned over to find the girl sitting upright, in the middle of the bed again. Using her elbows to push herself up, Tess wrapped her arm across Molly's trembling shoulders and drew her closer.

"Shhh! It's okay, Molly."

Molly tucked herself into the crook of Tess's arm and sobbed for a few more minutes before dropping off to sleep once more. Wide-eyed and soggy from Molly's tears, Tess lay perfectly still and awake until the break of day.

BY THE TIME the taxi pulled up in front of her condo building, Tess was ready to call it a day. The problem was, it was barely past one o'clock. She'd gotten out of bed at six-thirty when a pert and lively Molly, unscathed by the night's tearful episode, insisted on watching the Saturday morning cartoon shows. Tess had reluctantly joined her, offering her now empty bed to Nick whose adolescent sleep patterns demanded extra time.

Two hours later, when Nick finally arose, Tess staggered zombielike to the street below in search of supplies for breakfast and lunch.

"I said I wanted Corn Pops," Molly had whined at her return.

Nick had merely eyed the health food store granola that Tess was holding and had grumbled, "Even Cheerios would've been better."

The trip to Lincoln Park Zoo had been more successful. Molly seemed enchanted by everything she saw while Nick's mood grudgingly improved at the familiar presence of junk food. But Tess quickly realized that the delights of the zoo and the warm, sunny day couldn't compensate for lack of sleep or the strain of strangers being thrust together. She found herself checking her watch at frequent intervals, all the while wondering exactly when Alec Malone would arrive. At one point, after breaking up a noisy exchange between brother and sister, Tess had an alarming thought— *What if he doesn't even come?*

When the taxi rounded the corner of her street, Tess almost swooned in relief at the sight of her building. She longed for her weekly routine of reading the Saturday papers ensconced in the downy comfort of her new armchair, a cup of freshly brewed coffee at hand and the latest Dave Matthews CD pulsing softly in the background.

Then Molly dug her elbow into Nick's ribs because he'd accidentally stepped on her foot and Tess's mental replay of her typical Saturday morning unspooled. Tess thrust a handful of bills at the taxi driver and marched around the front of the cab to yank open the rear passenger door.

"Enough already!" she cried, her voice a notch louder than she'd intended.

As a pinch-faced Molly struggled out, her foot caught on part of the released seat belt and she tumbled out of the cab. Tess rushed to catch her before she hit the pavement, but, frightened by the near accident, Molly began to sob.

Nick slid from the car and, realizing his sister hadn't been hurt, berated her for being such a baby. That set off another round of sobs. Tess stood helplessly beside them and, aware that her morning fantasy was never going to happen, raised her palms to her face.

"Long morning?" a deep, male voice drawled from behind.

Lowering her hands, Tess whirled around, registering

Nick's grin and Molly's shriek of delight all in the same instant. They rushed to the man's side, Molly wrapping herself around a solid frame well over Tess's own height of five-eight and standing, legs astride a canvas duffel bag, a few feet away. Nick gave him a friendly tap on the shoulder.

"Alec! Alec!" cried Molly, her tumble completely forgotten as she danced around the man and his luggage. Nick, now the image of benign tolerance, moved farther apart so she could squeeze in closer, latching on to Malone mid-thigh.

"Hey, hey. Let me say hello to your sister," he said, laughing as he pried his leg loose from Molly's clutch and gently clasped her hand in his. Then, taking a big step forward, he extended his free hand to Tess and said, "Miss Wheaton, I presume?" at which Molly giggled and Nick snorted.

Tess, still tuning in to the fact that the word *sister* had meant her, merely stared dumbly. His big hand touched hers briefly, then let go. He took off the baseball cap he was wearing, releasing a shock of thick, sandy-red hair. His hazel eyes, swirled with bits of green and amber, swept over Tess from head to toe. When they returned to her face, their expression shifted ever so slightly, she thought.

"Looks like everyone—including you—is ready to call it a day," he said.

On cue, Molly complained, "I'm hungry and Tess doesn't have any good food."

Nick, however, got straight to the point. "When are you taking us back, Alec?"

Without taking his eyes off Tess, Malone replied, "Guess that's up to Miss Wheaton here, Nick. How about if we go inside and talk things over?"

Knowing she was being put on the spot, Tess felt a rush of annoyance. She glanced at the children, their faces turned expectantly toward hers. As if she would be announcing a decision about their future that very instant, she thought. She decided the man was as impossible in real life as he'd been on the telephone.

"Of course," she mumbled and made for the front door of her building.

"What about lunch?" cried Molly.

Her back to them, Tess paused long enough to hear Alec Malone say, "There's a submarine sandwich place just around the corner. I'll go get some while you go inside with your sister."

"I'm coming with you," Nick quickly said.

"Me, too," added Molly.

Tess half turned to catch an expression of helpless amusement from Malone. "Do you mind?" he asked her.

"Why should I?"

His smile vanished. "Just asking. Would you like a sandwich?"

"No, thank you. I'm in number 601," she murmured and turned her back again to insert her key into the front door. She heard them chatting happily as they walked away and, stepping into the foyer, had the distinct sensation of being cut right out of the picture. Though why that bothered her, she couldn't explain.

CHAPTER THREE

TESS PRETENDED to be engrossed in the laptop screen when they returned, bustling into her living space as if they'd been part of it forever. A sudden resentment at their noisy intrusion flared up. She wondered how long it would take to sort out this situation and get on with her life.

"We brought you one, too, Tess. In case you changed your mind." Molly's voice was pitched high with excitement.

Tess glanced up from her computer and organized her face into a passable smile. Oblivious to the fact that she was trying to work, Alec Malone and Nick began to open paper bags and pull the tabs on soda cans. Tess bit down on her lip when Malone asked where she kept the plates. Before she could answer, Nick pointed to a cupboard above the sink. Tess rolled her eyes in exasperation. A full-blown invasion was taking place right beneath her nose and there wasn't a thing she could do about it.

She didn't realize Molly was standing in front of her until she detected a slight movement. The little girl's smile was less enthusiastic now.

"Aren't you hungry, Tess?" she asked. "We got you one with roasted vegetables and fatty cheese." She held a paper bag in her small hand.

"Feta cheese," corrected Nick.

"Whatever. Alec said you'd probably choose that one if you were there."

And what's that supposed to mean? That he's got me all

figured out? Or worse—that in his eyes I represent some kind of yuppy stereotype? The fact that his choice had been right on the mark made it even more galling.

Tess knew Molly was waiting for a response. The problem was, the only one she felt like making would be quite inappropriate. *Like telling them all to leave.*

"Maybe we should let Tess finish up there first, Molly. Why don't you put her sandwich in the fridge for now? The three of us can take ours over to the couch," Alec suggested.

Heat rose into Tess's face. Now he was answering for her! She clicked out of her program and pushed the laptop aside. "It's okay, Molly. I'd like that sandwich now, after all. We can eat here at the counter."

Alec paused midway from the counter to the couch area. The look he flashed Tess told her he saw right through her effort to gain control. Still, he turned and headed for a stool at the counter.

Nick was less accommodating. "I wanted to watch TV," he complained.

"Later, fella," Alec said. "We can talk—get to know each other."

Nick snorted. "What's the point? We already know *you,* and *she's* not going to be in our lives much longer anyway."

"*She* has a name, so use it. As for the other point, we haven't made any decisions yet."

Silenced, Nick sullenly picked up his sandwich and began to eat.

Tess stared at the wrapped sandwich on the countertop in front of her. Her appetite took a nosedive. Nick's retort stung, though she couldn't explain why. It was true that she wasn't going to be in their lives much longer and intellectually, she understood why he rejected the idea of getting to know her better. She herself felt much the same. What she couldn't fathom was the niggling doubt in the back of her mind. The sense that, somehow, she'd made two children unhappy and now it was up to her to make things better. *But how?*

"Not hungry?"

She looked up to find Alec Malone staring at her. The expression in his eyes was softer now. Tess shook her head.

"Want a coffee?" he asked.

She shrugged. "Sure. I can make some."

"No. I meant, would you like to go out for one? I noticed a place just around the corner."

"But the kids—"

"Will be fine. Right, guys?"

Nick and Molly nodded, glancing at the same time from one to the other.

"Maybe Tess won't mind if you eat at the couch—long as you're careful." He wrapped up the rest of his sandwich and got off the bar stool.

"What about your lunch?" Tess asked.

"Later. Right now, we need to talk." He watched Nick and Molly settle themselves a few feet away on the couch. "Alone," he added.

Although Tess knew he was taking charge again, she also knew he was right. And the talk had to be done away from the kids. "They won't—"

"Run away again? Nah. But just to be sure…" He headed for the couch and leaned over to whisper something to Nick, then walked toward the door to wait for Tess.

She put her sandwich in the fridge and went to the bedroom to get her keys and wallet. Nick and Molly were both engrossed in the TV when she joined Alec at the door. She paused. "There's frozen yogurt if you two want any dessert."

Nick glanced up. "Any ice cream?"

"No, but…it's strawberry yogurt."

He gave a half shrug, as if that was better than nothing, then turned his attention to the television again.

"I like frozen yogurt," Molly piped up. "Thanks, Tess." She waved her fingers and resumed eating her sandwich.

Tess locked the door behind them and followed Alec to the elevator. His stiff, broad back looked ready for inspection. If it weren't for his hair, thick and fringing slightly at the nape of his neck, she'd have pegged him for a military man. He didn't say a word as they waited for the elevator. Either small talk wasn't his style, or he was ticked off at her. His demeanor suggested the latter.

But as the elevator slid to the ground floor, he finally murmured, "The kids have been through a lot."

"I can see that," Tess said.

"Can you?"

"What's that supposed to mean?" she asked, offended by the tone of his question.

"Just that from your manner, it seems you can only see how their unexpected appearance has impacted on *you.*"

Tess felt her blood pressure skyrocket. Or perhaps it was the elevator, lurching to a stop at the condo lobby. Speechless, she tagged behind him out the main door and onto the sidewalk.

"That's the most unfair thing I've heard since—"

"Since what? Hearing your father was dead or finding out you had a brother and sister?"

Was her own face as red as his, she wondered? Was that why people were turning around to look at them? She strode ahead, making for the Starbucks around the corner. The familiarity of the place calmed her. This was her turf after all. She could be in charge again. By the time he caught up to her, she'd already placed her order at the counter.

She carried her cafe latte to her favorite table and watched him, secretly congratulating herself on avoiding a song and dance about who would pay. He was speaking pleasantly to the female counter clerk, laughing about something she'd said. Behaving as if he hadn't been on the verge of exploding moments ago.

When he turned to walk toward her, Tess also realized for the first time how good-looking he was. Not her type, of course. Too athletic and rugged. But she noticed how the clerk's eyes tracked him to where Tess was sitting, then shifted away in obvious disappointment as he took the seat across from her.

"First off," he began once he'd set his mug of regular coffee down. "I apologize for what I said back there. I was out of line."

Out of line? He *must* have been in the military.

"None of this is your fault—any more than it's Nick or Molly's." His tawny eyes met hers briefly, then lowered to his coffee. He blew gently on the brew, sipped carefully and set it on the table.

Giving her time to come up with an opening line, she asked herself? Tess forced herself to outwait him, thinking she'd rather see where the talk was going to go.

"I can appreciate how your world's kinda been flipped upside down the last twenty-four hours," he said.

Kinda? I guess.

"Finding out your father's dead and all."

"As far as I'm concerned, my father died twenty-five years ago when he walked out of my life."

His eyes flicked abruptly from the coffee mug to her face. "Sorry. I didn't realize when I spoke with you yesterday that he'd basically abandoned you. I just assumed...you know...that your folks had divorced."

"Well, they did eventually I suppose, because he went on to marry someone else." She paused. "And don't be sorry...please! I've managed to put all that out of my life."

"Until yesterday."

It was her turn to stare down at her coffee, still untouched.

After a moment, he said, "I guess that explains your reluctance to get involved."

Reluctance? How does refusal *sound?*

He went on. "But unfortunately, the past has reared its ugly head, as the saying goes. Nick and Molly are your family now."

Tess raised her head. "I haven't had a family for several years, Mr. Malone. At least, not the family most people mean. My mother spent most of her life after my father left us in and out of psychiatric hospitals until her death. When I was fourteen my guardian applied for legal custody."

"Call me Alec—please." He reached across the table and placed his hand on hers.

Startled by the sudden contact, Tess quickly pulled hers away.

"Look, I'm sorry about what happened but it's got nothing to do with Nick and Molly. They may not seem like family to you, but they're your flesh and blood."

"Half siblings," she muttered.

"Half is more than enough," he said, lowering his voice. "I think I should fill you in on some of what the kids have gone through these past few weeks. So, enjoy your latte and listen up."

Not wanting to know, yet accepting that she needed to, Tess reached for her drink.

"I guess by now Walker has given you the details of the accident—hasn't he?"

She shook her head. "I haven't spoken to him directly yet. I just got the letter on Thursday and yesterday..."

Alec pursed his lips in disgust. "Yeah. The kids turned up on your doorstep. Walker could've handled the whole damn thing with a bit more sensitivity, but that's not his style. Anyway, Richard and Gabriela—his wife—were killed when their car went off a mountain road outside Boulder. That was the end of March."

"The twenty-eighth," Tess said.

He nodded. "The police investigation didn't turn up anything—you know, like drugs or alcohol—and concluded Richard had lost control of the car for some reason. Maybe to avoid an animal. It happened at night and it was snowing."

Tess blew an audible sigh. She wished he'd get to the point, rather than dwell on an accident scene she'd rather not envision.

"Okay, sorry. I'm wandering. Bad habit of mine. Some trucker found the car the next morning and called the police. Apparently both kids had sleepovers that night and didn't find out until afternoon, when police finally tracked them down. Boulder County Child Protective Services—where I work—got involved as soon as they learned there was no next of kin. Both kids went to the same foster home but that's a temporary arrangement. I've done my damnedest to find a place that'll take both of them, but so far haven't been able to." He hunched forward, wrapping two large hands around his half-empty mug of coffee.

"When I first met Nick and Molly, they still had that shocked appearance most trauma victims have. Ashen-faced with haunted eyes. They were passive, almost apathetic in their grief. Clutching one another and not really speaking to anyone else for the first week. Friends of the family and some neighbors made funeral arrangements on Walker's instructions. He's the family lawyer."

An expression of such contempt crossed his face that Tess had to comment. "What is it between you and Jed Walker? On the phone yesterday you made some negative comment about him, too."

"It's a long story and it's personal so I guess I'd better stick to the facts here. Until a week ago, Walker didn't know you even existed." He paused, adding, "Which means, of course, that you weren't mentioned in the will."

"I'd have been more than surprised if I had been."

His eyes fixed on hers a moment longer before he continued. "Right. So when the kids learned about you, they saw you as a lifeline. Someone to keep them together."

Dry-mouthed, Tess sipped the dregs of her latte and searched frantically for the response she knew he was waiting for. *C'mon girl. Pretend you're negotiating a price for an ad campaign. He's a social worker from Colorado. How hard can it be to convince him the kids are better off where they are?*

"You have to understand—"

"Oh, I do," he interrupted. "For twenty-five years you've lived under the impression that Richard Wheaton was gone for good. In less than forty-eight hours you discover that not only has he just recently died, but he's also left behind two children who happen to be your half brother and sister. Who *also* happen to be minors."

Tess frowned. Was he implying she was legally bound? "I don't think there's a law, is there? That I have to take them in?"

Alec leaned back against his chair. Tess winced at the pitying look he flashed her.

"No," he said, his voice so low she had to lean forward to hear. "I doubt it. Although I think there's definitely a moral responsibility."

"If they need money," she rushed to say, "I can certainly help with that."

He shook his head from side to side. The pitying look shifted to one of utter despair. As if, she thought, he'd given up on her.

"They have money, too. The estate is worth quite a lot. Another reason why they need family to supervise things, rather than some hotshot lawyer like Jed Walker."

"Then..."

"They need a *family,* Tess. They need to feel part of something. Their whole lives have been blown apart. Molly's only six years old."

Tess stiffened. "I was barely eight when my father left. I know what it feels like."

"But you had a mother."

"A mentally ill mother. I practically raised myself."

He blew out a mouthful of air and forked his fingers through his hair, making it stand up in thick clumps. "We're getting off track here. The point of the matter is that unless you intervene—become their legal guardian—those two kids will be split up and could eventually lose each other completely. Molly has a good chance of being adopted, but Nick…few people are willing to take on a boy just entering his teens."

Exactly what Nick had said, Tess realized. Still, she couldn't let the fact influence her. The matter had to be settled. She straightened up, ready for the negotiation. "Look," she began. "About six months ago I was promoted to Vice President of Marketing at the company where I work. It's a demanding job. I work basically anywhere from ten to twelve hours a day. I take work home and spend most weekends working."

She paused to let that register, but he didn't look impressed. "I couldn't physically be there for them, much less emotionally. Frankly, they'd be better off in a family context, even if an adoptive one."

"Family context?" He sneered. "Sounds like something out of a sociology textbook."

Tess felt her face heat up, but decided to play her next card. "I'd be willing to visit once or twice a year."

"Wonderful. That should really keep the family context concept alive and kicking."

"There's no need for sarcasm. I thought we were trying to negotiate something here. To nail down a deal."

Alec rubbed a hand over his face and groaned. "Omigod, you really do see it that way, don't you?"

She had a sense of floundering in deep water. It was an

unfamiliar feeling—that she might be handling the matter all wrong—and she couldn't think of a smart comeback.

"Doesn't it occur to you," he went on, "that sometimes we have to give things up for the sake of others? That we have to put on hold our own dreams so that we can help out someone else?"

Tess drew a blank. Was he talking about her or himself? "Are you asking me—"

"To give up some of that time. Yes! A good nanny can manage the daily routines, but take off one day a week and the weekends."

Blood pounded in her ears. "I can't possibly do that," Tess said. "My job is all I have."

The persuasion in his face vanished. He shook his head sadly. "God," he said in a low voice. "I'm so very sorry for you. Your own childhood experience has obviously made it impossible for you to look at this situation another way."

Tess bristled at the pity in his voice. "Apparently you are unable to view this in any other way yourself." And that, Tess realized, pretty much ended the conversation.

NICK TURNED off the television as soon as they entered the condo. He took one look at them and slumped back into the couch cushions. Guessing, Alec figured, that no decision had been made. Or no *deal*, as Tess would have put it. He felt sick at the thought of breaking the news to the kids, but then realized at once that he wasn't going to give up so easily. Their return flight to Denver wasn't until four o'clock the next day. He still had a little more than twenty-four hours to convince Tess Wheaton it was in her best interests to basically rearrange her whole life.

Yeah, right. In spite of her damn good looks, she was definitely no pushover. Not as soft inside as she appeared on the out. And no wonder, given the childhood snapshot she'd shown him. Still, that was no excuse for shirking one's duty to family. That was something he himself had finally learned, after a rocky adolescence and reality-checking career in the armed forces. The one thing you could count on at the end of a long hard day—whether your job was slugging it out in a factory or dropping bombs for NATO—was family. So maybe Tess Wheaton didn't know that yet, but there was no reason why she couldn't learn.

"Okay, guys," he said, hoping his voice didn't sound as hollow as it felt. "Ready to hit the arcades?" He saw Tess frown, not knowing what he meant. Maybe afraid she'd have to get involved in yet another project. Just itching to turn that laptop back on again. He felt a surge of anger, but stifled it. That wasn't the way he'd win the battle.

"Before we went out for coffee," he explained, "I told Nick I'd take him and Molly to play some games."

She looked blank.

"You know," Alec explained. "Computer games. Shoot-outs and all that."

"Oh, those things," she said, dismissing them with a slight upturning of lip.

For a second, Alec wondered if he was on the right track with his idea to get her back to Colorado. She didn't know kids at all. Except for the offer of frozen strawberry yogurt, she'd struck out completely. And even that had been more of a walk than a real hit. Maybe she wasn't cut out for the role of surrogate parent. She definitely didn't look the part. Her slender, tall frame, jet hair and dramatic green eyes suggested a fashion model rather than the shrewd businesswoman she must be to make the executive echelon at her age.

Nick was on his feet and halfway to the door before Alec had a chance to remind him about returning his empty plate to the kitchen area. He went back to the couch and got Molly's half-eaten sandwich and pop can, too. Eager to please, Alec realized. Wanting to get something out of the trip to Chicago, even if only a couple of hours in a games arcade. Before he had to go back to Boulder and face a bloody awful future. Resentment against Tess flowed through him. *I'm not giving up yet.*

"Coming, Molly?" Alec asked.

She was sprawled against the cushions. Her face, usually rosy-cheeked, was pale against the navy-blue-and-white-striped fabric. "I'm tired," she said.

Alec glanced across at Tess, hovering near the kitchen counter. He passed her what he hoped was a meaningful look and finally she got it.

"Molly can stay and have a nap on my bed, if she wants."

Generous of you. "Okay, Molly, catch forty winks. When we get back, there's dinner out and maybe a movie."

The small face broke into a heartbreaking smile. How could Tess not be moved by that wattage, he asked himself? But when he turned his head her way, he saw that she was raising the lid on her laptop. Alec sighed. *Twenty-four hours.* He hoped he was up to the job.

"WHAT ARE forty winks, Tess?" Molly asked as soon as the door closed behind Nick and Alec.

Tess pressed the On button of her computer. "It's an old expression, meaning to take a short nap. People don't say it very much anymore."

"Except Alec," giggled Molly. "He says lots of funny things."

"I bet," murmured Tess as she clicked open her file. Then she looked across the room. "I thought you were sleepy."

"Aren't you going to tuck me in?"

"For a nap?"

Molly struggled up and perched on the edge of the couch. "Someone always tucked me in whenever I got into bed." Her voice trembled.

Tess had a sudden flash who that someone must have

been. Her mother or father. Personally, she couldn't recall either one of her parents doing that for her. But Mavis had, when she'd moved in with her. For at least the whole first year. "All right," she said, minimizing the window on the laptop screen. "Tuck-in time!"

Molly giggled again. "Is that like nap time?"

Tess shrugged. "I guess."

"You say funny things, too. Like Alec."

That name overrode the mild pleasure at being called funny. Tess motioned toward the bedroom. "C'mon, then."

Molly followed her into the bedroom and was on the bed before Tess had the comforter pulled back. When the small dark head hit the pillow, Tess said, "Okay, how does tuck-in go?"

Molly grinned. "You really don't know anything about kids, do you?"

"Who said that?"

"Alec did, at the sub place. He said we had to give you some time and space 'cause you didn't know anything about kids."

Tess sniffed. "Huh. And I suppose he's an expert, having a hundred of them at home himself."

Molly's laugh rang out. "He's not even married, silly!"

"That's not surprising," Tess muttered under her breath. "So now you're tucked in, I'll go do some work."

"Wait!" Molly's smile disappeared. "You're not finished yet."

"I'm not?"

A shake of raven curls. "Nope. First you kiss me, then you sit for a few minutes until I feel sleepy."

Okay, Tess. You can do this. Shouldn't take more than another five minutes.

She sat on the side of the bed and leaned over to kiss Molly on the cheek. The girl's eyelids fluttered as she popped a thumb into her mouth. She must have taken in Tess's expression for she pulled it out long enough to say,

"It's okay. I'm giving it up later, when things are back to normal."

Tess couldn't help but smile. "A good idea," she murmured.

Molly nodded. She withdrew the thumb again. "It was Alec's. He said as long as I'm not sucking it when I'm walking down the aisle, I'll be okay. I don't know what he means but if he says it's okay—"

"It must be," Tess agreed. In spite of the reminder that Alec was, once again, proven to be such a superhero, she had to admit he obviously knew more about kids than she did.

The thumb was returned and Molly closed her eyes. Tess stared down at the heart-shaped face, small and delicate against the oversized pillow. She was a beautiful little girl, she thought. They both had Richard Wheaton's thick, dark and curly hair and bright-green eyes. For a moment, she wondered what else they shared in common.

Tess waited while Molly fidgeted restlessly, getting comfortable. She reached out a hand to brush back a tendril of hair from Molly's forehead and began to gently stroke the smooth skin in a circular pattern. When she pulled her hand away before getting up to leave, Molly's eyes fluttered open.

She withdrew her thumb just enough to be able to say, "Daddy does that, too."

Tess froze. She had a sudden memory of lying in a bed herself, someone bending over and stroking her brow. Had that been Richard? Or was her memory playing tricks on her?

Molly fidgeted some more, then Tess resumed the stroking until the girl was fast asleep.

"I'M STUFFED," announced Molly, plunking her fork onto the plate of half-eaten pasta. She leaned forward to ask, in a dramatic whisper, "Do they do doggie bags here?"

Tess laughed, catching Alec's startled expression out of the corner of her eye. She wanted to make some gibe about having a sense of humor after all, but sensed it might spoil the neutral ambience of the evening so far.

Dinner at the funky Italian restaurant she and Mavis had discovered years ago had been a success. Her first of the day, she thought, and was surprised how that pleased her. Even Nick had shown—though not verbally—obvious enjoyment of the noisy restaurant as waitstaff and cooks hollered orders back and forth. The eclectic array of items decorating the walls, along with the clotheslines strung from wall to wall and festooned with photographs of various celebrities who'd dined there, had been the subject of most of the dinner talk.

"They do doggie bags," Tess replied. "Believe me. I've taken many home from here."

When the bill arrived she and Alec had a brief debate over who was paying. He insisted that his expense account would cover it, but Tess was skeptical.

Nick and Molly were busily examining some of the decor on their way to the door when the waitress returned with change.

"You have a nice family," she remarked.

Tess felt her face redden but Alec acted as though he hadn't heard. As they walked out behind the kids, she had the odd sensation of being part of a group. Although the feeling didn't take long to evaporate.

Out on the sidewalk, Molly and Nick were already bickering. Tess grit her teeth. She didn't have the faintest idea how to get them to stop and suspected her impulse to scream would be deemed totally inappropriate.

"It's been a long day for them," Alec said in her right ear.

"Hasn't it for all of us?"

"Yes, but they're only kids. This is how they deal with

stress." He paused a beat before asking, "What do you do about it?"

She shot him a questioning look.

"Stress," he repeated.

"Sometimes I go for a run—if the weather's good."

"Never felt inclined to snap at people?"

She stiffened at the indulgent smile in his face.

"No. Why should I? Sometimes the orders I give out are a bit more...brusque."

"Ah, well. I suppose when you're at the top of the heap, there's no objection to...*orders.*"

Tess found his grin irritating. Why was he always trying to bait her? What had she ever done to him? Self-pity surged through her. She knew what it felt like to be abandoned.

"What time will you be picking up the children tomorrow?"

The grin vanished. "I...uh...I thought maybe I'd come round early. Bring breakfast with me."

"If you like," she said and, turning her back to walk up the steps to the condo, heard him say good-night to Nick and Molly.

"I'll see you two at breakfast, okay?"

"Aren't you staying here, too, Alec? We were supposed to watch videos."

For a tense second Tess froze on the steps, afraid one of the children would ask if he could, but fortunately Alec quickly said, "No, I've got a hotel room near the airport. And I think everyone's far too tired for videos tonight, Molly."

Relieved, Tess continued on inside, holding the door open while the children waved to Alec as he climbed into a taxi. Then they turned and walked, slump-shouldered with disappointment, toward Tess.

Once upstairs, Nick sullenly set to making up his bed on the couch. Molly didn't ask to be tucked in, but lay silently staring up at Tess, her unblinking eyes tracking her every move until Tess switched off the light. She made for the bathroom and a hot shower, happy to have the day come to an end at last. She just wished she felt better about their leaving the next day.

CHAPTER FOUR

SOBS TORE INTO the quiet night, wrenching Tess from sleep. She sat up, disoriented, searching the darkness for a familiar landmark. She found one almost at once—the pale marine glow from her laptop monitor on the table beside her.

She'd fallen asleep in the easy chair opposite the couch. The draft of a report lay strewn on the floor at her feet and the shape now rising from the dark space occupied by the couch must be Nick.

They both hit the bedroom door at the same time. Tess had left one of the bedside lamps on when she'd said goodnight to Molly and was glad she had. Otherwise, she and Nick could have crashed into the bed, frightening even more an already distraught Molly.

"I want my mommy and daddy," she cried. She was sitting huddled in the center of the bed, wiping at her eyes with both fists.

Tess reached Molly's side first and bent over to wrap an arm around her shoulders. But Molly pushed her arm away with a strength belying her delicate frame. "I want Nick," she wailed, her voice pitching to near hysteria.

Nick crawled up the bed from the end where he'd been standing and pulled Molly against him. Tess stood back, watching brother and sister in a scene that must have occurred many times since their parents' death.

"Shhh! It's okay Molly. Just another bad dream. I'm here."

"Don't leave me, Nick. Promise you won't leave me," she sobbed, tucking her head into the crook of his shoulder.

He lowered his face to the top of her head and murmured, "I won't leave you, I promise."

He was still comforting her, repeating those words over and over, when Tess left the room, softly closing the door behind them. She returned to the chair and sagged into it, covering her face with her hands. Thinking. Remembering again the day her father walked out, leaving her behind. Did she seriously think she could do the same?

As soon as he walked in the door, Alec sensed that a change had taken place. He couldn't put his finger on it, because everyone seemed just as subdued as they'd been when he'd left last night. Molly didn't rush to greet him and Nick was blasé about the box of Krispy Kreme doughnuts Alec was holding, along with two large coffees and a bottle of orange juice.

Tess was tidying up things at the kitchen counter and, in spite of dark circles beneath her eyes, gave him what could have passed for a friendly greeting in the real world. A spark of indignation fired deep inside Alec as he wondered if her improved mood had anything to do with the fact that they'd all be out of her life in a few short hours. Or maybe he was ticked off because the greeting wasn't quite as friendly as he'd have liked it. He dismissed the notion at once. Wanting to establish a warmer relationship with the woman was natural, given his objective of bringing her around to taking the kids. It was just that a small part of him—a part he was unable to ignore the more he was in Tess's presence—wanted her to like him.

"Hi," she said. "We had cereal, but it was first thing this morning."

Alec set the purchases down on the counter and looked across the room at the two kids, huddled together on the couch. Molly was sucking her thumb and Nick looked as though he'd been up most of the night. He glanced back at Tess. Matter of fact, they all did.

"What's happening here? You all look like zombies."

Tess managed a wan smile. "We didn't get much sleep."

He frowned, but waited for her to continue.

"Molly had a nightmare and Nick spent a long time getting her back to sleep."

Alec wondered what Molly would do when Nick wasn't around. Resisting the thought, he shoved it aside at once. Part of him wanted to blame Tess, who stood there, calm and detached. As if she didn't hold the solution to all their problems. But he knew that was unfair. She'd made a successful life for herself and, even though it wasn't one he envied in any way, he couldn't fault her for being reluctant to change it. Still...

"These look good," Tess said, opening the box of doughnuts.

Alec bet she'd never tasted one. He watched her plop one on a plate, lick her fingers and pick up one of the coffees.

"Thanks for the treats," she said and wandered to the easy chair. "Better get one before I eat them all," she warned the kids. They stared at her with the same open-mouthed surprise that Alec had. "I don't *always* eat granola," she said by way of explanation.

Molly was the first to bounce up and run to the counter. Alec second-guessed her request for juice and poured a glass. Nick was a bit slower rising to the bait, suspecting what the treats were all about, but eventually sauntered to the counter and deposited two doughnuts on his plate.

"Hey!" Molly gave a weak protest, not really minding.

"Growing boy," Alec said and winked at Nick, provoking a semblance of a smile. He retrieved his own coffee and perched on a bar stool with it.

"No doughnut?" Tess commented.

"Have to watch my waistline," he said, suppressing a

grin at her chagrined expression. So, she'd taken one to be a good sport. Great show of unanimity, he thought, even if it was completely meaningless.

He sipped slowly on his coffee, trying not to be too obvious about his study of her. She was a ringer for Molly, but her skin coloring was paler. Molly had inherited her Italian mother's olive tones while Nick, with his father's paler skin and mother's chestnut hair, was a different blend. He wondered if Tess's iron will and fierce determination was from her father or her mother. Whatever, he just hoped she could be bent.

When everyone had finished eating, Alec got off the stool and said, "How would you two like to go down to the lakeshore, check out the park?"

"We went there yesterday," Nick said. The look in his face defied a suggestion to return.

Alec shrugged. "Okay. What about a movie?"

"At ten in the morning?"

Alec figured the kid was doing his best to rein in his attitude. He had guessed where Alec was going with this and wanted none of it. No amount of entertainment and junk food could make up for the hard fact that he and Molly were heading back home—mission unaccomplished.

"What time does your flight leave?"

Startled, Alec turned sharply toward Tess. *Jeez.* Did she have to be so blunt about it? No subtle whisper to him when they were alone?

All eyes in the room were riveted on her face. At least, Alec noticed, she had the grace to seem embarrassed.

"Because I—I've been thinking maybe I should go back with you. Just, you know, to make sure the kids are settled and check out this Jed Walker. Make sure he's doing right by the kids." Flushing, she stared down into her coffee cup.

Alec was speechless. He tried to process what she'd said. Not a commitment to anything, that was for certain. He wondered what had made her change her mind. Whatever it had been, luck was now on his side. The door had opened a crack and she'd stuck her foot through. And he'd do his damnedest to make sure the door was wide-open very soon.

Molly was thrilled, unaware of the nuances of what Tess had said. "I can show you my room and my pet hamster."

Nick was more doubtful. "How do you know you can get a flight?" he asked.

"I can try." She looked over at Alec.

"I'll call the airline right away," he said before she could change her mind. Fifteen minutes later, thanks to a last-minute cancellation, she was confirmed. "We should be at the airport by two, at the latest," he said.

She rose from her chair. "Then I'd better get busy with the phone calls I need to make."

But she stood there, as if the reality of what she'd promised had just hit home. Alec quickly filled in the gap. "Guys, how about if we go for a walk while Tess makes her phone calls and gets ready?"

Molly skipped around the room while Nick, feigning indifference, shuffled toward the door.

Alec couldn't blame him for being skeptical about the whole thing, but the kid didn't realize what an opportunity Tess had given them. All they had to do now was to persuade her—somehow—to *stay* in Boulder. Not an impossible task, Alec decided. But, surveying the upscale loft that represented her success as he joined Molly and Nick at the door, definitely a challenging one.

As SOON AS the door closed behind them, Tess sank back into the chair and trembled all over. The emotional drain of last night had ceded, and she couldn't help thinking that she could just as easily have made a different decision. She could have simply accompanied them to the airport and waved a goodbye with promises to visit soon. In time, she knew that squirm of guilt inside would have disappeared and she could resume her normal life again with a vow to keep in touch.

She'd made her move—no turning back now. She decided that she'd make it clear from the start that her trip to Colorado was only a visit, to ensure the children were dealt with fairly by the lawyer and the authorities. And surely there must be one family in all of Boulder willing to foster two children!

She got up and headed for her computer to e-mail Carrie, but realized a phone call would be necessary after all so that Carrie could reschedule an early Monday meeting. She started the conversation off with an apology for calling on a Sunday afternoon, then explained what she'd decided to do.

"No kidding," Carrie kept saying until Tess's teeth ached from clenching.

When Tess had eventually finished what she'd chosen as her official story—estranged father dead, leaving behind two children who were her half siblings—Carrie had jumped to the ending. "So instead of going on a cruise next week, you're heading for Denver?"

"Something like that, assuming my vacation leave is still valid."

"It is unless you canceled it when you canceled the cruise."

She hadn't. Was that an intentional oversight on her part? An unconscious desire to get away, if not with Doug Reed, then by herself?

After Tess relayed the rest of her requests, Carrie asked, "Will you be in Colorado the whole two weeks of your vacation?"

"Heavens, no. I hope to finish what I have to do in less than a week."

There was a slight pause before Carrie asked, "And will you be bringing the kids back here to Chicago?"

Tess closed her eyes. She hadn't come up with an official

story for this part. "I really don't know how it's going to play out at this stage," she said.

"Yeah?" Carrie's voice was full of disbelief. "But obviously you're their next of kin so…"

"It's not that simple, Carrie," Tess snapped back. "Look, I've got to go now. You can get hold of me on my cell phone if you need to."

"Sure, Tess. Say hi to the kids for me and have a good trip."

Tess hung up, drained from the questions that she knew were merely a beginning. She decided not to phone Mavis until her answers were more practiced. Mavis would be a tougher interrogator. Instead, she finished other calls, leaving messages to cancel a dental appointment and reschedule a massage, which she figured she'd need once she returned from Colorado. Then she tidied up and did a load of laundry. When the buzzer rang she was finally on the phone with Mavis, who had just returned from her visit to Sophie.

"Hold on, Mavis. They're back—I'll just buzz them in." Tess muttered on her way to the intercom. She'd hoped to have the call with Mavis finished. When she returned to the phone, she said, "Look, can I call you when I get there? I'll know more by then what's going on."

"But, Tess love, what's going to happen to the wee ones?"

A vision of Nick came to mind. "They're not so wee, Mavis. At least, Nick isn't. He's just turned thirteen and looks as though he'll be tall."

"Like your father."

"Yes, I suppose. At any rate, I'll see if they can be fostered out to the same family. This Alec Malone said—"

"Tess! What's this talk about fostering? You're the next of kin. I don't understand why you're blathering on about settling them in and so on. You should be going there to pack them all up and bring them back to Chicago."

"To stay where?"

A slight hesitation. "If not with you, then—"

"Mavis, please. Be realistic. There's no way you could manage. Not that I don't appreciate your offer but—"

"Well, I was going to say you could all move in with me. Sell off that pricey condo and live mortgage free. You'll be inheriting my house, anyway."

Tess closed her eyes. God, this was getting complicated. "Mavis, I don't want a commute every day. You know my hours. That's why I decided to live close to downtown in the first place. And this place isn't appropriate for children."

There was a heavy sigh from the other end. "Sounds to me like you're trying to convince yourself you're doing the right thing here, Tess."

"I *am* doing the right thing."

Another sigh. "Not by a long shot, my girl. But hopefully you'll work that out once you get to Colorado."

Tess recognized an impasse when she saw one. There was no way that Mavis would see her side of it. She was too old-fashioned and had never understood the importance of a career to Tess. "As I said, I'll call you when I get there—let you know where I'm staying."

"You do that, love. And Tess?"

"Yes?"

"Don't be so quick to write those kiddies out of your life. They may be just what you've been looking for."

"What I've been looking for? *Two children?* Hardly."

"Not just two children. Your brother and sister." She paused. "A family."

Tess set the receiver down as the others walked through the door. Mavis's parting words were still screaming in her head. Perhaps she had wanted a family years ago, when she could have still benefited from one. But not anymore.

Alec must have sensed something when he saw her because the first thing he said was, "Everything all right?"

"Of course," Tess replied and got up to take her laundry

out of the dryer. Molly watched her open the door to the
compact cupboard that contained her apartment-size combination washer and dryer.

"Cool," she said. "I was wondering what was in that
closet."

Alec laughed. "Didn't you think to look?"

"Oh, no," Molly said. "It would have been rude."

Tess smiled, her gaze meeting Alec's for a few seconds
longer than she'd expected. It was Nick's snicker at Molly
that brought her back to task.

"All right then," she said, quickly changing the topic
before Nick set off Molly. "Alec, why don't you get some
cold cuts and bread out for a lunch while I finish packing?"

She saw at once from his expression that he was pleased
at the way she'd diverted a potential quarrel and gave herself a mental pat on the back. She'd had lots of experience
at steering clear of hot topics and deflecting hostile attitudes
in business dealings. How much more difficult could it be
managing children?

TESS WAS FORCED to rethink that question once they were
settling into seats on the plane. Both children wanted a
window seat, which might have worked if all four were
sitting together. But Tess was seated way at the back in the
center while the others were in a row of three seats on the
side. Fortunately, that left Alec to settle the seating dispute.
She contentedly leafed through a magazine until a flight
attendant came by after the plane had finished climbing to
its cruise altitude and asked if she'd like to join her family.

Tess shot her a blank look before noticing that Alec was
craning his head to the back of the plane.

"Your husband said you might like to join them and
we've got a no-show in the row behind. I think with some
rearranging we can seat two of you in one row and two
behind. Would that be all right?"

"Uh, sure." Tess followed the hostess to the front of the

plane. As she took the seat next to Alec, Tess flushed when the hostess said, "We can't have a family separated like that."

Molly swiveled round to flash a quick grin at Tess before getting back to her crayons and coloring book while Nick, plugged in to the audio system, didn't even notice she'd moved.

"When I found out there was a vacant seat in this row, I asked if you could move up. Hope you don't mind."

Tess, certain the reference to *husband* had been an assumption of the flight attendant's, said, "No, no. I hate the claustrophobic feel of the center section anyway."

"Me, too. My knees seem to be propping up my chin whenever I get stuck there."

Conversation stopped there as drinks and snacks were served. Their seats were so close Tess figured she might as well have been sitting on his lap. His thigh pressed against hers and every time she went to lean on the armrest, his arm was already there. What bothered her the most, she hated to admit, was the unexpected tingling sensation that shot down her arm when her hand accidentally landed on top of his.

Until now, interaction between them had been confrontational and the almost intimate proximity was suddenly stifling. Tess had never been good at small talk so she was relieved when he didn't seem bothered by the silence.

But when the snack trays were removed, he turned his head toward her and asked, "This may seem too personal, but is there a man in your life right now?"

Tess stared at him, not sure at first what he was saying. Then she felt heat rising up into her face. "You're right, it is. Why do you ask?"

"Sorry to be blunt, but it may be important should you—" he lowered his voice "—decide to apply for legal guardianship."

Her first reaction was to check if the children had heard.

Then she hissed, "I hardly think this is the time or place to be having this conversation."

He had the grace to redden. "You're right. Sorry. I guess I'm just trying to find out if there's any chance at all—"

"I made it clear why I was coming. To see that they're settled."

He leaned his head back against the seat and closed his eyes. After a moment, he turned to her and said, "We'll be seeing a lot of one another over the next few days and it makes sense for us to be as amicable as possible with each other. Doesn't it? Even if we're both coming at this problem from totally different perspectives?"

"Fine...Alec." Tess raised her tray and rummaged in her handbag for the paperback she'd brought to read on the plane. After reading the first sentence three times, she gave up. Swiveling her head back to him, she added, "For your information—not that it's relevant—there *is* someone in my life and I was supposed to be going on a cruise with him this very week."

"Oh...well...sorry, I guess this has altered your plans slightly."

"Slightly," she repeated with emphasis. The fact that she was misleading him nagged for only a second. And the arrival of Nick and Molly certainly had altered her plans! Plus, there was always the remote possibility that she and Doug might get back together again...someday.

"So this guy you're seeing—what did he say when you told him about Nick and Molly?"

Tess stared down at the novel on her lap. "I haven't told him yet. He's been busy and we haven't had a chance to talk." She could feel his eyes boring through the side of her face, but didn't have the courage to turn his way.

Finally he said, "Sounds as though your relationship might not be the type to accommodate a couple of youngsters."

That really got to her. "What gives you the right to draw inferences about my personal life?"

"Sorry again. I just keep puttin' my foot in, don't I?"

If his grin was meant to disarm, it failed. "You're no backwoods hick. Please don't insult my intelligence by pretending to be."

That got to him, she noticed with some triumph. Instant sobriety fell over his face like steel mesh. When his eyes flicked back to her, Tess saw by their expression that she'd pushed him further than she'd intended.

"My job is to ensure that those two kids are safe, healthy and reasonably happy. It's a tall order, given their circumstances. If you can't grasp the inarguable fact that you're their best option here, then…I'm sorry." His eyes swept over her, dismissively. As if she were some kind of strange and repulsive insect. "So," he went on, "we'll agree not to discuss this again until you've had a chance to check things out for yourself. Okay?"

Feeling suddenly graceless, she could only shrug, wondering how she always ended up faring so badly in their talks. He turned his head aside to peer out the window, then suddenly swung back to her.

"One last thing. I'm curious—did you have a chance to talk to Nick about your father?"

Blood roared into her head. Her tongue flapped uselessly against the palate of her dry mouth. Tess was certain her eyes were going to eject from their orbs.

But the expression in his own face was inscrutable. After the slightest pause, he murmured, "I didn't think so," and shifted his gaze back to the window.

Tess waited until the pounding against her rib cage eased up before silently slipping out of her seat and making her way to the washroom. When she bolted the door behind her, she plunked onto the seat and burst into tears.

HE ALMOST EXTENDED an arm to stop her and apologize again for behaving like such an insensitive jerk. But his anger hadn't subsided enough and besides, he knew he'd crossed into the kind of territory where apologies counted for little. The problem was, she was in denial about everything. And Alec knew from hard experience that you didn't reach people in that state with kid gloves. Usually they needed a jolt. Like dumping a bucket of cold water over the head. He figured he'd just done that—figuratively—to Tess Wheaton. His regret at having to do so was minimal compared to his worry about what was going to happen to Nick and Molly.

Nick unexpectedly craned his head around from the seat ahead. His earphones were still clamped on but Alec hoped the kid hadn't been tracking their conversation. He managed a smile and gave Nick a thumbs-up sign. The boy responded with a wobbly grin, confirming Alec's suspicion that he probably had picked up some of what had been going on behind him.

He sighed, knowing that the quarrel had been more his fault than Tess's. If only he could learn to be more subtle. Surely he could have extracted all the information he wanted from her without raising hackles. If he'd taken the time to cultivate her, he might even have brought her round to at least acknowledging another point of view. Malone closed his eyes and sank back against the headrest. It all boiled down to time—and there just wasn't enough of it.

TESS PEERED OUT the window at the desolate terrain below. At least, to a big-city resident, what appeared empty, vast and very brown countryside. According to the pilot, they'd be landing at Denver International Airport in fifteen minutes. Could have fooled me, she thought. I don't even see a city down there, much less the state capitol. Just a featureless landscape patchworked by peculiar dark-green circles and squares.

When she'd finally returned to their seats, she saw with

relief that there had been a change. Nick was sitting with Alec and the window seat next to Molly was waiting for her. Molly gave an excited wave, which made Tess feel even more miserable.

"You were gone a long time," the little girl said. "I was worried. Nick wanted to talk to Alec and I was going to take the window seat 'cause it was my turn, but I thought you might want it 'cause you've never been to Denver before." Taking a quick gulp of air, Molly added, "Have you?"

Tess shook her head and smiled. "Thank you." When she settled in, the seat belt warning flashed. She helped Molly buckle up and then surveyed the place she planned to visit for the next few days. Not exactly the Caribbean, she was thinking.

Okay, get real, Tess. You weren't going on that cruise anyway. As for Doug…he hasn't garnered a second's thought since you saw him at work on Friday. Two days ago. God. Seems more like a week. Or a lifetime.

"Tess?"

"Hmm?" Tess turned from the window to Molly.

"We'll all be staying at our house, won't we?"

"Our house?" Tess drew a blank, then caught her drift just as Molly was explaining.

"Where Nick and I live…used to live…you know, before…" Her voice trailed off. Tess's instinctive paranoia mode switched on. Had Alec Malone put Molly up to this? "I guess Mr. Malone and I'll decide where to stay when we get there. Okay?"

Molly looked doubtful. "It's just that my hamster is at the house where I'm staying in town and if we go back home, then I'd like to get her. She must be missing me a lot."

"What's her name?"

"Squiggly." Molly flashed a gap-toothed grin. "When I first got her, she was squiggling all over my lap and in and out of my shirt so I got the giggles. Daddy said we were a good match because she was squiggly and I was giggly. That's how she got her name.'' Her high-pitched voice lapsed into silence again, lost in sudden remembrance.

While Tess, who couldn't recall the last time Richard Wheaton had made *her* giggle, turned her attention back to the window.

THE SUN BEAT DOWN on them as they waited for a chance to cross the lanes of traffic leading into the terminal. Shuttle minivans, taxis and city buses vied for space to disgorge or pick up passengers. It was a lot less congested than O'Hare, Tess noticed, but hotter.

"Anything like you expected?" Alec Malone asked as he led them toward the parking area where he'd left his car.

"Not at all. I was thinking mountains. Fir trees. Greenery. And cool air."

"This is actually a desert plain or plateau—hence all the sand and scrubby vegetation. Mountains are over there." He pointed toward the thick haze that hung over Denver in the distance. "It's not usually this hot this early, but we've had a drought in these parts for a few years and the seasons don't seem to synchronize the way they should."

Hmmm, Tess was thinking. *Something you can't control.*

He turned back to where Nick and Molly were lagging behind. "The kids are tired and it's almost dinner. Boulder's about an hour away, but if you don't mind I thought we'd stop at a service center off the highway to get a bite to eat."

"That's fine with me," Tess said. Ten minutes later they were loading their luggage into Alec's Bronco. "It's big enough," Tess mumbled, hitching up her skirt to climb into the front passenger side.

"You need a four-wheel drive here, especially in the winter," Alec said, closing the door behind her. When he came around to the driver's side, he added, "I hope you brought some casual clothes, as I suggested. Folks in Boulder are pretty laid-back and informal."

"I did. But as Mavis always told me, you never know when you'll need a skirt."

Alec grinned.

"Who's Mavis?" Molly asked.

Tess couldn't recall if she'd mentioned Mavis or not, but said, "She's my guardian."

"What's a guardian? Someone who stands on guard?"

Another sound from Nick.

Ignoring him, Tess said, "Yes, something like that. When my mother couldn't look after me anymore, Mavis became my guardian. Then she took care of me until I was an adult."

"Your mother?" Molly's voice was puzzled. "But I thought we had the same parents."

"Oh, God," moaned Nick. "You are so stupid."

"I am not!"

"Guys, we're heading for dinner right now. Cool it, okay?" Alec suggested as he steered the Bronco out of the airport area onto the highway.

Wanting Molly to understand, Tess explained, "We had the same father but our mothers were different."

"Oh. Then since we don't have a mother and father anymore, will Mavis be our guardian, too?"

"Ah jeez," muttered Nick.

"Molly, it doesn't work that way," Alec said.

He shot Tess an exasperated look as if, she thought, he wished she hadn't mentioned the whole matter in the first place.

"Well, then how about if Tess is our guardian?" Molly persisted.

Tess glanced across at Alec, whose expression read, *See what you got yourself into now?*

But in spite of the smug look on his face, Alec bailed

her out. "Why don't we save some of those questions for later, Molly? When we've eaten and after we get back to your house."

"Sure," she piped up.

Tess, half turning to the back seat, caught Molly sticking her tongue out at Nick. As she faced the front again, not wanting to get involved in what could be another dispute, she saw that Nick was gloomily staring out the window, oblivious to his little sister.

LESS THAN two hours later, the Bronco was approaching the outskirts of Boulder. They'd eaten silently and quickly at a fast-food place in a service center on the way. Watching them, Tess wondered what was going through their minds. Some anxiety, perhaps, about being in their own home again? While they were waiting for their orders, Alec had suggested that he drive them straight home. No doubt he would be relieved to drop them all off with a brief good-bye and continue on to his own place—wherever that might be—and his own life.

She bet that Molly was excited about getting her hamster back and showing Tess her old bedroom and her toys. And Nick? His face registered bland indifference, but Tess noticed that his body language told a whole other story. He had hunched over his meal and jiggled his right leg constantly until Alec jokingly told him he was cut off all cola drinks. He responded with a polite half smile but when they rose to leave and Tess brushed past him, Nick cast her a look of such contempt a shiver zipped up her spine. *Obviously no indifference or small courtesies where I'm concerned.*

The Bronco sped past the Welcome to Boulder sign and continued on the highway.

"Hey," said Molly, "aren't we going to the Sullivans'?"

"I know you want to get your hamster, Molly, but it's

getting late and Tess and I thought we should go to the house first.''

"But I wanted to show Squiggly to Tess!"

"Quit whining," Nick complained.

Tess waited for the rejoinder, but none came. From her peripheral vision, she saw Molly's forehead scrunch in a frown, but otherwise, the girl kept quiet. Tess breathed a sigh of relief. "I'll see Squiggly tomorrow, Molly. Not to worry. How far out of town is their place?" she asked Alec.

"About fifteen miles. It's on the road to Estes National Park."

"Oh? Is it in the mountains then?"

"Not quite, but pretty close."

Tess looked out the window as they bypassed Boulder. "It's not a very big place," she commented.

"Nope. It's a university town basically, but there are a few good nightspots and so on."

"Do you live there or…?"

"Yeah, I've got an apartment in town. But my sister and I share ownership of our parents' ranch, close to Lyons.'' The Bronco turned off the paved road and entered a long, gravel drive lined with trees.

"This is it," Alec said. "You won't be able to see the house until we're almost at the end of the drive, but it's in that stand of firs and aspens over to the right ahead."

"Aspens?"

"The most common deciduous tree here in Colorado is what's commonly called the trembling aspen. When the wind blows, its leaves shake and tremble, rather than flutter like regular trees."

"I see it! I see it!" Molly yelped from the rear.

The Bronco made a sharp right and there, tucked into a thicket of trees, was a blue-gray frame ranch-style house in the shape of a large L, with two smaller outbuildings behind.

Tess stared at the place where, according to Alec, her

father had spent the last fifteen years of his life. For the first time since she'd received Jed Walker's letter, the reality of her father's death struck. Until a month ago, she thought, he was here. *Alive and well. With a family of his own.*

CHAPTER FIVE

IT TOOK HIM a minute to realize what was happening. In the bustle of the Bronco doors opening and slamming shut, Alec hadn't clued in to the effect of arriving home on the other three. The silence was the first signal.

Molly no longer burbled on about showing off her room, but hung back in the drive. When Alec turned around from unlocking the front door with the key he'd obtained—after some persuasion—from Jed Walker, he noticed Nick standing at the rear of the Bronco, kicking its tire as if he had nothing better to do. Tess was leaning against the front right bumper, staring, transfixed, at the house.

At first, Alec had assumed she was silenced by its beauty, because even for the trendy suburban areas of Boulder, the house was simple but stunning. Especially the gardens around it, where native wildflowers blended in with strategically planted succulents and hardy perennials. But the pallor of her face hinted at more serious emotions than awe.

Then he swore at himself. He had been so intent on getting everyone here that he hadn't considered how they would react to seeing the place again. The kids hadn't stayed in the house since the night their parents were killed. Tess's father had disappeared twenty odd years ago and now she was confronted with the very tangible proof of his recent existence.

He didn't know how to make the moment easier for any of them, so he merely began to unpack the Bronco and let them wander in when they felt up to it. By the time he'd opened a few of the windows inside, Molly and Nick were drifting around the living room. Tess stood in the foyer, staring at the large oil painting hanging to her left.

"One of your father's," Alec commented as he came to close the front door behind her.

She seemed at a loss for words so he added, somewhat foolishly he realized in retrospect, "Recognize it?"

Her face turned slowly toward his. Her eyes were blank and her voice hollow. "Should I?" she asked.

Alec gave himself a mental kick. He looked at the painting again, avoiding her eyes. "Just that I assumed it was Molly, but I guess it could have been you, at her age."

After a moment, she murmured, "When I was her age, my father couldn't afford to paint on canvases this size. He used wood."

Then she moved past him, into the living room. Alec hesitated at the entrance to the large room that formed the short arm of the L of the house. French doors led out to a terrace that ran all along the interior and longer branch of the L. The kids had already disappeared into that wing. Checking out their rooms, he guessed. Perhaps wondering if any facsimile of their former lives would ever be possible. And probably concluding—at least from Nick's point of view—likely not.

Alec sighed. "Look," he said, getting her attention from the stone fireplace and the oil portrait of Gabriela Wheaton that hung above it. "There's something I have to tell you." He hesitated at the instant narrowing in her eyes. "Just that I have to get permission from the Sullivans—the current foster parents—for the kids to stay here with you. They know I went to bring them back but no one was certain whether or not you'd be coming, too."

"Staying *here?* I...I assumed I'd be staying at a hotel in Boulder. I thought we were coming to pick up some of their things."

"Well...uh, we could do that I suppose. I haven't really made any commitment with the kids but I've got a feeling they might want to stay here with you." He saw right away that she didn't like that idea and quickly added, "I think it would be better for them to be together in a familiar setting."

"But won't it be painful?"

"Yes, it will be. But not as painful as going back to the Sullivans', wondering how much longer they'll be together."

She wiped a hand across her face. "I'm afraid if we all stay here together that...that certain expectations will be raised."

Of course they will, he was thinking. And if you're the decent person I think you are—under that executive skin—you'll make sure those kids won't be let down.

He watched her back toward the front door, as if making her escape. *Slow down, Malone. You're pushing her into a corner. She has to work things out for herself.*

"We could ask the kids what they want to do, but let them know right up-front that it's only going to be a temporary arrangement."

She was shaking her head. Wishing she'd never agreed to come? he wondered. "I'll ask them right now," he said before she had a chance to kill the idea. He swiftly made for the hall leading to the rest of the house, sensing her eyes tracking him out of the room.

As he'd suspected, Molly was all for the plan and Nick saw through it at once. "Aren't we just putting off the inevitable?" he mumbled.

Alec crouched beside the bed where Nick sat. "Look fella, you have a point. But it doesn't have to be that way. You could get to know her—bring her around to the idea of having a family again."

A faint scowl crossed Nick's face. "She's not into kids."

He was no fool, Alec had to admit. And he was justifiably cynical. "But she may eventually come round to the notion of having two kids in her life. Think about how you can help her change her mind," Alec said quietly as he stood up.

"Nick," Molly said, placing a small hand on her brother's knee. "What's Alec talking about? Do we have to go back to the Sullivans' after all?"

Alec headed for the door, afraid he'd be tempted to swoop her up into his arms and promise she'd never have to leave. He heard Nick whisper, "No, Mol. Not yet anyway." Then, in a more resigned voice, "Okay. We'll stay here until she decides."

"What about Squiggly?"

"We'll get her in the morning," Alec turned around to say. On the way to the living room, he mentally repeated Nick's last words. *Until she decides.*

Not Tess, but she. He couldn't help wonder how long the thirteen-year-old would be content to let others control his future.

TESS HAD NO IDEA what time it was, but suspected daylight was still a long way off. She had the other twin bed in Molly's room and hadn't slept at all. In spite of her size, Molly could toss, turn, grind her teeth and snore as well as any man sleeping off a binge. You could have had the master bedroom, Tess reminded herself. And shivered again at the notion. *Sleeping in her dead father's bed.* Of course, Alec had tried to reason with her.

"It's not as if you really knew him as a father," he'd said.

Which had stung. "I had eight years of him," she'd countered angrily. "The most impressionable years of my life." And when she'd seen that look in his face, she knew he was sorry but didn't care. She didn't need his pity.

Tess rolled onto her side and stared bleakly into the dark. She shouldn't have agreed to come. Staying here with the kids merely compounded the mistake of her decision. If she'd stayed at a hotel as she'd planned, she could have kept the whole family thing at arm's length. Driven off to the airport in a few days with a friendly but casual goodbye. Instead, she could feel herself sinking into the whole mess as if she'd played some part in it all along.

She didn't know this family. She didn't want to know it. She simply wanted to go back home and continue with her life. *Yeah, right. Get real, Wheaton. It's not going to happen that easily.*

Tess swung her legs off the bed and sat up. I've got to start making some decisions of my own, she thought. Otherwise Alec Malone will manipulate me to the very place he's been trying to put me since he arrived on my doorstep in Chicago. Then he can close his case with the satisfaction of a job completed. While I...she closed her eyes, unwilling to face even the remote possibility of a future in Boulder, Colorado.

She eased off the bed, careful not to disturb Molly, though she doubted her slight movements would. Tess smiled. At least the girl was getting a good night's rest. Surprisingly, there'd been no sobbing episodes tonight. Tess had been prepared for something, but after prattling on about what they could do in the morning and getting Tess to tuck her in again, Molly had cheerfully gone to bed as if nothing painful had happened in her short life.

Perhaps Alec was right about their need for a familiar context, Tess grudgingly admitted. Molly could be sleeping well because for the first time in weeks, she's home with people she knows and trusts. *Even if one of those people will probably have to break that trust.* Tess pushed the thought aside and headed first to the bathroom, then to the kitchen for a glass of cold water.

Standing at the sink, she stared out to the terrace, lit by a moon that was almost full. The house had been carefully designed so that every room faced the terrace side of the

L and had a stunning view of the foothills and mountains in the distance. A long hallway illuminated by skylights was the artery connecting the rooms. And of course, there was art everywhere—on the walls, with sculptures and pottery on shelves and tabletops. The latter was the work of Gabriela, as Nick had nonchalantly informed Tess. She set her empty glass on the porcelain drain board and rubbed her damp fingers across her forehead.

What am I doing here? she asked herself for the umpteenth time since stepping foot in Richard Wheaton's home. Which only begged the next question—how am I going to gracefully leave? She sighed. There was no win-win here for her. That much was certain.

She turned to head back to the bedroom when a shadow appeared in the kitchen doorway. "Nick?" she whispered.

"No, it's me. Alec. I heard someone prowling around and wondered if Molly was sleepwalking."

He stepped forward until the moonlight caught him in its grasp. Tess was grateful that her own face was in shadow. Clad only in boxer shorts, he hardly represented the image of a social worker. At least, not any she'd ever known and there'd been a few in the years before and just after Mavis took her in. But then striving for a professional ideal was definitely not his style, otherwise he would never have agreed—at Nick and Molly's pleading—to stay overnight.

"Couldn't sleep?" he asked.

She shifted her eyes from the well-toned smoothness of his broad chest to his face, aware that she'd been staring. "No. Molly's a restless sleeper and I was thirsty. What's this about sleepwalking? Does she?"

"Her foster parents reported one incident, but it was her second night with them and no doubt an anomaly, rather than part of a pattern."

Well, she thought, he can *talk* like a social worker when he wants to. He didn't continue the conversation and she was tired. It was time to go back to bed, except Alec's body filled the space between the door and the hall beyond.

Finally, he said, "Thirsty? Feeling out of breath and headachey, too? Takes a few days to adjust to the altitude here. Drink lots of water."

"Right," she murmured, wondering if he ran a medical clinic on the side, too. She moved toward the door. "Guess I should get back to bed. No doubt Molly will be up early."

"No doubt."

But he didn't stand aside and when Tess was close enough, he reached out a hand to her forearm, stopping her. "Thanks for agreeing to stay a few days, Tess."

Her eyes traveled from his hand, along his arm, back to his chest and eventually settled on his face. His body radiated heat, embracing her in an unexpected intimacy that was suddenly overwhelming. When she edged away, he let go of her, averting his face slightly so that he seemed to be talking to someone behind and to her right.

"It means a lot to the kids," he went on, "and it'll make things easier for you, too, helping them go through the estate stuff. Walker seems to be in a hurry to do that, for some reason."

Tess cleared her throat, trying to focus on what was supposed to be business talk. Except the air around them sparked with an energy that she figured some madcap genie had gleefully released into the room. The skin beneath her own Joe Boxer shorts and camisole literally tingled. She'd known this man scarcely forty-eight hours, had sparred constantly with him during that time and now—for some perverse reason—the sight of him in undershorts had her in a tizz.

Annoyed at this fickle betrayal of her body, Tess purposely nudged past him into the hallway. "Good night," she said, forcing nonchalance into her voice, and without a backward glance, made her escape.

HE DIDN'T MOVE until she left the room. Then he headed for the sink and poured himself a glass of cold water. *What was that all about? A perfectly normal conversation suddenly zapped by some kind of charge.* Alec chugged the water and set the glass back on the drain board. Who was he kidding? He'd known all along it was Tess wandering about. Her tread was heavier than Molly's and Nick's room was at the far end of the hall, next to the master bedroom suite. So what crazy impulse had levitated him from the family room sofa to the kitchen?

Probably the same one that had compelled him to break more rules than usual since he met Tess Wheaton. Alec swiped a hand through his hair and scratched his scalp. *What the heck is going on, fella? Sure, you can spout all the right jargon to convince everyone that what you're doing is essentially part of your job but hey, let's be real. It's not like you offer to camp out at any other client's house to supposedly help someone over a rough spot. So get those hormones in check and go take a cold shower. But do something quick, before you ruin everything. Like Nick and Molly's best shot at having a normal life again.*

As Tess had predicted, Molly was awake at the crack of dawn and ready for breakfast.

"I don't think there'll be any food, do you?" Tess asked, yawning and rubbing her eyes at the same time. "Didn't Alec say he'd take us grocery shopping today?"

"There's usually stuff in the freezer," Molly said. "You know, like orange juice and waffles. We used to have syrup." Her voice was wistful.

Tess turned her head to look at Molly, sitting cross-legged on the twin bed across from her. An expression of profound sadness filled the small face. *She's thinking about other things they used to have, too. Like parents.*

"Okay. Give me five minutes in the shower and we'll put on our winter hats and mittens and go exploring in the deep freeze."

That brought a smile. "See," Molly said, "you can be funny, too. Like Alec."

"Whoopdeedoo!" Tess cracked, which elicited a giggle. She retrieved a robe and fresh underwear and headed for the door. The hall was still in semidarkness and the rest of the house quiet. Tess padded along the gleaming hardwood floor and stopped at the linen closet right beside the bathroom. The kids had directed her to it last night when they'd been searching for sheets and extra blankets.

It was a large, double-sided closet, the envy of any homeowner. Tess wondered what kind of wife and mother Gabriela had been. The decor of the house suggested two artistic spirits had worked together, blending simplicity, elegance and comfort. And her portrait, obviously a work of love by her husband, revealed a woman of stunning beauty. Tess pulled out a lush bath towel from the neatly stacked pile, closed the doors and went into the bathroom.

In daylight, it was even more magnificent. Most of one wall was window, looking out to an alcove of the terrace that had been partitioned off by latticed modesty panels. The centerpiece of the alcove was a miniscule waterfall of fieldstones, which spilled into a tiny pond edged with the same type of wildflowers she'd seen in the front gardens. Beyond, an expanse of field stretched toward the foothills and the shadowy peaks on the horizon. The toilet was tucked away in a corner of the room, but the round whirlpool bath and glass shower stall next to it were perched on a ceramic tiled platform, affording an even better view of the distant hills.

Tess figured it was as close to bathing outside as she'd ever been. After peeking out to ensure that the lattice framing the windows did provide privacy, Tess stepped into the shower. But her enjoyment of the bathroom's luxury was tempered by the sobering reminder that while her father had been enjoying the perks of affluence, Mavis McNaught had scrimped to pay their bills. *Keep that in mind, Tess, whenever you feel too sorry for those kids. At least they've been left with an inheritance.*

As she stepped out of the stall, there was a tap at the door.

"Tess?"

"Yes, Molly, what is it?"

"We don't have to go exploring after all. Alec got up early and drove to town to get food for breakfast. He wants to know if you're ready for coffee yet."

"Sure. Okay." Tess heaved a frustrated sigh. There seemed to be no end to Alec Malone's involvement in whatever she planned. Then, realizing the childishness of the thought, she sighed again. She'd have to stop being annoyed at everything the man did. Reaching some kind of amicable agreement with him about the kids was paramount. That, she resolved, was the main goal. And one of the most important rules of business was to always keep an eye on the goal.

She bumped into Nick as she left the bathroom.

"Sorry," he mumbled hoarsely.

He looked exhausted, Tess thought. "It's okay. Apparently breakfast is ready in the kitchen."

He peered at her from swollen eyes. "Is it even daylight yet?"

She smiled. "Just after that, I think. Molly was up early."

He nodded. "Yeah, she's always up first."

"That'll change when she's a teenager."

"Yeah. Guess so." He managed what could pass for a friendly smile and edged past Tess into the bathroom, softly closing the door behind him.

She stared at the door a second longer, thinking she could probably call the exchange an improvement, but knew it was still a long way from a conversation. By the time she dressed in jeans and a loose, long-sleeved white shirt, breakfast was well underway in the kitchen. The kids were at the round table set in front of glass sliding doors that opened onto the terrace. Alec was standing at the stove.

"Tess!" cried Molly, her full mouth spewing out bits of food. "Bacon and pancakes. With blueberries."

"Swallow first," Alec warned. He winked at Tess and pointed to a chair.

"And guess what?" Molly went on. "We found the syrup, too."

"Great," murmured Tess, wondering how anyone could be so cheerful at such an hour. She looked across the table at Nick, still in his pajamas, who was tucking steadily into a stack of pancakes. Now that's concentration, she decided, admiring his ability to just hunker down and get to business. Alec set a mug of coffee in front of her.

"The works?" he asked, spatula in hand.

"Hmm? Oh, sure," she said, catching his motion toward the pancake griddle on the stove top. "Why not? I think there's a long day ahead."

He flipped two pancakes and a rasher of bacon onto a plate and as he passed it to her, murmured, "For all of us."

Tess glanced sharply up at him, catching his more ominous interpretation of her comment. Fortunately, the kids were focused on eating and had missed it. While Tess, who'd merely been referring to an early rising, figured she might as well put her other foot in her mouth and chew on it, rather than pancakes. Some combination of her plus Alec seemed invariably to lead to misunderstanding.

Choosing the safer route of eating than talking, Tess finished her breakfast quickly. When they'd finished, Alec surprised her by asking Nick to show her around the property while he and Molly washed the dishes.

"We've got a dishwasher," Nick pointed out.

"Then we'll rinse and stack. Go get dressed."

The tone of Alec's voice ruled out argument and Nick

pushed back his chair and shuffled from the room. He returned scarcely five minutes later clad in jeans and a sweatshirt.

"Take a jacket. It's a bit chilly today, even for early May," Alec advised Tess.

By the time Tess had run to her room and retrieved a thick sweater from her suitcase, Nick was standing in the center of the drive at the front of the house. "Not much to see," he mumbled.

"Alec said your dad had a studio out back. Could we walk around and have a look?"

"He was your dad, too," Nick said.

"Yes," she said, "but when I was about your age, maybe a bit younger, I decided he must be dead or he'd have come back for me."

"You thought he was *dead?*"

"He and my mother had a big fight. I was eight at the time. They were always fighting—mainly about money. She told him to leave and he did. For a couple of years I waited for him to change his mind and come back to take me with him, but he never did. Never sent a letter, much less any money. So I decided he was either dead or had gotten himself a new family." Tess paused, taking a breath. "Which apparently he did."

He gave her a wary look. "So is that why you aren't so keen to take care of Molly and me? *We* didn't have anything to do with all that."

She stepped closer to him. "Nick, believe me, I don't blame you or Molly. This has nothing to do with you at all."

"But it does kinda, doesn't it? Like you got gypped out of a father and now you're angry at him because of what he did to you and your mother and that's why you're taking it out on Molly and me."

She ignored his language, focusing on the more important point he'd made. "I'm not taking out some kind of revenge on you two. Please believe me. It's just that mentally I got used to the idea of being an orphan a long time ago. My family is Mavis. She helped put me through school and did all the parent things. It was a struggle. I can't explain how hard it was for both of us.''

Anger flared in his eyes. ''Yeah, well at least you had each other. And that orphan part? Well, Mol and me are just getting used to that and it's pretty damn hard, too.'' He turned his back on her.

Tess knew he was crying but didn't know if trying to comfort him would make him feel angrier or more embarrassed. ''I'm sorry,'' she said. ''All that happened to me when I was a kid. I should be over it by now.'' Tess dug her fingertips into the pockets so she wouldn't be tempted to reach out for him. Arm's length, she reminded herself.

She took a deep breath and said, ''Nick, I haven't any idea what's going to happen while I'm here. But I can promise you that we'll all discuss things together—with Alec, too, if you want. We won't pull any surprises on you and Molly.''

He swung round to face her, wiping his eyes with the sleeve of his sweatshirt.

Tess knew at once how hollow that promise sounded. In fact, it was the kind of statement she'd make to a client whom she was stalling for time. And Nick recognized it, too, but he graciously dropped the subject.

''We can get to the studio this way,'' he said, setting out on the gravel drive that ran parallel to the long side of the house. A field stubbled with tufts of prairie grass and spiked plants stretched to the left of the drive that ended in a two-car garage behind the house. A hundred yards or so off to the right of the garage, nestled in a stand of fir trees, was a rectangular, single-story building sided with aluminum painted the same blue-gray as the house.

Nick walked up to a hanging planter suspended on a hook at the front door of the studio and rummaged his hand through it, pulling out a key. "Dad hated getting out here and having to go back to the house for a key, so he always kept one in here. Even though Mom asked him to stop, after the fire."

"Fire?"

"This is brand new. His old studio was all wood and burned down almost a year ago. We don't know how the fire started—maybe a short circuit in Mom's pottery kiln. They both worked here." He unlocked the door and stood aside for Tess.

The interior was breathtaking. Floor-to-ceiling windows ran along the side facing the distant foothills. The floor was ceramic tiles of mottled green and the roughened plaster walls were the color of pale buttermilk. Large wooden beams with units of pot lights transected the ceiling. Plants and trees outside the windows gave the impression of a greenhouse in reverse.

"Dad went for the aluminum siding for the new studio because of the fire. Mom's pottery studio is down there," Nick said, pointing to the end wall of sandalwood red bricks. "That part's original—the only wall left standing after the rest burned down."

Tess stood in the center of the single room studio, aware of Nick's quiet study of her. As if waiting to measure her response to the place. She wished she'd come in alone, because there were some half-finished canvases and she wanted privacy to examine them. Searching, perhaps, for some clue to the past. Some hidden message that would reveal why Richard Wheaton had forsaken her all those years ago and gone on to lead this other life.

Surprising her, Nick blurted, "I guess it's hard to get used to the idea that my dad and yours was the same person." He paused for a moment, then asked, "Was he a painter then, too?"

"That was his dream but he wasn't making any money at it. He worked in an office during the day and painted nights and weekends. When I was five or six, he had an exhibit at a friend's house. I remember how excited he was when he sold his first piece.''

Tess scanned the room, thinking how different the workplace was from the tiny room off her bedroom that he'd used when she was a kid. There, his paints had been stacked haphazardly on an overturned crate. Here, everything was methodically arranged on a long Formica-topped island complete with two sinks.

''It looks like he went on to become very successful.''

Nick shrugged. ''I guess so. I only remember living here and him painting all the time, but Mom told me once that he lived as a poor starving artist for many years. Before they met.''

Tess smiled to herself. The expression was one her mother had used a lot, too. Usually in an accusing way. As if Richard would rather be poor on his own than with a family. Maybe she was right after all, Tess thought.

She noticed some canvases stacked neatly against empty wooden packing cases. ''Have these been sold?''

''Maybe. That's usually how he got things ready. Mr. Walker—that's Dad's lawyer—came to have a look a couple of days after they…after the accident. He said he'd find out who the buyers were and arrange to have them shipped off.''

The business side of Tess kicked in as she bent down to have a closer look at the pieces. There were at least a dozen, she figured. ''What kind of prices did your father get for his work?''

Another shrug. ''A lot, I think. I don't really know. I never paid much attention.'' Nick averted his face and mumbled, ''Never had to.''

Tess stood up. It was time to go back to the house, she realized. Touring the studio was proving to be an emotional trial for both of them, for very different reasons. ''Come on,'' she said briskly. ''Alec said he'd take us grocery shopping into Boulder and you kids will have to help me. I don't have the faintest idea what you like.''

Nick swiped at the end of his nose with the back of his hand. He gave a faint smile. ''Not granola and stuff like that. But you can get some for yourself,'' he added magnanimously.

''That's generous of you,'' she teased and followed him out the door. Just as he was about to tuck the key back into the planter, she impulsively said, ''Why don't I take that? The stuff in there may be too valuable to risk someone else finding the key. I don't think that hiding place is very original.''

Nick hesitated briefly, then plopped it into her palm. ''There aren't many people around here,'' he said. ''Our nearest neighbors are a quarter mile down the road.''

''Well, I'm a big-city girl and we lock up everything there.'' Tess pocketed the key and headed for the drive.

''There's a back door to the house over there, at the end of the hall. There's also a door leading outside from my parents' bedroom. That was so they could work late at night and come back into the house without bothering anyone. But both doors are probably still locked. We could knock and see if Molly or Alec hear us.''

''That's okay,'' she said, ''we'll go back to the front.'' She headed to the drive. Nick lagged behind, as if reluctant to have to continue carrying on a conversation with her. She was almost at the front of the house when a bright-red pickup truck roared up the drive from the highway, raising a dusty wake in its path. It braked to a stop just behind Alec Malone's Bronco and a tall husky man wearing a white Stetson climbed out.

''Mornin','' he said, tipping his hat. He nodded at Nick, but turned his full attention to Tess. ''I'm Larry Stone. My wife, Marci, and I have a spread down the road. Noticed the car and guessed you'd arrived.'' His big face broke into a warm grin. ''Boulder's called a city, but it's really a small town. Especially out here. We all know each other up and down the highway almost to Lyons.'' He lowered his voice as he added, ''We were all pleased as punch when we found out there was family up north. These kiddies have been suffering.''

Tess glanced at Nick, who obviously had heard him and seemed more on the verge of scowling than suffering.

''Tess Wheaton,'' she said, placing her hand in his outstretched one and retrieving it as soon as he gave it a hearty pump. She estimated he was in his late forties and, from his ruddy, weather-beaten face, most of those years had been spent in the sun and wind. He removed his hat with his freed right hand and wiped the back of it across his brow. Long strands of gunmetal gray hair clung damply to the top of his head, forming a fringe around a small bald spot that glistened when he moved from the shade into the sun.

''Marci and I would love to have you pop over for a drink sometime before you all head back to Chicago.''

Tess's ears perked up at the last part of his invitation. *You all?* Was it merely a southwestern expression or did he really mean all of them?

Then he ducked his head closer to her, keeping his back to Nick and, in hushed tones, said, ''They've been through a lot, those kids. It'll be good for them to get away from here as soon as possible.''

Tess looked sharply at Nick, lurking in the background. ''I haven't made any plans at all yet, Mr. Stone,'' she said, her voice matching his in volume. ''I suspect there'll be some discussion with the family lawyer and other authorities.''

He gave a sheepish nod. ''Right you are, of course. Marci's always on my case about my tendency to blunder. But if there's anything we can do at all, please feel free to call. Our phone number's in Richard's book, I'm sure.'' He stopped then, nonplussed by his spontaneous reference to his former neighbor.

"Thank you," Tess quickly said. She turned toward the front door when it suddenly swung open. Alec Malone was standing in the frame.

"Thought I heard a car," he said, staring at the other man. "Hello, Mr. Stone."

"Mr. Malone," the neighbor said with a polite but stiff smile. "I'm surprised to see you out here so early in the day."

There was a short silence during which Tess waited for Alec to mention that he'd stayed the night. When he didn't, she said, "Mr. Stone dropped by to offer some neighborly help if we need it."

Alec nodded, keeping his gaze fixed on Stone until the man turned away to walk back to his vehicle. As he passed Tess, he paused long enough to mutter, "Keep your eye on that fella. He's got a lot of problems I hear." Then he climbed into the pickup, tipped the brim of his Stetson with his index finger, and backed out of the drive.

CHAPTER SIX

IT WAS LATE afternoon by the time Alec Malone's Bronco pulled up to the Wheaton house again and Tess was exhausted. The mini tour of Boulder, the stop at the Sullivan home to pick up more clothing and Squiggly the hamster, plus the grocery run at the very end proved to be more draining than her customary fourteen-hour day in Chicago.

Or perhaps it had been the brief visit with the Sullivans. They were a pleasant and obviously hardworking couple in their mid-thirties who had three young children of their own—all under the age of five, Tess estimated—and who took in foster children to, as Mrs. Sullivan honestly admitted, "make ends meet." It was also obvious to Tess that, although Nick and Molly would get good care, they would not be receiving much personal attention. In another not-so-subtle aside, Mrs. Sullivan said she'd love to keep Molly who was a wonderful playmate for her oldest child, but Nick was far too moody and uncooperative.

Placed in the unexpected role of having to defend Nick, Tess had acidly remarked that it must be difficult for a child who's recently lost his parents to be cheerful and helpful. She'd received a long, unblinking stare and the comment that maybe it was a good thing then, that next of kin had been found and the children could be together. Tess clamped her mouth shut at that point.

After unloading the groceries and helping to put things away in the kitchen, Alec took Tess aside to say, "I've got to go now. Forgot to ask before, but do you have a valid driver's license?''

"Yes, why?"

"You'll need wheels out here. There's a station wagon in the garage that Gabriela used to drive." He paused, then added, "Richard's Explorer was totaled in the crash and is still on a lot in downtown Boulder. The insurance company is probably going to settle with the estate, so that's another thing to ask Walker about when you meet him. I assume you'll be arranging a meeting as soon as possible. Or have you already done that?"

"It's a bit late now. I'll call him first thing in the morning. Besides, I had my secretary Carrie give him notice that I was coming to Boulder."

He nodded, then glanced beyond her to the kitchen door. "The other thing is," he lowered his voice when Nick came into the room to get something from the fridge, "the kids should go back to school tomorrow. Molly's bus picks her up at the end of the drive at eight-fifteen and takes her to an elementary school in Boulder." He waited until Nick left the room. "Nick's at a junior high there and his bus comes by a bit after that. He hasn't been too happy at school since the accident. I've had a couple of meetings with his homeroom teacher and the principal. His main problems are truancy and not getting assignments done, but just before they took off for Chicago, he got into a shouting match with another teacher over something. So he may try to persuade you to let him stay home longer."

Tess doubted she'd be any influence at all on Nick should he decide not to go, but kept that opinion to herself. She walked Alec to the front door and out to the Bronco. "Thanks again for all your help today," she said. "I'd have been completely overwhelmed if I'd had to organize things myself."

He shot her a doubtful look. "A big CEO like yourself? Today was a piece of cake."

"I don't think so." She couldn't hold back a sigh. "I've got a feeling looking after two kids and running a house is a lot harder work than what I've been doing."

He laughed aloud, crinkling the tiny lines around his eyes. "A lot of mothers would love to hear someone like you say that."

"Someone like me?" she asked.

He must have felt the chill in the question because he sobered instantly. "Someone who's been plunked into an extremely challenging position and who's measuring up to the situation very nicely."

Her gaze locked on his until, unexpectedly, a stain of color rose up through his face into the sandy-red hairline of his brow. His golden-brown eyes flicked away to the Bronco. "Best be going then," he muttered and opened the driver side door. One long leg was half inside when he turned to ask, "Not that it's any of my business, but what did Larry Stone have to say to you just as he was leaving this morning?"

Tess had almost forgotten the peculiar remark, but decided against telling Alec. "Not much. He was concerned about the kids and invited me for drinks some time."

Alec kept his thoughtful eyes on her a moment, then climbed behind the wheel.

"Why are you asking?"

He hesitated. "Just curious," he finally said, turned over the engine and shifted into reverse. Before he backed up, he stuck his head out the window. "I'll give you a call tomorrow. See how the meeting with Walker went." He thought for a second, adding, "One thing though. Keep in mind that the guy is like a lot of lawyers. Self-interested. No matter what he says about looking after the kids, his main concern is going to be what's in it for him."

With that, he reversed the Bronco, spun a U-turn and headed for the highway. Tess stood watching until the last plume of gravel dust disappeared. She didn't have the faintest idea what Larry Stone had meant by his remark about Alec Malone, but it was obvious that Malone, too, had some kind of personal agenda. When she returned to the house, Molly greeted her in the open doorway, holding Squiggly in her hands.

"Nick won't let Squiggly and me watch our favorite TV show and what are we having for dinner? I'm getting hungry."

Tess closed the door behind her. "I don't know, Molly. Shall we go have a look at the food we bought today?" She headed for the kitchen with Molly trailing behind.

"But what about my TV show?" she whined. "It's going to be over soon and Nick's had the remote for an hour now."

Tess ran the cold water and poured herself a glass. She ignored Molly, hoping the girl would forget her complaint. When she set the glass down, Molly repeated, "Tess? Can I have the remote now? It's my turn. Will you go tell Nick?"

Okay, Tess, she told herself. Calm down. Alec Malone is gone and you're on your own with two kids. God only knows for how long.

"Tess? Did you hear me?"

Tess peered down into Molly's pinched, unhappy face. She summoned a smile, though really felt like going to her room and shutting the door. "Let's let Nick finish his show, okay? Then at—" she glanced up at the kitchen clock mounted on the opposite wall "—six o'clock, it's your turn."

Molly frowned. "There's nothing on at six but the news. And won't we be eating dinner then? It's not fair, Tess. It's supposed to be my turn."

Tess walked toward the hall, with Molly clinging to her heels like plastic wrap. "Tess? Are you gonna tell him? Where are you going, Tess? *Tess?*"

Tess spun around and snapped, "The washroom, Molly. Now be quiet and wait in the family room."

Molly's dark eyes grew bigger but she turned and went back along the hall to the family room adjoining the kitchen. Tess stepped into the bathroom, closed the door and perched on the edge of the toilet. She didn't know whether to laugh or cry. But she did know she needed help.

DINNER WASN'T quite a disaster, Tess figured. The pasta was slightly undercooked and the canned tomato sauce bland. Molly began to explain how her mother used to make sauce and abruptly burst into tears. While Tess took the girl onto her lap to console her, Nick stole away to his room, closing the door behind him. Tess didn't see him again until long after she'd helped Molly bathe and get into bed.

When she came out of the bath herself, she saw a glimmer of light beneath his door and tapped on it. "Nick?" After the third attempt there was an audible grunt from inside that could have been a response. Tess slowly opened the door to see Nick reclining on his bed, reading a book.

"Nick, I just want to remind you that you'll need to get up early for school in the morning. Alec mentioned that he'd talked to you about going back."

"What's the point? The school year's almost over."

"It's only the first week in May. When does school finish here?"

He shrugged, ignoring the question. "Besides, I'm failing anyway."

Tess sat down on the edge of the bed, forcing him to grudgingly move his legs aside. "No one's going to be concerned about grades this year, Nick. I think the important thing is to try to get back to some kind of routine."

"Why bother? You'll be gone in a few days and then the routine will change again." He moved the book higher, covering his face.

Tess couldn't think of an answer because he was perfectly right. She *did* hope to go back in a few days—maybe a week max—and was still clinging to the illusion that everything would be sorted out by then. Now, she realized what a fool she'd been to even imagine the possibility. After a long uncomfortable silence, she stood up and quietly left the room.

She was beginning to realize that she couldn't physically take care of the children and run around trying to settle things at the same time. Even though they'd be in school—at least Molly would be—there'd be all the household chores to manage. Chores she'd never had to do for another person but herself. Chores that Mavis had done for her when she was young.

Mavis. Tess remembered that she'd promised to call her when they arrived in Boulder. She checked on Molly, already fast asleep, and headed for the telephone in the kitchen. Mavis picked up the phone after half a dozen rings. Worried that she'd roused the older woman from bed, Tess greeted her with an apology.

"Not to worry, love. Just took me a while to get to the phone, you know how it is," Mavis said.

Once the brief exchange of small talk was finished, Tess plunged right in with her problems. "There's so much to do here, Mavis. More than I expected. The kids hate my cooking and there's all this laundry. I think a lot of it is from before the accident. It's as though they just closed up the house after it. Then there will be meetings with the lawyer and helping to oversee packing up stuff. Perhaps even the sale of the house. The kids will be in school all day but someone needs to be here when they get home and…and make meals and that."

"You'll be busy, but I've lots of faith in you, love."

Tess closed her eyes. That wasn't quite what she'd hoped Mavis would say.

"How're the kiddies doing? Are they happy to be home again?" Mavis asked.

"Well, yes and no. Molly is but Nick is pretty moody."

"Have you made a decision yet about bringing them back to Chicago?"

"Uh…no. But I think that would be very problematic."

"There are nannies and housekeepers to be hired here, too, love. Anything can be worked out."

"That's not the point, Mavis. The kids need to be with a family."

An impatient sigh sounded along the line. "They need to be with people who care for them, Tess. Remember that." A slight pause, then, "Don't forget you're all those wee ones have. Keep that in mind over the next few days and feel free to call me any time."

Tess said goodbye and replaced the receiver. Then she paused, hearing quiet movement in the hall just outside the kitchen door. "Molly? Is that you?" There was no answer. Seconds later, a door clicked shut. *Nick.* How much had he heard?

Tess headed for Molly's room where she'd planned to spend the night again. The little girl was snoring peacefully and Tess, realizing she'd be lying awake for at least part of the night, picked up pillows and the lightweight quilt covering the other bed and retreated to the family room sofa. The very place vacated by Alec Malone earlier that morning. For some reason, the thought was oddly reassuring.

TESS BIT DOWN on the smile that threatened when she shook hands with Jed Walker. He wasn't at all the cowboy she'd imagined when she'd received his telephone message in Chicago. In fact, he could easily be one of the many executives she met with daily. Designer business suit with impeccable coordinated accessories, including a Rolex watch. She couldn't see his feet on the other side of the mahogany desk but doubted he was wearing cowboy boots.

And his face suggested he hadn't been riding the range any time lately, either. Early forties at the most, she guessed, with a hint of pampering in the skin and well-trimmed blond hair. He was good-looking, with the kind of face that turned heads, and he exuded a charm that appealed to Tess instantly.

As soon as she perched on the edge of her leather chair, he asked, "Coffee?" and before she'd finished saying please his secretary appeared with a tray. When she'd poured for both of them and left the office, Walker leaned back in his leather swivel chair and said, "It was fortunate I had some time to spare this morning. And by the way, thanks for having your secretary give me notice that you were coming. Frankly, I was expecting a return call from Chicago."

Tess felt heat rise up into her face. "Sorry about that. But I just got your letter late Thursday and then Mr. Malone called the next day. At the same time the children showed up."

He nodded, accepting what Tess knew was a lame excuse about her failure to call him back. "Mr. Malone phoned me as soon as the children went missing. There was a bit of a panic here, as you can imagine. Fortunately, everything turned out all right." His icy blue eyes passed over her.

Accustomed to frank appraisal from businessmen, Tess nevertheless felt herself fidgeting. She sipped her coffee, at a loss for a reply.

When she set the cup onto the saucer, he said, "I was Richard Wheaton's lawyer for ten years and never had an inkling that he had another daughter. Especially one so—"

"Grown-up?" she asked, smiling.

His white teeth flashed. "Precisely. And perfectly grown-up, if I may add."

Tess straightened in her chair. "How did you find out about me?"

"Actually Nick did. He was apparently going through some of your father's papers and found some letters with your name and an address in Chicago."

A stillness fell over her. "I'm sure my father didn't have my address in Chicago. I last saw him when I was eight years old. There's been no other communication since."

"The letters had been sent to you several years ago and most had been returned unopened. The address isn't your current one so I had to contact an investigative agency in Chicago. I realize I could have sent the letter to your home address but thought the work one was a better gamble in case you'd moved in the meantime. Having an unlisted phone number at home was a drawback for us." He flashed a smile. "But we made contact. That's what matters. By the way, I've got the letters here in a filing cabinet. Remind me to give them to you before you leave."

So her father had written after all. *And who'd returned them? Mother, of course.*

"Shall we get down to business then?" he asked, finishing his coffee in one swallow. "I'm executor of your father's will and I'm happy to go over the main points with you. It hasn't been probated yet, because once we learned of your existence, we decided to locate you first."

"We?" Tess asked.

"Oh, that social worker and I. Malone. He seemed real anxious to get hold of you before I started proceedings to have the kids adopted."

"Is it normal for a social worker to have such influence?" She couldn't help asking.

"A bit. But Boulder's a small place and your father was very well known here. It wasn't just Malone, but people in your parents' circle of friends were concerned about what would happen to the children."

"Though not enough to take them in."

Walker averted his gaze to the desktop. "No, I guess other obligations made that impossible." Then his eyes came back to her. "Although now that you're here I assume things will work out for them."

"If you hadn't found me," she said, changing the focus, "what would you have done with Molly and Nick?"

"The will instructs me to set up a trust fund for them until they both reach the age of twenty-one. I would naturally try to have them adopted by the same family—or, in a worse case scenario—be kept in foster care. I'll go over the will now, if you like. It may answer some of your questions." He opened a drawer in his desk and withdrew a legal-size manila folder.

Tess tuned out the preamble and its wordy legalese, paying attention when he got to the main points. The estate was tentatively assessed at a million dollars, all of which was to be established as a trust for Molly and Nick.

"Of course, the sale of the house, its contents, the land and any unsold works still in the studio and gallery will be factored in," Walker was explaining, "which may push that total up another half a mil." He paused. "You look surprised."

"My father left before he became successful. He sent nothing to my mother and me. We had to survive on her disability pension and welfare."

He frowned. "Are you planning to make a claim on the estate? If so, that'll definitely delay probate and may cause unnecessary suffering to your brother and sister."

"Of course not," Tess snapped. "I'd never do that. When my father left, he left for good. He didn't want us and we...we didn't want him anymore, either." Her voice dropped off. She'd unwittingly parroted her mother's very words. "I certainly wouldn't have expected to be included in the will."

"Oddly enough, I received a codicil to the will just a week before Richard died. It was just a typed sheet of paper informing me that one of his paintings should go to a Theresa Margaret Wheaton.'' He studied her from across the desk. ''I assume that's you?''

Tess nodded. She wondered if the painting Walker was referring to was the one Richard had finished days before leaving her and her mother. The one he had under his arm the afternoon he walked out of the house.

''When I got the codicil, I tried to call Richard to clarify his relationship with...well, with this new person but we never had a chance to touch base about it before the accident. Since the bequest was a piece of property rather than cash, I wasn't too worried. I knew I could track you down eventually. The fact that you're next of kin to the children was an added bonus—for them.''

Tess squirmed in her chair. Was the whole town of Boulder in on a conspiracy to force her to take the kids back to Chicago? ''I suppose as executor, you have the additional responsibility of liquidating the estate and so on?''

''Yes, I do. But now that you're here, I'd appreciate whatever assistance you can provide closing up the house before you all return to Chicago.''

There was that word again. *All*. ''Of course I'll help. But I should inform you that I've made no decision yet about taking on guardianship of Nick and Molly. Although they're my half siblings, the fact is we don't know each other. We don't share a family history. Plus, I've a more than full-time job in Chicago and living accommodation that's not appropriate for children.'' She paused, gulping a mouthful of air. Best to lay all the cards out at once. ''They should be with a family and I'm basically here to oversee that. If possible,'' she added.

He didn't respond at once. ''Certainly you're under no legal obligation to take the children. Of course, there is the moral decision and I'm sure you're more than capable of reaching the correct one there.''

Speechless, Tess merely nodded.

He went on. "Perhaps if I summarize the main points of the rest of the will? Richard basically left everything to Gabriela and the children. He didn't specify what should happen to the children, other than a trust should be established. Gabriela was much younger and presumably, he never imagined she would die before him. Or at the same time," he murmured.

Tess tried to concentrate on the business part of the talk, rather than the horrifying mental image of a fatal car crash. "You mentioned a gallery earlier."

"Oh, yes. Richard's agent, Tomas Kozinski, owns a gallery here in Boulder that often exhibited Richard's work."

"Wouldn't that have been a conflict of interest?"

"Yes and no. They were friends a long time and managed to handle things all right. Tomas hung your father's work and held occasional exhibits. He also helped to negotiate sales. Believe me, your father was an adept businessman as well as a wonderful artist. He was very involved in all sales and transactions. If you like, I can take you over to meet Tomas."

"Thank you. I'd like to see the gallery. And the painting left to me?"

Walker thought for a moment. "Kozinski will know about that. How about if I have my secretary give him a call to make sure he's available?" Walker turned on his intercom and relayed the message. Seconds later, his secretary advised that the gallery owner was free until lunchtime.

"Shall we go now?" Walker checked his Rolex. "Then perhaps you'll be my guest for lunch?"

"Thanks, but I've a lot of errands to do and promised to drop by Molly's school this afternoon."

"So the children are settling all right?"

"For now. Alec...that is, Mr. Malone," she amended, catching Walker's slight frown, "advised a return to routine as soon as possible."

"That's wise, though considering they may be uprooted soon anyway, that hardly seems too important."

He was beginning to sound like Nick. "At least until we...or you, as executor, decide what to do about the house," Tess said.

Walker shrugged. "Not much deciding there, I'm afraid. If you don't stay, we'll sell it before we set up the trust." He rose from his chair and came around the desk to where Tess was sitting.

"At least let me drive you, then I can bring you back here for your car. Are you driving Gabriela's, by the way?"

"Yes. Alec thought that would be okay."

He smiled indulgently. "Well, if Mr. Malone is in agreement..."

Definitely an edge there, Tess decided, as Alec had implied. She stood up and moved past the lawyer toward the door, catching a glimpse of his imported leather shoes on the way. *No cowboy.*

THE GALLERY WAS SITUATED on a side street off the Pearl Street Mall, which Jed Walker pointed out to Tess as his Mercedes angled into a parking space in front.

"There's one like it in Denver," he said. "Draws the tourists and is great for business, in spite of some opposition initially. Did you stay over in Denver on your way here?"

"No," she said, climbing out of the car as soon as he turned off the engine. "Alec had left his own vehicle at the airport so we drove right here."

Jed walked around to the sidewalk and placed a hand at her elbow to steer her toward some brick steps a few yards away. "What do you think of this Malone?"

Tess hesitated, struck by his use of the word "this." "I don't know," she began, feeling unexpectedly defensive. "He's certainly committed to doing the best for Nick and Molly."

"True enough. Though I can't help wonder about some hidden motive on his part."

"What? After all, he's only their social worker, not their…" She stopped.

"Lawyer?" He tipped his head back and laughed. "Guess I walked into that one. I don't know, he just seems to be a little too personally involved. But hey, that's only my opinion and I'm only the family lawyer." Another laugh.

Tess simply smiled but saw that he had a point. Hadn't she been mumbling to herself about the very same thing for the past two or three days?

She let him guide her toward an alcove in a courtyard clustered with trendy shops and boutiques. From the outside, the redbrick gallery appeared unimpressive but when Tess stepped through the double glass door, she realized that the two-story building was topped by an enormous skylight. The interior was a large atrium. Tess stopped to stare upward into the second story, enclosed only by a wrought-iron railing. Natural light showered through from the roof. Tall potted plants lined the iron staircase and native art hung from walls that had been splotched with pale yellow and terra cotta to resemble the interior of an old European building.

"I was aiming for Tuscany," piped a voice from the second floor, "but couldn't resist the native touch. Hence the slightly eclectic look."

Tess spun on her heel toward the voice, coming from behind her. Leaning over the rail was a tall, thin man with short, bleached-blond hair spiked in a current fashion trend. He waved his fingers and strolled down the staircase as if an audience were watching every move.

Up close, Tess noticed he was at least ten years older than the figure he'd cut from above. Fine lines wreathed startlingly blue eyes—his best feature, she thought—but his tanned skin failed to hide old acne scars. He wore a creamy linen suit paired with a cornflower-blue shirt opened at the neck. A thin gold chain lay against the base of his throat and, other than a single gold cross earring in his left earlobe, was his only jewelry.

"Tomas Kozinski," he said, dangling a long thin hand toward her.

"Tess Wheaton."

"A Wheaton indeed! You've got your father's dramatic coloring. That pale Irish skin coupled with raven hair. The Black Irish, isn't that what they're called?" He uttered a throaty laugh. "As opposed to the redheads, I suppose."

Tess heard Walker sigh impatiently behind her. "Miss Wheaton is interested in seeing any of Richard's paintings that you might still have."

The charming facade slipped momentarily. "Miss Wheaton, I'm so very sorry about Richard. We were not only business partners but very dear friends for many years."

Tess withdrew her hand from his moist grasp. "Please. Both of you call me Tess."

"Well then, Tess, let me show you around," Tomas said, extending his elbow for her in a gesture she found embarrassingly old-world and familiar.

But she was pleasantly surprised at the tasteful and, as Tomas had said, eclectic displays of art. The southwestern influence was predominant, but she saw some abstracts that would have exhibited well in Chicago or New York. The few pieces he had of Richard Wheaton's were on the second floor.

One look told Tess that her father had been a truly gifted artist. There were six pieces in all, of varying sizes. Most were mountain and desert scenes, although two portrayed people in solitary poses. There was a dreaminess in these that touched her, drawing her closer to examine them.

"A lot of people do that," Tomas remarked. "Move right up to the piece. Whenever we had a show of Wheatons, there was always this strange hush in the crowd. Not the usual buzz over cocktails and canapés." He edged closer to Tess in front of a woman in shadow at sunset, wrapped in a native blanket and looking out into the desert.

"That's Gabriela," he said. "He used her a lot in his portraits." He sighed. "She was a striking woman."

Tess couldn't help calling up a memory of her own mother, who had been beautiful once herself. Long before mental illness and a failed marriage had removed the warmth from her eyes. She felt an unexpected rush of pity for her mother, who'd never been able to cope with life. Tess turned away, feigning interest in another painting to conceal the emotion she knew was etched on her face. After a moment, she noticed a price tag on one of the larger canvases and was shocked.

"I didn't realize my father was so...so commercially successful. Will you actually find a buyer for this at that price?"

"Oh, yes. In fact, after his studio fire last year, most of his pieces doubled in price."

"Really?"

"Because so many were lost in the blaze. In fact, it was almost a turning point in Richard's career. He'd been written up in a lot of catalogues and had received tremendous reviews from critics outside Colorado just before the fire. This came after years of local success and shows in Denver, Aspen and so on. When it was reported that many of his pieces had been destroyed, interest in his art skyrocketed. Along with the prices." Tomas stepped closer to Tess and added, "Now of course, prices will go right through the roof."

Now that he's dead. The business side of Tess lost out to her natural revulsion at the unconcealed excitement in Tomas's eyes.

Realizing he'd made a faux pas, he prattled on. "That's the silver cloud in this whole tragedy and one that will certainly benefit the children."

He was quick on his feet, Tess had to admit. "If you don't mind my asking, I'm curious about Richard's share of the price."

"Uh, well...our terms were very fair," he stammered, giving Jed Walker a furtive glance that intrigued Tess. "He took seventy-five per cent and I got the rest."

"Is that standard?" she asked. "Just that I've no idea how the art world works."

"Arrangements vary with artists and dealers. Richard and I started out together years ago when we were both setting up shop, so to speak. In those days he basically sold on consignment. Then as his success grew, he was able to pay me a percentage as his manager."

"So with his death, your take will also increase."

Tomas frowned. "Certainly. But my dear, one doesn't celebrate the death of the golden goose. If you get my drift."

She did. And for some reason, for the first time since she'd learned of her father's death, Tess felt a pang of sadness for her father. He'd sometimes talked about being rich and famous. And when both were finally in his grasp, he was killed. Such talent, gone forever.

"Mr. Walker—Jed," she amended at the look in his face, "tells me that one of my father's paintings has been left to me. May I see it?"

Tomas pursed his lips, regret in his face. "It's being cleaned at the moment, I'm afraid. Richard brought it in just the week before he died. It's one of his early ones, you know."

"Perhaps when it comes back to the gallery you can let me know?"

"Of course, of course." He placed a hand at the tip of her elbow and led her to the staircase. "Would you two like coffee?"

"No, thanks," Tess quickly said. "I've got to finish some errands and then visit Molly's school."

"I suppose you'll be taking the children back to Chicago with you?"

"I doubt it. I think they'd be much happier staying with friends and in a place that's familiar to them."

"Oh, I just assumed—"

"I noticed some canvases in my…Richard's studio at the ranch," she said, changing the subject. "Would you happen to know if they've been sold or not?"

Tomas looked flustered. "Oh? I thought I had all his work here."

Tess turned to Jed Walker. "I thought Nick told me you saw them when you visited the studio, after the accident."

Walker frowned. "I vaguely recall some canvases but didn't inspect them." He cut his eyes to Tomas. "If there are more, I'll collect them for you. Anyway, I'll need to go over an inventory of Richard's unsold works before liquidating the estate. Shall I come round here some time and do that?"

"Please do," Tomas murmured.

Tess paused at the front door of the gallery. Neither man seemed to be aware that she was waiting to leave.

"Thanks again," she said to Tomas. He gave a preoccupied nod while Jed Walker followed her out the door.

Now she wished she'd brought her own car, rather than having to make small talk on the way back to Walker's office. She wasn't in the mood to discuss business or her future plans for Nick and Molly. They were almost at Walker's car when a voice called from behind.

"Tess?"

She spun around, vaguely aware of a small hiss of air coming from Jed's pursed lips. Alec Malone was walking toward them.

"I was in the area at a meeting and just thinking I'd have to call you," he explained as he caught up to them. His eyes flit from Tess to Walker and narrowed perceptibly.

"Walker."

"Morning, Mr. Malone. Tess and I were thinking of going for lunch. Care to join us?"

Tess felt her eyes widen. She was about to correct the lawyer when Malone swiftly added, "Another time, then. Give me a call, will you, Tess?" He handed her a white business card. "At home, too, if you like."

He was already disappearing into a group of shoppers when Tess found her voice. "I thought I told you I couldn't make lunch," she said.

Jed gave a sheepish grin. "Guess I hoped you'd change your mind. No? Ah well, my bad luck. Come, let me drive you back to your car anyway."

Sensing her mood, he didn't attempt small talk and as soon as his Mercedes was parked behind her car, Tess leaped out of the door.

"I'll call you as soon as the will goes through probate. If you decide to return to Chicago before then, will you let me know?"

"Yes, I will. Thanks for taking me to the gallery. We'll be in touch." She got into the station wagon and pulled away from the curb before he had a chance to say another word. All she wanted to do was to go someplace quiet and try to conjure up faded memories of Richard and Hannah Wheaton.

CHAPTER SEVEN

DINNER THAT NIGHT was more successful, although Tess doubted that frozen meals qualified in any cooking sweepstakes. Molly babbled on to Nick about Tess's visit to her school, but other than an occasional nod of his head, the boy was silent. He was also evasive when she asked how his first day at school had gone. It wasn't until after the two had gone to bed that Tess realized she'd received no more than a gruff "okay" to her question.

After she tidied the kitchen and prepared lunches for the kids for next day, Tess sank into one of the armchairs in the family room and clicked on the television. She was exhausted and wondered how much longer she'd have to stay. When she'd talked to Mavis the day before, she'd been tempted to ask her outright to come to Boulder and help. But Mavis's arthritis and other minor health problems deterred Tess. Besides, she figured she ought to be able to look after the needs of two children for the few days it would take to settle affairs.

Tess mindlessly browsed through the channel selection before giving up on the television. The telephone jolted her out of her vegetative state and she ran for it, half hoping that Mavis was calling to say she could come and help. Her hello was a breathless one.

"Everything all right there?"

Alec Malone. "Fine. I…uh, ran for the phone, thinking it might be someone else."

"Like?"

"Mavis."

"Oh, sorry. Just me. Were you able to finalize things with Walker this morning?"

Tess hesitated, wondering why he was asking. His curiosity about her affairs seemed to cross the line of professional interests and she decided to remind him so, as subtly as possible. "There's a lot to discuss with the lawyer, the Sullivans and your department. I assume you'll be assisting me with the last two, won't you?"

He cleared his throat. "Yes, of course. That's why I'm calling. I got a message from Nick's school at the end of the day. Apparently he never showed up after the lunch hour. They didn't know you were in charge temporarily and so phoned Mrs. Sullivan who contacted me."

Tess closed her eyes. That explained the "okay" from Nick at dinner. "I see," she said.

"So I've arranged for the two of us to meet with the school principal tomorrow afternoon. The appointment is for one o'clock if that's all right with you." He gave her directions to the school, adding, "It might be better not to mention this meeting to Nick just yet. I don't want to make him feel cornered. He may not go to school at all if he thinks there's going to be a deputation waiting there for him."

"He has to face the matter sooner or later," Tess said, "but if that's what you want, okay by me. I'll see you at one."

She was on the verge of hanging up when he said, "A word of advice. Don't let Walker try to persuade you to do something your instincts warn otherwise. He can be a very smooth character."

Tess was tempted to say the lawyer's manipulative skills were no match for Malone's. Instead, she said, "He's a very charming man and you'd be surprised to know that he's just as anxious to have the children go back to Chicago with me as you seem to be."

"Really?"

His voice was a mix of surprise and incredulity. And something else that Tess didn't identify until he rang off. *Suspicion.* Definitely that, too.

SHE WAS FIVE MINUTES late but her entrance was so damn self-assured no one minded at all. Especially the principal who was on his feet in an instant, hand outstretched and saying, "Ted Capshaw, Ms. Wheaton. Glad you could come."

Alec simply nodded from his chair across the room. Though he was aware that all of his senses perked up when she walked in. She was wearing a short, straight, olive-green skirt that just skimmed the tops of her knees and a matching jacket that, swinging open as she leaned forward to shake Capshaw's hand across his desk, revealed a form-fitting creamy blouse. Her cheeks were flushed, though Malone doubted it was embarrassment from being late. She didn't strike him as the type who would care. Besides, he bet that executives like her made a practice of it.

Capshaw got to the point right away, opening the file the school had already documented for Nick since the accident a little more than a month ago. "What concerns us most, Ms. Wheaton, is that Nick's scholastic record has thus far been excellent. He's been a straight A student since starting here a year ago. This is a Junior High and he's finishing grade eight. His teachers are understandably worried that the truancy and behavioral issues will affect his success not only this year, but in grade nine as well. He's had a couple of sessions with the school psychologist and of course, Mr. Malone here has been in touch regularly. But all of us feel that part of Nick's problem is fear of the unknown. His future is frightening for him so he's obviously doing his best to avoid dealing with it."

Malone noticed that she didn't murmur or interrupt once during the long report. Another good strategy, he thought.

Letting someone else do all the talking while you do all the thinking. Then make your pitch clearly and succinctly.

When she did speak, he felt almost smug at his prediction, which had been spot on. "You're quite right, Mr. Capshaw. And believe me when I say that I, too, am worried about Nick. My job as next of kin is to ensure that both Molly and Nick stay together in a supportive and caring environment."

Environment. An image of some kind of plant habitat came immediately to mind. Alec pretended to brush something from his cords. At least she hadn't used the word *context* again.

But the principal appeared to like her terminology, beaming as if she'd just quoted some article on the latest in child development. Malone half listened as they talked about needs and issues. His gaze shifted from one to the other before settling on Tess. She was on the edge of her chair, explaining something about her career demands in Chicago. The topic obviously enthused her, for her impossibly green eyes sparkled. Can people really have eyes that color? he wondered.

Then he couldn't listen any longer. "Excuse me," he interrupted. "We all understand the why of Nick's behavior. Let's get to how we can change it. Support and encouragement are fine enough—" he nodded to the principal, letting him know he was on his side "—but what he really needs at this very moment is some assurance that he and Molly will not be split up and that he can recapture some semblance of family. I think he knows all too well that his life has irrevocably changed. What he needs to know now is that it can still be safe and secure. Perhaps even happy again." He leaned back into his chair.

Capshaw gave him a blank look as if to say, *Isn't that what we've been talking about here?* But Tess paled, fixing him with an expression that almost sent shivers down his spine.

"What do you suggest then, Mr. Malone?" she asked.

"I hope—in fairness to Nick and Molly—that a decision can be made as soon as possible with regard to their future care. All the rest—the trouble at school, nightmares, thumb sucking and bed wetting—will be resolved eventually." He saw Tess raise her brows at the bed wetting and felt a tiny pang. Actually, there'd been only one incident and that had been Molly's first night at the Sullivans', but he wanted to emphasize the children's post-traumatic symptoms.

"So basically you're suggesting I should make a decision about the children as soon as possible?"

The fire in her eyes belied the calm in her voice. She was royally ticked off at him, he thought. And rightly so. It had been unfair of him to raise the point again in front of Capshaw. But he was hoping the man would concur, strengthening Alec's side.

"Mr. Malone has a point, Ms. Wheaton," the principal began. He glanced from Alec to Tess and flushed. "At least," he backtracked slightly, "one that needs to be considered as quickly as possible. Though I understand you've only just arrived in Boulder and so may need to investigate the situation here and at the Sullivans'."

Tess pursed her lips and shot Alec a triumphant look. The discussion went nowhere from there. They agreed that both Tess and Alec would talk to Nick again about attendance and keep in touch with the school. Tess was on her feet, out of the office and almost to the front door by the time Alec caught up to her.

"What was the meaning of that in there?" She rounded on him at his approach.

"I'm sorry if I put you on the spot. But my job is to look out for Nick and Molly, not to worry over the niceties of conversation."

"But it was mean. It was backstabbing. You know my position on this. I don't understand why you have this compulsion to be always in charge."

"And you don't?"

The color in her face deepened, but she said nothing. Instead, she turned away and kept walking, through the tall wooden doors of the school and onto the sidewalk. Alec noticed the Volvo wagon parked a few feet away. She'd be in it and gone if he didn't act quickly.

"They need you, Tess. I know it's difficult for you to understand that, but they do."

She stopped and turned around. "They need an adult to be in charge and take care of them. Any decent and caring person will do. I'm sure there are plenty around. Just because I'm connected to them by blood doesn't mean we have a relationship. Nick knows me less than...than he knows Mr. Capshaw. It's your job to find someone to take them, Alec. Please don't foist your responsibility onto me."

He couldn't think of an answer to that, but simply watched her get in the Volvo and drive off. You've really screwed up now, he told himself. Pushed her right over the edge.

THE CALL CAME after ten and Tess knew right away who was on the other end. Alec Malone. Checking to make sure she'd had her talk with Nick. Which she hadn't.

"Look," he began without preamble, "I'm sorry for this afternoon. I know how it appeared—that we hadn't discussed the matter before—and I didn't intend to be so confrontational. I just couldn't stand listening to you and Capshaw talk about the kids as if they were part of some case study in a textbook."

"Mr. Malone, if that's how it looked to you, then I'm sorry. Because nothing could have been further from the truth."

"Please—it's Alec. Is it too late to resume a friendly relationship here? For the sake of Nick and Molly?"

If she hadn't realized how much she still needed Malone's assistance, Tess might have been more frank.

"I agree that a more amicable business relationship is necessary for us to do what's best for the kids," she said.

"Fine," he said, in a resigned voice. "That's definitely the bottom line here. One last thing before I let you go—have you had a chance to speak with Nick yet?"

"No, but if he's not asleep I'll talk to him now. Otherwise, in the morning."

He cleared his throat. "Just that, the sooner the better. If he knows we're on to his shenanigans and are prepared to set appropriate consequences, he might think twice before cutting school."

"Agreed."

There was a pause. "Okay. Fine then. Perhaps I'll give you a call tomorrow night and find out how your talk went." Another pause. "Do you mind?"

"Not at all. Talk to you then. Bye."

She hung up before he had a chance to say goodbye himself and mentally patted herself on the back for effectively taking charge of the conversation. Although she wondered why she didn't feel upbeat about the fact. Before turning out the lights for the night, she padded down the hall to the bathroom. Passing Nick's room, she noticed his light was still on and wondered if she ought to speak to him now or put it off until morning. She was tempted to opt for the latter, wanting to avoid another confrontation. But knowing how hectic mornings were, she decided there was no time like the present. She tapped lightly on the door before opening it. He was reading by his bedside lamp, but its dim glow didn't conceal the scowl on his face when he saw her.

"Nick? I need to talk to you about something," Tess said, walking into the room. She sat on the edge of his desk chair and told him about Alec's phone call.

In the beginning, he hotly denied skipping school. Then his guilt switched to anger, that she had been checking up on him. Worse still, that she and Alec had participated in a meeting that he ought to have been invited to. Tess had conceded that point, explaining that Alec hadn't wanted him to feel on the spot. He'd be included in the next one, she'd said.

Slightly mollified, Nick reiterated his rant about being uprooted and not knowing what his future would be and, last, what was the point of it all anyway? Tess had let him rave, knowing arguing would be futile. When she finally said good-night, she asked only that he make a good effort for Molly's sake as well as his. And feeling a bit guilty at using the little girl—knowing how protective Nick was of his sister—Tess had slipped out of his room. When she came out of the shower half an hour later, she noticed that his light was still on.

Even at the risk of being too tired to go to school in the morning, at least Nick would have the chance to do some thinking. And thinking kept Tess awake as well. She tiptoed into Molly's room but as soon as she lay down, sleep eluded her. Tess gave up. She crept out of bed and wandered into the living room.

It was a room the family obviously rarely used, judging by Nick and Molly's attraction to the family room and its television set. But staring at the portrait of Gabriela Wheaton in the spillover of a full moon, Tess felt a peculiar tranquillity, in spite of her stressful talk with Nick. She sensed that the real reason she wanted to rush to settle things was because to stay longer would make leaving difficult. If not impossible.

Studying Gabriela's portrait was no less difficult. There was love in that face, Tess thought. What more would a mother want for her children than to know they, in turn, were loved? And how likely was that if they were adopted or placed in another foster home? Yet, she was ashamed to confess that she doubted the feelings she had for the children had anything to do with love. Concern, definitely. Because they were children. Compassion, too, because they were orphans and she could relate to that. But love?

Tess got up and walked over to the full-length picture windows fronting the house. The moon was behind the house, but still lit up the bushes and trees dotting the land between the house and part of the drive. Beyond, all the way to the paved highway, the countryside was pitch-black. In spite of the privacy curtain of the stands of trees clustered around the house, Tess knew from her first night there that headlights of passing cars could occasionally be seen from the living room.

That thought pricked her attention when she saw needle-point beams of light approaching from the direction of Boulder and then suddenly, disappear. As if, she thought, the night simply swallowed them up. She waited a moment longer for the lights to reappear on the other side of the stand of trees, but they never did. After another ten minutes, and guessing that she must have missed them, she decided to go back to bed.

She made a stop in the kitchen for water and headache pills—another consequence of her chat with Nick—and was turning away from the kitchen sink when she caught a flash of light in the field stretching out from the terrace side of the house. It was a quick stab of light that at first made her think she must be mistaken. But then she saw it again, bobbing erratically in the dark. Certain that she wasn't having hallucinations or migraine aura, Tess moved swiftly along the hall to the back door at its end.

The yard behind the house was still and full of moonlight. No strange bobbling lights here, she thought. She unlocked and opened the door, standing behind the outer screen door, waiting. *There.* Was that a flash? She tensed, then pushed open the door and called out, "Hello? Anyone there?"

Silence. *Of course, fool. What were you expecting? Some polite voice to say, "Sorry for bothering you, but just thought I'd check out your property while you're all sleeping?''*

Tess waited a few more seconds, her anxiety level rising to the point where she doubted she'd hear a reply even if one were offered. The blood was pounding so violently in her head. She started to close the door when she noticed the hanging planter suspended from the corner eave of the studio. In spite of the utter lack of wind that night, the planter was swaying gently back and forth.

Puzzled, Tess quietly closed the door and carefully locked it. Why would the planter be moving? The planter that had hidden the studio key. Which was now on top of the bureau in Molly's room.

CHAPTER EIGHT

TESS DECIDED not to mention the strange incident of the planter and the lights to the children for fear of alarming them. By morning, she had questioned her interpretation of events. Perhaps the light in the field had been a reflection from something or had been much farther away than she'd thought. Some nocturnal bird or animal might have leaped onto the planter and set it swinging.

To her surprise, Nick arose on time and wordlessly helped her pack the lunches she was making when he came into the kitchen. After breakfast he accompanied Molly to the end of the drive to wait for her bus. Tess decided not to remind him about his behavior at school. The ball was in his court, she figured. As Tess watched the kids walk down the drive, she couldn't help wondering which parent had usually stood in the doorway doing the same thing. Gabriela or Richard? Maybe both. The sense of filling in for one of them was strange, though not unpleasant.

After tidying the breakfast dishes—and praising dishwashers—Tess called Jed Walker. She was taken aback by his insistence on driving out to the ranch. "I promised Kozinski I'd have a look at those canvases you mentioned and perhaps the two of us can decide what things you and the children will want to keep and which items should be sold with the house."

"Okay," Tess agreed, but as she hung up, she couldn't help but feel that she was being shepherded into a decision in spite of herself. Yet, she reasoned, isn't this the very impression you left him with the other day? That you wanted to get back to Chicago as soon as possible?

She was in the middle of taking an inventory of the food stock in the kitchen when he arrived. He was dressed more casually, minus a tie and jacket, but still appeared to have stepped off the set of a photo shoot for some fashion magazine. In spite of their almost cool parting the day they met, he greeted Tess with a warm smile.

"Since we missed out on our lunch the other day, I thought I'd bring some with me." He held aloft a plastic shopping bag from a well-known gourmet food chain. The end of a French baguette was visible, as well as the top of a bottle of wine.

Tess stifled the urge to correct his reference about lunch because he looked so pleased with himself.

He followed her into the kitchen and set the bags on the table. "Shall we go out to the studio first?"

"Fine." She led Walker along the hall to the backyard and the studio. The key was in her pocket but she hesitated at the locked door, curious to find out if Jed knew about the planter hiding place. He didn't appear to, but stood patiently waiting until she dug into her jeans and pulled out the key.

"Did the investigation into the fire here turn up any evidence of arson?" she asked.

He seemed startled by her question. "Uh, no, I don't think so. I believe Richard and Gabriela felt it had something to do with faulty wiring in her pottery kiln. Apparently it was an old one, about to be replaced. Of course, all of the paint thinners, solvents and rags on the premises ensured a strong blaze."

Tess stepped inside, Walker at her heels. "How lucky no one was hurt," she remarked.

"Hmmm." Jed was in the center of the room, giving it a panoramic scan. "It happened when the family was away for the weekend. Lucky for them, but on the other hand, it meant that the alarm wasn't raised until too late.''

"Who called it in?''

Jed turned his head her way, frowning. "I'm not sure. Probably a neighbor. Why all the questions?''

"Just curious." She pointed to the canvases propped against a worktable. "Those are the pieces I mentioned.''

He knelt down and using his index finger flicked quickly through them. When he stood up, he brushed off the knees of his trousers and said, "I'll take them with me, if you've no objections. Kozinski will know if they've been sold or not and can assess their value for the estate." He peered around the room. "If there are no more art pieces here, why don't you take whatever you want and then pack the rest up? We can sell off the whole lot in bulk.''

"Won't Mr. Kozinski want anything here?''

Walker's brow knotted together. "Like what?''

"Well, he's an art dealer with a gallery.''

"True, but he just handles the finished products.''

"What about Gabriela's work?" Tess pointed to the other end of the room and the collection of pottery on shelves and in display cabinets.

He gave a dismissive shrug. "As I said, take what you want. I know she sold some stuff locally and donated some to charities for raffle prizes, but…''

She wasn't in Richard Wheaton's league and so her work should be cast aside. Oddly, the implication rankled Tess. "Then the children and I will decide.''

"Sure," he said. "Shall we go back into the house and check out the rest of it?''

"Okay," was all she said, though her discomfort level had risen dramatically. What she really wanted to do was to put off any more sorting and sifting, as Mavis called it, for another day. Another time when she could tackle the task alone.

But he was keen to finish the job and as soon as they

entered the back door, he jerked his head toward the master bedroom. "Have you had a chance to go through their personal effects?"

Heat rose up into her face. "No, I haven't. I didn't think I ought to."

When she turned her head, she saw that he was studying her. "An understandable response," he murmured, "and I suppose you felt too uncomfortable doing it as well."

Tess glanced away. "Yes, I did. To tell you the truth Mr. Walker—Jed," she added at the prompt in his eyes, "I still haven't gotten used to the idea that my father was alive these past twenty-five years. Mentally, I'd written him off as dead. So you see..."

He reached out and took her hand. "I do. Sorry, I should be more subtle. This is a difficult job for any grieving person, let alone someone in your position." His eyes were kind and sympathetic and he pulled her toward him. Then, he abruptly pulled away.

"Would you prefer to go through the things in the master bedroom on your own?" he asked, getting back to business.

Tess nodded, baffled by the unexpected embrace.

"There is one thing," he said. "If you find any legal papers or documents regarding the estate, Richard's art sales—whatever—you'll need to pass those on to me. For the rest, I'm sure there are pieces of jewelry or other valuable items that you may want to have set aside in trust for Molly or Nick. Shall we agree on a timeline? Maybe you could set aside what you think should be kept and what sold. Then I'll come back here and make an inventory."

Tess felt as if she'd just hopped onto a speeding rail car. Dazed, she said, "All right."

"Speaking of papers," Jed exclaimed, "I've got those letters I mentioned the other day in my office. The ones Nick found, that had been sent to you years ago? I'll go out to the car and get them." He started to turn away when he paused to say, "Why don't you set up our lunch while

I'm doing that?'' Then he retreated along the hall to the front door.

Tess watched him go, thinking he had Alec Malone beat in the management department. And she also wondered if she'd left her own take-charge skills behind in Chicago.

Tess had to restrain herself from sneaking a look at the elastic-wrapped bundle of letters Jed handed her. She took them into the bedroom she shared with Molly and tucked them under her pillow. Reading them would require time and privacy.

By the time she returned to the kitchen, Jed was opening cupboards to search for wineglasses and plates. She thought he was surprisingly adept at making himself at home and wondered if he'd enjoyed a social relationship with Richard and Gabriela as well as a professional one. Somehow, she couldn't see her father being friends with someone like Jed. Although, she reminded herself, the father she'd known at eight years old was likely not the father Nick and Molly had known.

She sat opposite Jed and raised her glass of wine when he said, ''Cheers! To a satisfactory ending for all.''

The toast was a peculiar one, she thought. The ''all'' obviously included him, but did it extend to the children? Still, she found the food delicious even if the atmosphere in the room seemed contrived. Jed Walker was not an easy person to categorize, she thought. Unlike Alec Malone, whose character could be summed up in three words. All starting with the letter C. *Caring, conscientious and controlling.*

''Enjoying the food? You were smiling,'' he said at the question in her face and she instantly blushed. Not that she'd been thinking anything wonderful about Alec Malone, but later, as she followed Jed to the front door, she wondered why the social worker had crept into her mind at all.

Jed loaded the canvases into the trunk of his Mercedes and came around to say goodbye. "Maybe we could have lunch—or dinner—in town the next time. Alone."

Her reply was cut short by the approach of a vehicle driving up the gravel lane from the highway. Tess squinted, trying to identify it in the cloud of dust. It wasn't until it pulled to a halt, dust settling on its hood and bumpers, that she recognized it as Alec Malone's Bronco. And Nick was sitting beside him in the front seat.

The driver door swung open and Alec stepped out. He didn't look happy.

His glance took in first Jed, then Tess.

"Sorry for the interruption," he said, "but could I talk to you for a second, Tess?"

"I'll be off then," Jed stated. "Call you tomorrow, Tess. Thanks for lunch," he said as he climbed into his car and turned over the engine.

Tess was waiting for Alec to speak but he was staring at the Mercedes as it drove toward the highway. Then he turned back to her. "Lunch with the family lawyer?"

"Why is Nick with you? What's happened?" she asked, ignoring him.

The irritation in his face gave way to something else. *Caution*, Tess thought. *Another word for the list.* But that failed to provoke a smile this time, as Tess listened to Alec's summary of a brawl at school, culminating in a two-day suspension for Nick.

"The other kid got a week, Tess, before you jump to any conclusions about who started what. The school has a zero tolerance policy for physical fighting. Nick said for some reason this other boy had been picking on him since the accident. He said he'd been managing to handle the situation, but apparently the kid made some crude remark about Gabriela and Richard and Nick lost it." He looked at the Bronco and Nick, hunched in the passenger seat.

"Nick did say he was sorry to disappoint you," he added, looking back at Tess.

Tess was still trying to sort out the gist of Alec's account but his tacked-on last sentence, said almost reproachfully—as if she didn't deserve such consideration from Nick—stung. Rather than reply, she walked around to the passenger door and opened it.

"Nick?" she asked, bending down to talk to him. "Are you okay? Did you get hurt?"

He raised his face to expose a large red mark on his right cheek. Tess must have gasped for Nick's face cracked in a faint smile. "You should see *his* face," he whispered.

But the boast was a hollow one, Tess knew. "Come inside and I'll see what I can do for it."

Nick got out of the Bronco and on his way into the house turned round to say, "Thanks for coming, Alec. Sorry again. I'll hold my temper the next time."

Tess waited until he was inside before turning her attention back to Malone. "Did you take him to a doctor? Why didn't you call me?"

"Whoa! The school nurse had a look and said he was fine. A bruise or black eye will be his only penalty, next to the suspension."

"Well it sounds like this other fellow is responsible."

"He is, but the problem is that Nick has to learn not to get drawn into fighting."

"Has this happened before then?"

"The first week after the accident. No one blamed Nick, but he was obviously too quick to lash out. And the other boy has a history of bullying, but Nick isn't entirely blameless. Male adolescent taunting accounts for a lot of fighting in schools."

Tess sighed. Something else to worry about. She was about to follow Nick into the house when Alec said, "Not that it's any of my business, but what was Walker doing out here? Besides having lunch with you?"

She wheeled around. "You're absolutely right, it isn't any of your business. But because I ought to feel grateful for your helping Nick this afternoon, I'll tell you." She took a deep breath to calm herself. "Jed came to discuss the sale of the house and its contents. He brought some letters that Nick had found, from my father to me. And he also brought lunch. Anything else on your mind?"

His eyes never wavered from her face, in spite of the dark stain of color that rose into his own. "I know that you resent my interference, although I'm not sure why. You're right, I ought to have called you first. Nick asked me not to because he didn't want to alarm you. The school called me because Nick asked them to. That ought to suggest something to you, Tess."

She waited, knowing he was going to tell her that something whether she wanted to hear it or not.

"Nick doesn't yet consider you the adult caregiver in his life. He doesn't trust your commitment to him or to Molly." He paused a beat. "I think he's afraid of being hurt all over again. So it's safer and easier to fall back on someone he knows."

She opened her mouth to speak but couldn't put together anything rational to say. Instead, she started toward the door.

"I'm sorry if I hurt your feelings," he called after. "But facts have to be faced. These are just two kids here, Tess, and you're the adult."

She kept on walking, closing the door behind her without once looking back.

ALEC STARED at the phone on his desk. Each time his hand reached for the receiver, he snatched it back as if it had a mind of its own and couldn't be trusted. For the third time, he read through the first paragraph of the report he'd just printed out, forcing himself to concentrate. But the day hadn't gone well and he had a feeling in his gut that it wasn't going to end any better.

It had started with a request from his supervisor for a meeting. She'd received a complaint that he'd overstepped professional limits as a caseworker. That he'd become too personally involved with the Wheaton case and what was his explanation? When he'd asked who'd made the complaint, she'd flushed and admitted there had been an anonymous call.

But his dismissal of the call didn't quite go down with her. Was there anything to it? she'd asked. And if so, then perhaps he ought to review the matter and consider handing the file over to another worker. Alec had managed to keep his cool, all the while wondering who'd made the call. He convinced his supervisor that the call was nonsense but that he'd watch his step. When he left her office, he knew she'd be keeping an eye on him and the idea rankled. His friendship with his supervisor had allowed him to cross a lot of lines in his job and he'd always appreciated her faith in him. He didn't want to lose that confidence, but at the same time, knew that it was impossible to do his best without ignoring some of the arcane and arbitrary rules that bureaucrats seemed to love.

He knew he had talents and skills to offer, especially to teenagers. His successes with his caseload had prompted the "blind eye" attitude his superiors had adopted with him. Yet he knew it was a matter of time before some new guy on the job would want to go by the book. He just hoped he could sort out the increasingly complex Wheaton case first.

Alec checked the time. Almost seven. He'd been hard at it all day, wanting to clean up some outstanding reports. He'd had to admit—to himself—that his boss did have a point. The Wheaton file was taking more of his time than it ought to. Time that ought to have been spent on other cases. He was grateful that his boss hadn't asked for his log book because she'd have noted that at once and demanded an explanation. And what would he have said?

That the Wheaton case was more challenging and demanding than his others because—*let's face it, Malone*—he was drawn to Tess Wheaton like a moth to light. He couldn't keep his mind off her. And even though some of his thinking about her had initially been negative, he was beginning to realize that she was handling things fairly well. Her response to Nick's fight had been guarded and cautious, but she hadn't automatically inferred Nick had been the instigator. She'd saved the fiery part of her reaction for him, which he reluctantly admitted he probably deserved.

The other thing that bothered him was why he kept finding excuses to call or drop in. Not that he had to search hard for a reason, what with Nick providing plenty of opportunities. The fact was that too many of his thoughts seemed to drift from work to the shifting color of her unworldly green eyes. Or the way she bit her lower lip when she was troubled by something. Or the way her head tilted slightly to one side when she was listening attentively. Or the way she carried herself when she walked into a room. That graceful flow of her long, slender limbs and torso. A kind of natural undulation that was mesmerizing to watch.

So, he breathed aloud, that was his problem in a nutshell. *Fixation. Obsession. Preoccupation.* Call it what you like. He couldn't pry his mind from the subject of Tess Wheaton any more than he could walk away from Nick and Molly. And that brought him full circle back to Tess and Jed Walker.

His anger at seeing the two so cozy together at the Wheaton ranch had alarmed him. At the time, he wanted to lash out at the lawyer, at her. Of all people for Tess to become friendly with in Boulder, Walker was the worst possible choice in many ways. The main one being Alec's unbridled loathing of the man. Fantasizing about getting to know Tess

Wheaton on a more personal—and intimate—level was bad enough. Imagining that Jed Walker might be the one to actually fulfill the fantasy was unbearable.

Alec tossed the report aside and groaned. He massaged the tension at the back of his neck and stood up. Time to go home, grab a late dinner and hit the sack. His route to his apartment in the university area took him past Walker's office building and he couldn't resist craning his head to check out the place, noting that lights still blazed inside. The Bronco was idling at the intersection a few yards beyond the building when Alec became aware of raised voices.

He checked the rearview mirror and saw two men out on the pavement. Alec cranked down the rest of his window and turned around for a better look. Walker and another man, whom Alec didn't recognize, were having a heated argument about something. Probably yet another poor sucker who's just lost his home or business to the guy, he thought.

The man raised a fist angrily in Walker's face then pivoted round, walking Alec's way. To Alec's surprise, the unknown man sprinted across the intersection in front of the Bronco just as the light was changing. The close-up didn't help with identification, but Alec figured there couldn't be too many middle-aged guys in Boulder with spiked, bleached-blond hair.

Curious, he thought, as he took his foot off the brake and continued on home.

TESS HAD BEEN watching the clock all night. Not because she had an engagement, but because she'd promised herself to delay reading her father's letters until everyone had gone to bed. That way, she'd have the long hours of the night to digest what she read.

By the time dinner was finished, Tess had acknowledged that a large part of her reaction to the afternoon's quarrel with Alec Malone really stemmed from his parting words. She didn't understand why she'd been hurt, rather than angered, at what he'd said.

She'd thought perhaps he'd call and apologize. When he failed to do so, she decided she'd misjudged the man. Obviously, he could be petty and insensitive. Nick hadn't attempted an apology either, which bothered Tess more than she expected. When he finished helping clear the dishes, he'd mumbled something about homework and had disappeared into his room.

"Does Nick still have to do homework even if he's spended?" Molly inquired as Tess was tucking her into bed.

"Spended? Ohhh. *Sus*pended. Yes, he does."

"I hope I don't get spended," Molly whispered. "Sometimes I feel like getting into fights at school, too."

"You do?"

"Yes, but I haven't yet. But some kids are mean to me. Yesterday Tiffany called me an orphan. Am I really an orphan, Tess?"

"Of course not," Tess murmured, her reassurance belying the pounding at her temples. She kissed Molly on the cheek and paused at the door a minute longer, watching her settle in for the night, her stuffed rabbit under one arm and her thumb popped into her mouth. Then Tess turned out the light wishing, not for the first time, that Mavis McNaught was just down the hall.

Later, when the children were both safely asleep, Tess retrieved the bundle of letters from under her pillow in Molly's room and headed for the living room. Curled up on the sofa next to the fireplace and beneath Gabriela's portrait, she began to read.

The first letter, a scrawl of almost indecipherable writing, was dated a week after Richard stormed out of the house.

My beautiful Tess,
I'm so sorry you had to see that argument with your Mommy. I know it frightened and confused you. I also

know that in your short life you've seen too many fights between us. That's one of the reasons why I decided I should leave. Children shouldn't have to live in a house of hate and fear. Your Mommy and I once loved each other very much. She was beautiful then and sweet. I don't understand when or why we changed. Just that it happened and none of it is your fault. You've got to remember that. If things were different between your mother and me, I could have stayed and followed my dream there in Chicago. But my dream and hers are no longer the same. When I get settled, I will save enough money for you to come and visit me. No matter where I am! Would you like that? Until then, I will write as often as I can. And I will always always keep you in my mind and heart.

Love, Daddy.

Tess finished the letter, though the last few lines were a blur. She set it down on her lap and dug into her robe for a tissue. The letter had resurrected a vivid memory of her father. His smile and gentle way of teasing her. She could almost hear his voice in the words that were so typical of him. She picked up the next letter, noticing that it had been written two weeks after the first one, and began to read.

Later, when daylight was creeping into the house, Tess folded up the very last letter and carried the bundle, like newfound treasure, into the bedroom. Molly was snoring softly and Tess tucked the letters into her suitcase and crawled into bed. She knew she'd never sleep, but closed her eyes anyway, going over in her mind every word again. Just as she'd read every letter twice and some, a third time.

She shied away from the awful realizations the letters had revealed. That her father had made many attempts over several years to communicate with her. That Hannah had spitefully returned every letter unopened until there were no more. For the first time, Tess felt a surge of hatred for her mother. How could she have been so cruel as to deprive her of a father? Finally, Tess had discovered that the only message Richard had received from Hannah the first year after his departure had been a request for a divorce, sent through a Chicago lawyer. Richard had kept it and a copy of the Decree Nisi packaged together with his unopened letters to Tess. As if, she thought, he was parceling up his old life before going on to the next.

CHAPTER NINE

TESS SLEPT IN and missed seeing Molly off to school. When she rushed, frantic, into the kitchen, she saw that Nick had walked the girl down to wait for the bus and then come back to tidy the breakfast dishes. She didn't dare say a word, just poured water into the coffee machine and sneaked glances at Nick as he finished loading the dishwasher and then slouched through the door back to his bedroom.

She felt hungover from the letter reading last night. Or, she mentally corrected herself, the hours she'd spent afterward lying awake and thinking about what might have been if Hannah had given her Richard's letters. How she might have experienced a father in her life after all. She made some toast and poured a coffee, wanting desperately to talk to someone about the letters. But there was only Nick and she hesitated to bring up her past with him. He had enough trouble dealing with his own situation. There was, however, always Mavis.

Tess looked at the clock. Just after nine. An insomniac, Mavis would likely have been up since dawn. Tess poured herself a second coffee and reached for the phone.

Mavis expressed the same shock Tess had felt when she heard about the letters.

"There are about two dozen of them, Mavis. He wrote almost every two weeks the first year he was gone. The last few had been sent after we moved in with you. The post office returned them address unknown. That must have been when he gave up trying to make contact.''

''So the rest were obviously sent back by—''

''Mother.'' Tess heard a soft cluck on the other end of the line. ''She had no right to do that!'' she blurted. ''I could have had some kind of relationship with my father all those years.''

''But she was angry, hurting and not in her right mind. I'm sorry to say she wasn't thinking of you at all.''

''It was spiteful and mean. She deprived me of a father.''

There was a heavy sigh. ''True enough, lass. But there's no putting it right now, is there?''

''No.'' Tess toyed with the telephone cord.

''I'm curious, did the letters give you a better picture of your daddy? Did you remember more of him?''

Tess felt tears well up in her eyes. ''Oh, I did. They were…enlightening. They made me feel—'' she paused, searching for the right word.

''Good?''

''Yes. Simply good. I felt lighter somehow.''

''Got rid of some of the anger,'' Mavis said.

That was it, Tess thought. Just lifted right off my shoulders. ''Not all, mind you,'' she said. ''I mean, he could have kept on trying, especially after he became wealthy. He could have hired a private detective or something.''

''I suppose, love. But what's the point of all those 'could haves?' At least now you won't have to go the rest of your life hating him for completely abandoning you.''

And although Tess had believed she had put the past aside and gone on with her life, she saw now that Mavis was right. She'd merely let the anger seethe deep inside. At least something good was going to come out of this trip, she realized.

''Well, my love, what else is happening there?''

''Jed Walker, the lawyer I was telling you about, suggested I go through Richard and Gabriela's personal things.

I still haven't even taken more than a step into their bedroom and I don't know if I can go through with it.''

"You can, lass. You've just got to face it and do it. How about the young lad? Nick. Maybe he can help.''

"It might be too overwhelming for him.''

"He can always say no. But he may like the fact that you're treating him like a grown-up. I think you should ask him. Give him the choice. Listen, Tess, I'll let you go now. Let me know how things are going and…well, maybe it's time for you to walk into that bedroom. Time to talk to Nick, too, about his parents. He's probably been wanting to talk but afraid to.''

Tess rang off with the promise to call again in a couple of days and headed for Nick's room. She could hear the faint hum of music and had to repeat her knock, a bit harder this time. There was a brusque "Come in" and she opened the door. He was cross-legged on his bed, earphones clamped on his head and plugged in to his portable CD player. He grudgingly removed them when Tess walked farther into the room.

"Mr. Walker—the lawyer—wants to probate the will as soon as possible. He suggested that we sort out important and valuable papers and…and other things in your parents' room.''

Nick paled. "You mean, like, go through their drawers and stuff? Their clothes?'' His voice pitched on that last word.

"There may be some things, jewelry or pictures, that you and Molly will want to keep. And Mr. Walker needs to know if there are any legal papers he may have to deal with. If you'd rather not, Nick, that's okay by me. But I'd like to get your opinion on what's there.''

"I'll think about it,'' he mumbled and replaced the earphones.

Tess withdrew, closing the door softly behind her. Whether he helped or not, the job had to be done. She went back to the kitchen for some big garbage bags for the clothing. No doubt there were agencies in Boulder that could make use of most of it. Then she marched along the hall to the bedroom. *I can do this.* After all, it wasn't as if she really knew Gabriela and Richard. He'd been her father and her whole world until she was eight years old. Twenty-five years later, she told herself, he was little more than a vague memory attached to some sentimental letters. Thus steeled, she walked into her father's bedroom.

She stood in the center of the room, examining it close-up for the first time. It was as comfortably elegant as the rest of the house, though with a bit more clutter. She moved slowly around it, taking in the assortment of obviously treasured items. A scatter of etched silver boxes that looked Native American in design. A carving of some bird Tess couldn't identify. A small glass jar covered in gaily decorated tissue paper with Love Molly printed in dark block letters.

Then she picked up a pewter-framed photograph of the four of them. Judging from Nick's size, it was a recent one. They looked like they were returning from a holiday. Tanned, happy faces. A small collection of luggage around their feet. Tess focused most of her study on her father. He looked vaguely similar to the image in her memory, though the more she looked at the photograph, the more bits and pieces of him emerged from the past. Thick wavy hair, still worn long, but streaked with gray, and a few more lines etched his face. A bit more flesh on his tall frame. But otherwise, the familiar grin and sloped shoulders magically erased the twenty-five-year gap. She set the picture back onto the bureau, unable to look at it any longer.

When she raised her eyes, she saw that Nick had slipped into the room. He stood silently in the background for almost ten minutes before wandering over to the bureau that Tess was standing in front of.

"My mom had some nice jewelry that Molly might like to have someday. It's in that carved wooden box there."

Tess picked it up and handed it to him. "Let's keep the whole thing, okay? How about if you put it in Molly's room?"

"She's too young to be responsible for it now."

"Yes, but we'll have Mr. Walker put it in a safety deposit box or something for her. Okay?"

He nodded and took the box from her, setting it gently on the bed.

"You'll want the things in the studio, too, won't you?"

He shrugged. "I'm no good at art."

"But maybe someday—"

"Sure," he said.

"This is very difficult for you, I know," she said.

He didn't say a word, just scanned the room with a vacant look on his face.

"Why don't you put that jewelry box in Molly's room while I pack up some clothes. Unless you want to help with that?"

He shook his head fiercely, alarm in his eyes. Then he picked up the box and, without a word, left the room.

Tess watched him, understanding his reluctance to touch the personal garments he'd all too recently seen his parents wearing. Then she set to work, opening closets and pulling out drawers. The couple had obviously not been interested in ostentatious displays of wealth, she noted. Some of their outfits were expensive, even formal, but most were casual. Reflecting a semirural, western lifestyle. Lots of jeans, jackets and tailored shirts and blouses. She had bagged all of the contents of both closets and was in the process of pulling out folders of papers from the bottom drawer of Richard's bureau when Nick returned.

"Want to have a look through these?" she asked, raising her head.

He nodded and shuffled toward her, took the folders and

perched on the bed. After a few seconds, he said, "These are pencil sketches Dad made last fall." He fell silent.

Tess sat down beside him. "They're lovely. I remember him drawing a rough outline in pencil first, before starting the real thing in oil. Where were they done?" she asked, riffling through the small pile.

"There's a place out past Lyons—that's a small town a few miles from here—where he'd go to sketch. Sometimes we all went with him and camped for a weekend. He liked it because he could see the valley where Boulder is and also the Rockies behind him."

"If these sketches are anything to go by, it does look beautiful." Nick was staring at the drawings so wistfully that Tess impulsively asked, "Would you like to go there sometime? Show me around?"

He thought it over, gave a nonchalant shrug and said, "Sure. Why not?"

Tess decided that was as much enthusiasm as she was going to get. She suggested a break for lunch and they left the room together. When Tess closed the door behind her, she felt oddly light. As if she'd finally gotten rid of a terrible burden. Nick excused himself and popped into the bathroom while she made for the kitchen. He joined her as she was setting out the fixings for sandwiches. As he began to assemble one, Tess said, "Yesterday Mr. Walker gave me some letters he said you'd found. From my father."

Nick glanced up from his task.

"I'm curious, where did you find them?"

A pale pink rose up into his face. He considered her question for a moment and then said, "Remember how I told you I came to the house a couple of weeks after the accident and found Dad's new credit card?"

Tess nodded.

"I was just starting to think of a plan to run away with Molly and I knew I'd need money. I didn't have more than a couple hundred dollars in my own account and that wasn't enough.''

Imagining the two of them wandering the streets of some big city was painful. Tess forced herself not to react but couldn't quell the scary thought that they might try to do that again.

''So,'' he went on, ''I searched through their drawers and Mom's jewelry box but I didn't find any money. There was a box tucked away at the back of Dad's closet, behind some other stuff. When I saw it, I thought he must have hidden it for a reason and that there must be cash in it. Sort of an emergency supply, you know. If he couldn't get to the bank or something.''

Tess stifled a smile at Nick's take on the adult world.

''When I opened it and saw the letters, I almost put it back right away. But—'' the color in his face deepened ''—I was curious. I opened one of them and it didn't take long to figure out Dad was writing to…to, well, a daughter.''

''You must have been shocked,'' Tess said softly.

''I was. Dad never talked much about his past. He was older than Mom and I guess I always thought he'd just been a bachelor all that time before they met and got married.''

''So you decided to turn them over to Mr. Walker.''

''Kinda.'' Nick peered down at his plate and half-eaten sandwich. ''Actually, while I was there, Alec came looking for me 'cause I'd skipped school and he guessed I might be at the house. This was right after we found out that the Sullivans didn't want to keep both of us any longer and that I'd probably have to go to another foster place. Or even a group home.'' His head ducked lower.

Tess waited, knowing he'd go on when he was able.

''I didn't want Alec to know why I'd really come out to the house—to look for money—so I decided to tell him about the letters I'd found. I made up some excuse about looking for a copy of Dad's will 'cause I knew he'd accept that." He paused. "He did. I—I didn't feel good about lying to Alec," he said, raising his face to Tess. "He's always been straight with Molly and me. He's not like other grown-ups who pretend they're helping you when really they're only looking out for themselves."

It was Tess's turn to flush, though she wasn't certain he was referring to her.

"Anyway, when I showed them to him he said they were very important. That they meant there might be next of kin. 'Course, he didn't promise things would change for Molly and me, but I kinda worked it out." His eyes met Tess's. "If we did have an older sister, there'd be someone to look after us and we wouldn't have to be split up." At that, Nick pushed his chair back and left the room.

Tess stared at his half-eaten lunch and, after a long moment, rose from her chair and left the room, too.

HE'D JUST RETURNED from lunch when the phone rang. The call took him by surprise. At first, Alec thought maybe Tess was calling to explain the situation yesterday. But he realized almost immediately that she wasn't the type to backtrack or come up with phony excuses about her actions. If she'd screwed up, she'd probably get to an apology right away. That is, he thought wryly, if she ever considered she might be wrong.

He was doubly surprised when she said she'd like to take Nick out to the mountains to some campsite the family had used to visit.

"Nick found some sketches of the place and I thought he might like to take a drive out there. What do you think?"

Alec was speechless. Not merely because she was asking his opinion about something, but that she'd figured out the place was important to Nick. "I think it's a great idea. Why not go for the whole weekend? Make it a camping trip."

"*Camping?*"

She made the word sound foreign, if not downright alien.

"Yeah. You know—tents, sleeping bags, that sort of thing."

"I know what the equipment involves," she said. Somewhat snippily, he thought. "Camping also means no beds, no showers and usually a lot of bugs. Not to mention larger animals. Aren't there snakes and other predators out here in the southwest?"

"All kinds of them. Unfortunately, most of them are the two-legged variety." No response. He tried again. "The thing is, the outing might give you a chance to make a breakthrough with Nick. He needs some time alone with you, Tess. Away from Molly and the house."

"I'll have to think about it. Besides, there's Molly. Someone would have to look after her."

"Let me work on that," he said, his mind racing. He didn't want to discourage her from acting on what he considered a brilliant idea. Good for Nick, sure. Even better for Tess to share an experience with Nick beyond looking after his needs at home.

More silence, followed by a drawn out "Well" that told him she was considering the option. "Maybe we could take Molly, too. Could you come out here later and show me how to set up the tent, when we find it?"

The request was totally unexpected. He knew—and he bet she knew, too—that Nick could show her just as well. Then he had a thought. The idea gained a lot more credibility the more he considered it. Though he knew if his boss found out, she'd be on him like a ton of bricks.

"I'll go you one better," he said. "Would you object to my coming, too? As a sort of guide and—" he searched for a casual line "—protector from predators, two-legged and otherwise?"

"You want to come *with* us?"

Incredulity there, he noted, but not disapproval. "Sure. Unless you think Nick might mind."

"Oh, he won't mind. In fact, I haven't even talked to

him yet about staying overnight. I simply suggested a drive and that obviously pleased him so I thought—"

"Your instincts were right on. This is exactly what he needs. Look, I'll see if my sister can take care of Molly. We could take her, too, but I think Nick needs grown-up time on his own. I can finish up here by four. I'll pick up some supplies in Boulder and be out at the ranch by five or five-thirty. If we leave right away, we can get to my sister's place outside Lyons in time for dinner. We could spend the night there and head for the campsite early in the morning."

There was a long enough pause for him to think she was going to change her mind. Then she said, "Isn't that a lot of trouble for your sister? Not just taking care of Molly but staying overnight, too?"

"It would be better than trying to find this place at dusk."

"Or we could just leave early tomorrow morning."

"True, but a while ago I promised Molly a visit to my ranch. I think she'll love the adventure."

"This is getting really complicated," she said.

She sounded like she was seriously having second thoughts. "My sister loves to have company," he quickly said. "Trust me on this. I'll call her right away and check it out. If she gives the slightest hint of not liking the idea, I'll call you back and we'll organize something else."

"Okay," she said doubtfully.

"Hey! Where's your sense of spontaneity? It'll be fun!"

"Right," was all she said.

Alec had a hunch her lack of enthusiasm stemmed from the knowledge that he might be running the show, rather than her. He quickly said goodbye before she *did* change her mind, and hung up. Relinquishing some control in her life might be just what Tess Wheaton needed.

It was shortly after five when Alec pulled into the drive. Molly ran from the garage to meet him.

"Nick and Tess are in there getting the camping stuff."
She gazed up at him. "I wish I could go," she said plain-
tively.

"Another time, Molly. Promise. Besides, my sister is
hoping you'll help her with the horses."

Her face lit up. He'd made the right decision. "C'mon,
let's go see if we can help." He took the small hand she
extended and walked with her to the back of the house.

The big garage door was open and Alec could just make
out Tess bending over something inside. She looked up
sharply at the sound of their approach and swiped back the
tendril of damp hair that had fallen over her eyes. As he
got closer, Alec saw the relief in her face.

"Thank heavens," she said. "Nick and I've been having
a hard time getting this stuff down from there." She
pointed behind her to a high shelf that ran the length of the
garage. There were a couple of oversize plastic containers
on the shelf and one lying opened at Tess's feet.

"Is there a ladder?"

"Of course there is," she snapped. "We got that far,
believe me." She jerked her head to a ladder propped
against the wall farther on.

It was Alec's turn to color. He ought to have noticed,
instead of jumping to conclusions about her ability to handle things. He caught Nick's expression confirming just
that. "Why don't you take Molly inside and finish packing?
Nick and I'll get the rest of this together."

"Glad to," Tess declared and walked out with Molly in
tow.

Alec watched her march straight-backed to the house.
When he turned around to the mess on the garage floor, he
saw Nick staring at him with some bemusement.

"Blew that one," the boy remarked. Alec could only
shrug. How very right he was.

BY THE TIME the Bronco turned off Highway 36 onto the
side road that would take them to the Malone family ranch,

Tess had calmed down enough to actually enjoy the ride. She was sitting up front with Alec, and Nick and Molly were in the back. Tess stared out her window, taking in the rapidly changing landscape. The flat, sandy scrubland around the Wheaton ranch gradually gave way to meadows of wild grass and flowers. Alec had explained that the Malone ranch was off the highway just beyond Lyons, a small town of less than fifteen hundred people.

"In the peak of summer, the population more than triples. Especially in July, when there's a bluegrass festival. Lots of Denver people have summer homes up here. The town's called the Double Gateway to the Rockies, over there." He'd pointed to the northwest as the Bronco turned off the highway.

Tess had looked, but the sky was too hazy to see the Rockies themselves. Coming from Chicago, she thought the foothills were pretty impressive on their own.

"There's the start of the Malone property," Alec said, gesturing to a split-rail fence on his right.

"How come your sister lives here?" asked Molly. "Isn't it your place, too?"

Alec craned his head to the rear and smiled. "Yep, it is. When my folks passed away, my sister and I inherited it. My job makes it easier for me to live in Boulder, but Karen and her husband work the place."

Molly thought for a long moment before asking, "Are you and Karen orphans, too?"

Tess didn't dare look at Alec, afraid what she might see in his face. He finally broke the silence by murmuring, "Yes, sweetie. I guess we are."

Molly was satisfied and resumed looking out the window. Ten minutes later, the Bronco swung onto a gravel drive that cut across grassy fields and ended at an old two-story stone farmhouse with a gingerbread-trimmed veranda that ran along its width. A white picket fence that needed a fresh coat of paint bordered a small section of lawn, separating it from the planted fields beyond.

"It's like the olden days!" Molly squealed.

As soon as the SUV braked to a stop, the front door opened and a woman stepped out onto the veranda to greet them.

The family resemblance was striking, Tess thought, as Alec introduced her to his sister. Same sandy-red hair, though Karen's had more red in it, and she also had a faint smattering of freckles across her nose and cheeks. She was tall like her brother, too, but only an inch or so more than Tess. Her warm manner in welcoming all of them was gratifying, setting them at ease right away.

She gave them a quick tour of the historic homestead that was clearly well loved. "Ken—that's my hubby—and I've been living here for seven years now, since my dad died. Alec probably told you we share the place. We're still waiting for Alec to find the right person and move out here, too. But I don't think that's going to be anytime soon." She rolled her eyes. "What a guy! No one can please him. Not since Sherry."

"Sherry?"

"His high school sweetheart. They were engaged and going to be married. But when Alec came back from his stint with NATO, he was really different. Made a whole lifestyle change. One that didn't include Sherry. Not that I minded, personally, because I found her a bit…hmm… demanding. A real princess. The marriage would have been a disaster."

Tess was torn between an interest in learning more and the realization that she'd probably heard far more than she ought to have. Still, curiosity won out.

"What was he doing for NATO?"

"Bombing bad guys in Kosovo. You know—in the late nineties. He'd always loved flying but that tour of duty finished it for him. He's never really talked about it."

Karen lowered her voice as they entered the kitchen from the backyard. "We all expected him to make the Air Force a career but when he came home, he said he wanted to spend the rest of his life doing good things for people. Especially children. I think he saw some horrific things over there."

Karen's story explained a lot about Alec, Tess thought. Like his intense commitment to his job. Unwilling to pry further though, she asked, "Can I help you with something? Will your husband be here for dinner, too?"

"Yes. He had to pick up some supplies at the co-op in Lyons. He should be here any second. But instead of helping this time, why don't you check on how the kids are settling in? I've put you in the master bedroom and given Molly my old room. Nick's bunking in with Alec in his old room. Okay?"

"What about you and your husband?"

"Oh, Ken and I are staying in our mobile home about half a mile from here. That's where we planned to build our dream home. Until the bank came down hard on us." She began to wash and chop vegetables as she talked.

"I thought you two were living here."

"We are for now, while Ken finishes the planting. But although we share the land and assets, the actual house went to Alec. Which is just as well, 'cause Ken's condition means we're going to have to live in a single-story home one day. That's why we wanted to start building."

"His condition?"

"He has MS," she said, her voice matter-of-fact. "Multiple sclerosis. He was diagnosed two years ago and so far, with medication and proper rest and so on, he's been doing very well. We're just planning ahead." Karen looked up from where she was working. "When you see Alec, could you remind him to keep an eye out for his arrival? He'll need help getting the seed bags and fertilizer out of the truck."

"Sure. I'll go look for the rest of them now," Tess said. As she walked along the narrow, dark hallway to the front of the house and the voices emanating from there, she realized how much Alec Malone had on his personal plate. Yet his even-tempered manner and devotion to his job had not hinted of any personal worries.

The children and Alec were coming downstairs when Tess met them at the bottom. "I was just going to take the kids out to see the horses and chickens."

"Great," Tess said. She felt suddenly embarrassed looking at him directly, knowing that she had just heard so much of his personal history. She smiled at Molly, who was hopping about on one foot at the front door. Nick still wore his wary expression, but there was a glimmer of anticipation in his eyes.

"I'll stay and see if Karen needs any help. Oh, and Alec, your sister asked me to remind you that when Ken comes back, he'll need help unloading the truck."

"Sure. If we're out back, come and give us a shout. Nick can help, too. Right, fella?"

Nick shrugged and followed his sister out the door. On his way through, Alec paused and turned around to say, "My sister's a real talker. I hope she didn't bore you."

"Oh, no. It was all very interesting." She smiled at the puzzled frown in his face and headed back to the kitchen.

MUCH LATER, when the crystal-clear night sky lit up with a billion stars, Tess wandered out the kitchen door into the backyard. She'd spotted a wooden swing there earlier, and thought it would be the perfect place for a moment's solitude. It was the kind of swing she'd seen on the porches of grand houses in home decorating magazines or in old movies set in small towns. She sat down on the torn and weathered cushions and let the big swing gently rock back and forth with her weight.

A night-light glowed in the kitchen for anyone who

wanted a midnight snack, Karen had joked. Though after the evening meal, no one would need to eat for another two or three days. Now silent, the kitchen had been filled with the hubbub of talk, laughter and the clinking of cutlery on plates. The experience of dining with an extended family unit was a new one for Tess, though she vaguely recalled having a similar meal with the family of a high school friend. At times, the noise had been overwhelming, but it seemed that whenever she was feeling lost, she'd catch Alec's eye and he'd wink or grin. Even Nick forgot himself occasionally and let slip a big smile.

After everything had been cleaned up, Karen took Molly upstairs and Alec and Nick went to help Ken with the animals. Tess chose to enjoy the night air, in spite of its coolness. Stargazing in Chicago was an exercise in futility. Here, that much closer to the mountains, the sky was magical.

She was leaning against the back of the swing, eyes focused on the canopy of stars, when she heard the rumble of an engine from around the side of the house. Seconds later, a shadowy form walked toward the kitchen door, then stopped, hesitated briefly, and came her way. It was Alec.

"Was that Karen and Ken leaving?" she asked.

He sat down beside her, setting the swing rocking at a faster rhythm. "Yes. They'll be back to see us off at breakfast. Molly's already asleep and Nick's reading in bed. No television." Alec grinned. "I think he's preparing himself for tomorrow night."

"I hate to have Ken and Karen inconvenienced like this."

He turned toward her, his warm breath fanning across her face. "Don't worry about it, Tess. They love to have company."

His thigh pressed against hers, but moving over on the swing would shift the balance too much so Tess sat still, folding her arms across her chest.

"Are you chilly?" he asked.

"Nooo."

An arm came around her shoulders. "This will save your going in for a jacket," he murmured.

Tess felt herself resisting at first, then as his body heat wrapped around her, the tension eased. "This is a great swing," she said.

"Hmm?" He lowered his head to hear, accidentally brushing his mouth against the hair just above her ear.

When she started to pull back, his hand pressed against the nape of her neck, holding her head firmly in place against his shoulder. Then he brought his other hand around to tilt her chin and before Tess realized what was happening, his mouth set lightly down on hers.

CHAPTER TEN

TESS YAWNED and with bleary eyes, peered out the passenger window of the Bronco. She really wanted to check out the sandstone cliffs on the left but decided against that. Anything rather than worry about a face-to-face with Alec.

She'd tossed and turned all night, though not from any soul-searching about her reaction to his kiss. The kind of heat generated by his lips on hers pretty much ruled out all rational thought. It had been so unexpected that, after the first nanosecond of shock, she'd yielded completely to physiology and responded in kind. And it was that totally unfettered response that had kept her awake much of the night. Along with the nagging question that still tormented her—*What the heck did it mean?*

When he finally loosened his grip on her, he didn't condescend to apologize. That would have shattered the whole two minutes of bliss. Nor did he resort to any half-baked explanations. Instead, he'd simply closed his eyes and groaned a very satisfied, ''Hmm,'' as if savoring some rare delicacy. It was only the sudden full illumination in the kitchen when someone—Nick?—entered it that was the deciding factor against another kiss.

Or so Tess believed when she saw the utter regret in his face as Alec stood up, held out a hand to her and murmured, ''Perhaps we'd better go inside.''

Tess closed her eyes and rested her forehead against the Bronco window. Of course, daylight had altered everything. Even her feelings about his lips on hers, tongue probing gently inside her mouth and tracing the outline of her own lips. Now the question of *What did it all mean?* had been expanded to include *What had she been thinking?*

"How're you doing back there?" Alec asked Nick, staring out the rear window. "Let me know when you spot the turnoff."

Nick gave a muffled grunt, concentrating on the scenery flashing by. Finally, he said, "I remember this crazy rock formation. It kinda looked like an old witch, hunched over. Dad always pointed it out to me just before we made the turn."

"Did you follow the river all the way?"

"No, it went in one direction and like, we went in another."

"To the west or east?"

"I dunno. On the right, I think."

He sounded frustrated, Tess thought. Maybe worried they wouldn't find the place and the whole trip would be canceled.

But suddenly he shouted, "There it is! I see it."

Both Tess and Alec craned round to follow Nick's hand pointing right, to the east. Alec slowed down, eyes searching the road ahead for the turn. They almost missed it. No more than a single lane of dirt and stone, the cutoff snaked away from the highway through a jumble of sandstone rocks. The Bronco bucked and heaved along the stony lane until it emerged from the rocks into a clearing of stubby fir trees.

Alec braked to a halt in the shade of some trees and they all climbed out. The first thing Tess noticed was the pungent scent of cedar and pine. The second was the absolute silence. Even the faint traffic noise from the highway had disappeared. Except for the wind hissing softly through the tree branches, the land was dead quiet. And very isolated, she noted. Not a rooftop or fence in sight.

Nick was charging through the trees.

"Slow down, fella," Alec called after him as he and Tess followed.

Nick waited impatiently a few yards ahead. "There's a trail here leading down. Don't worry, it's not very steep."

Tess realized for the first time that they were on the lip of a sandstone cliff that ceded gradually down a ravine to a tiny gem of a dark-green lake. From the top, she could just make out Lyons to the south but when she turned around to the west, she gasped. Snowcapped peaks jutted above the tree-covered foothills. The panoramic view was magnificent. Mountains and foothills to the northwest and a vista of meadows merging into Boulder Valley to the east. She could even make out the Flatirons, south of Boulder.

"Funny," Alec said, scanning the view with binoculars, "but I swear that area to the southeast is the very back end of our property."

"How big is your place, then?" asked Nick.

"Couple hundred acres. But the family hasn't used it all for years." He removed the binoculars. "Do you know who owns this part right here, or is it government land?"

"I'm sure my dad said we did. I know we've been coming up here since I was about eight or nine and I remember Mom and Dad talking about buying it. I'm pretty sure he did, a few years ago."

"Jed Walker would know," Tess said.

Mention of the name brought a scowl from Alec. "Yeah, right. Well, let's not spoil our outing just yet. Where did you usually set up camp?" he asked Nick.

"Down there," Nick said, pointing to the ravine and the lake. "The water is glacial fed, Dad said. Very cold and deep. You really can't swim in it. Dad used to paint up here and down there, too."

"It's beautiful," Tess exclaimed, breathing in the scenery. "I can see why your...why Richard loved to come here and paint."

Nick nodded, seemingly unaware that even now Tess had

difficulty calling her father Dad. She wanted to explain why, but the time didn't feel right. "Nick," Tess murmured, "thanks for letting us bring you here. It's a special place."

"Yeah," he said huskily and turned aside at Alec's approach.

"Shouldn't take more than a couple of trips to get everything down there." Alec glanced at Tess. "Up for it?"

"Of course," she said, tossing a nonchalant shrug. "Why not?"

She came up with a few reasons why not on the second trip. It was almost noon and the sun was relentless. In spite of the elevation and the cooler air, Tess had worked up a sweat by the time she was picking her way down the stony path with part of the last load. Panting, she sank onto a large boulder to watch Alec and Nick put up the tent.

When they finished, Alec strolled over to ask, "Ready for lunch? You must be starving after that climb."

Was he teasing or being sarcastic? "A bit," she said. "I thought my regular gym workout in Chicago would have prepared me for something like this."

"It's the altitude. Saps the oxygen right out of you. We're at least another thousand feet above Boulder." He squatted down next to the rock she sat on. "Check out Nick."

Tess followed his gaze to Nick, busying himself with sleeping bags and the fold-up table and chairs they'd brought. "He knows what has to be done," she commented.

"For sure. Done it many times, with his father. Okay, you relax while I help him get lunch organized. Then we'll go for a walk."

She was content to do just that—relax and watch them working. A sense of calm and contentment washed over her. No doubt brought on, she told herself, by the exhaustion of carrying down the supplies from the Bronco. Or maybe it had something to do with the quiet way Nick and Alec worked together. Each second-guessing the other's next move as if they'd been working together for years. In spite of her vow not to think about her decision regarding the children that weekend, Tess hoped that Alec would try to stay in contact with Nick even after he was placed somewhere.

Okay, Tess. Don't put a damper on the occasion by getting all serious. Time enough for that when we get back to the ranch.

When Nick motioned that lunch was ready, Tess practically leaped off the boulder.

HOURS LATER, Tess replayed the scene. Only this time she was sprawled in one of the fold-up chairs while Alec and Nick looked after dinner.

"Really," she protested. "Normally I have a lot more energy than this. Back home I can put in a sixteen-hour day if I need to."

Nick simply grinned but Alec said, "Yeah. Sitting at a keyboard."

Tess was feeling very mellow because she wasn't even tempted to rise to the bait. Instead, she gave an indulgent smile and watched Alec pump the propane camp stove. "No manly campfire?" she asked.

"Not here. Risk of forest fire. There was a nasty one a couple years ago. People in Lyons had to be evacuated." He turned up the burner and set a frying pan on it. "How do you like your steak?"

"Medium rare, please." Feeling guilty, Tess dragged herself toward the table. "At least let me make the salad."

Alec glanced up and grinned. "If you're sure you can handle it." He nodded toward a plastic bag. "Empty that bag into a bowl and the dressing's in that little plastic bottle."

"So it's all ready! Your sister's amazing."

"Yeah."

"How will they run the ranch when…after…?"

"He's wheelchair-bound?" Alec thought about that. "Right now, even *owning* the ranch by the time that happens is looking doubtful."

"Why?"

"There've been a lot of medical bills over the last two years, as you can imagine. Plus, there's been a drought here for a few years now. Ken once had a small herd of buffalo but eventually had to sell it off. Now they're down to a handful of horses, chickens for themselves and crops. So far they've managed to avoid selling off sections of land, but that may be inevitable. It was tough enough when he had his health. Now…" Alec turned off the stove. "Steaks are ready. Why don't you call Nick? He's over there, by the water." He gave a faint smile. "We can save the serious talk for later."

Tess took the hint, but hoped the talk wasn't going to include her future plans.

IT WAS ALEC'S TURN to watch Tess and Nick work and he had to admit, the sight was damn pleasant. Not so much the working part, but the chance to sit and study Tess without worrying about whether he was acting like a pervert or something. Though if thoughts counted…

He liked the way she rolled up the sleeves of her shirt and sank her hands into the plastic basin. Nick had fetched water and heated it on the stove and together, they got the job done without complaint or asking for help. Not that it was such a challenging task, but he knew a city slicker like her was more accustomed to rinsing under the tap and stacking in the dishwasher.

He also liked the way she used her right forearm to brush back a piece of hair that kept straying across her forehead. And the way she gave a half twist of her upper body to reach for the next dirty plate, creating a small gap between the buttons of her shirt. Enough of a gap for a flash of lacey undergarment that didn't look appropriate for a campout at all.

Oh, God, Alec sighed. This is what I've come to. Mooning over a woman while she's washing dishes.

When the dishes were finished, Alec got up to pour the last of the wine and brought a glass over to Tess, sitting a few feet away on a boulder that for some reason she'd taken a shine to. He looked back at Nick reading by the kerosene lamp. He'd been unusually chatty during the meal, even dropping his adolescent cloak of disdain and apathy. Bringing him here had been a stroke of genius and he admired Tess for not only having the intuition to recognize that the outing would be good for the kid, but to be willing to rough it herself. She was a good sport, under all that crusty business demeanor.

"What're you thinking?" he asked as he perched on the edge of the boulder, next to her.

She took a sip of wine before answering. "Just that it's so peaceful out here and if someone had told me three weeks ago I'd soon be camping in the Rockies, I'd have laughed or…or…" She gave a hapless shrug. "Well, I simply never would have believed it."

"Especially since you were planning a cruise somewhere. Weren't you?"

She nodded. "Yep. *A cruise*. God, it all seems so far away and long ago. Right now, I wonder why I even wanted to go on a cruise." She stared toward the lake, then said, "But that was Doug's idea anyway."

Alec's stomach muscles gave a little squeeze. "Doug?" Oh, yeah. The cruise guy.

"The friend I mentioned before, on the plane? At the time we booked it, I think we were already breaking up though we hadn't admitted it to each other."

A small whoosh of air at that. Shift the talk away from Chicago, he told himself.

But she did it for him, asking, "Have you ever thought about moving from town back to your family's ranch?"

"Briefly, when we first found out about Ken. But since then, Karen's convinced me to stick with my job in Boulder. For now, at any rate. We'll have to reassess the situation later, when Ken's not so mobile."

"You like your job."

"Yeah, I do." He laughed, recalling the initial reactions of friends and family after his return from Kosovo. "Though it's a long skip and hop from what I had been doing."

"In the Air Force?"

He turned his head toward her. "Karen told you about that?"

"A bit."

Alec looked away. He loved his sister but wished she'd be a bit more restrained when it came to passing on information. Still, perhaps she'd saved him the task. He'd never really talked about the NATO thing and now wasn't the time or place.

"You mentioned that they might lose the ranch?"

Conversation tonight wasn't going to be lighthearted after all. "They had to take a mortgage out on the place when Ken fell ill. My parents had paid it off years ago, but there wasn't a whole lot of cash lying about, if you know what I mean. Ken made some iffy business decisions, then was late with a few payments. The situation kinda snowballed before he and Karen could get a grip on it. The last two or three payments were missed completely. Unfortunately, they didn't tell me about it until just about a month ago. After they received a letter advising them that the mortgage holder planned to sell unless they could pay the arrears—with interest—by the end of this month." Alec downed the last of his wine. The urge to sip and enjoy now gone.

"By the end of May? But, that's less than three weeks away."

"I know. Short of their winning a lottery, it doesn't look good."

"Can't they persuade the bank to arrange bridge financing or something? Maybe they could have an auction and sell off—"

"What? The house? Then what's the point? Besides, they've tried all that, believe me. The holder will not be moved."

"And the mortgage holder is...?"

"Jed Walker." He didn't have to wait long for a response.

"I can't believe he'd be so mercenary."

Alec clenched his teeth. Believe it, he thought. Obviously no bias there. *No influence from the executor of your father's will or your current lunch date. God. Get a grip, Malone.* "What can I say?" He stood up and glanced back at the tent. Nick had gone inside, taking the lantern with him. "I see Nick's hit the sack. Not a bad idea, perhaps. Considering we'll likely be up early."

But she seemed reluctant to leave, gazing mutely at the dark water of the lake. When she did stand, she stumbled on a stone and lost her balance. Alec's arm shot out to stop her from tumbling. Once he got hold of her, he didn't want to let go. The air around him spun with the delicate scent of her body. He felt her heat closing round him like a fleecy blanket. And he knew—from the way she'd kissed him back last night—that the attraction was decidedly two-way.

His hands slid up the soft fabric of her sweatshirt, cradling her slender neck and gently drawing her head up close. She didn't pull back and when he found her lips— open and moist—excitement surged through him. He wanted to taste, then devour, as much of her as he could fit inside his mouth. Then he wanted to explore with his tongue the hidden crevices behind ears, at the base of her throat and the pulse points at her wrists. She pressed into him, her arms reaching up behind him. One hand forked through his hair and the other latched on to the collar of his shirt, holding him tightly against her.

It was all about sensation now. No time for thought much less second thoughts. When she began to move rhythmically into him, rubbing against his arousal, Alec ducked his head into her tousled hair and groaned. "Oh, Tess, Tess." He feverishly began a checklist of where they could go. The bushes? Too scratchy and maybe snakes. The Bronco? Uphill, but...

He slowed down, realizing that she'd begun to pull away. Her hands fell from his neck and she whispered, "Nick."

Then Alec heard, for the first time, the swish of the tent's canvas flap and the wheeze of the kerosene lamp being extinguished. The kid had decided to poke his head out at the wrong time. Alec bit down on his lower lip. Damn. What rotten luck. He held on a moment longer, letting the pain of unfulfilled desire dissipate. Then dropped his arms.

"I guess...I guess we should go to bed," she murmured. She gave a shaky laugh, just getting the irony of her suggestion. Seconds later, she vanished into the tent.

Alec sagged onto the boulder. The tremors sweeping through him were beginning to subside, but he stayed outside staring bleakly up at the night sky for a long time.

A CHILDHOOD GAME came to mind. She couldn't recall its name. It had something to do with taking steps forward and then back. The goal was to reach the person giving instructions at the front first and win the game. Tess sneaked a look at Nick, slumped so low into a corner of the family room sofa she could hardly see him in the dim glow cast by the television.

She had a feeling she was losing the game big time. There had been some progress with Nick at the start, then rapid deceleration as the weekend progressed. By the time they'd returned to the Malone ranch that afternoon, she figured she was almost back at square one.

There was no one else to blame but herself. First, for letting her body take charge without any consultation with her common sense the instant Alec Malone let his own impulses run wild. It was embarrassing enough knowing that Nick had probably witnessed the kiss last night. The passion ignited by Alec's touch had jolted *her*. How had the sight of it affected a thirteen-year-old who likely viewed any hint of sex between adults as disgusting? So, that was bad enough.

Worse still was her stress-induced tiff with Alec over coffee that morning. Her common sense was still running amok somewhere out in the desert for she'd foolishly mentioned the name most likely to arouse anger in Alec Malone. *Jed Walker.* Try again, she'd urged, to talk to him. Surely there was some iota of compassion in his lawyer's heart. Not that she really believed it herself, but what else could she say?

"Walker's got as much compassion as a rattlesnake honing in on a field mouse," Alec had muttered.

Tess closed her eyes, still cringing at her gaffe. Talk about jumping onto a roller coaster. Words and phrases bounced back and forth, disconnected from any thought or foresight. Culminating in his most hurtful taunt, so reminiscent of Nick's that she wondered if they'd exchanged bodies sometime in the night. *What do you care anyway? So long as your comfortable life in Chicago isn't ruffled?*

And the very moment that Nick walked around the side of the tent she had blurted, "So this is what that…that kiss was all about? Some kind of weird seduction to get me to change my mind about leaving the kids here, in a foster home?"

She could still see the expression in Nick's face. A blend of hurt and triumph. That he should have known all along how things were going to play out. Tess figured she'd taken at least six giant steps back.

Nick's show finished and he clicked off the set, even

though Tess was sitting in the chair opposite the sofa. Without a word or a backward glance, he headed for bed. Tess sat in the dark for a long time, wondering how she could possibly set things right. Or if it was simply too late.

IT TOOK A SECOND for Tess to realize the pounding was not just in her head, but at her door, too. It opened and Nick poked his head in. "Phone call. It's that Mr. Walker." He closed the door before Tess was fully awake.

Jed Walker. The person she blamed for yesterday's argument with Alec. Right now, the last person she wanted to speak to. But she dragged herself from bed, eyeing Molly's empty but made one. Someone—Nick?—had been at work while she slept off her guilt hangover. She staggered along the hall to the kitchen, half aware of the television blaring from the family room beside it. No school today, she wondered? Or did Nick go back tomorrow? Tess picked up the receiver, thinking she'd make a lousy substitute for a parent anyway.

"Tess?" Walker barked at her hoarse hello.

She moistened her lips, gave it another try. "Yes. Good morning," she said automatically, feeling there was really nothing good about it.

"I got the message you left Friday afternoon. About going through Richard and Gabriela's personal things. I wondered if you could bring in the list you made up of the items you think could be sold with the estate?"

"Uh, sure."

"You have a list, don't you?"

"Oh, yes," she lied.

"Great. I'm going to probate the will tomorrow and then I can get started on setting up the trust. I've a few ideas and would be willing to let you have some input, if you're interested."

God, she thought. Had she been in Boulder a mere week?

Felt more like a month. The fuzziness in her head vanished. "Yes. Yes, I am!" she exclaimed.

"Of course," he went on, "as sole executor I'm not legally bound to follow an instruction from you, but I understand as next of kin you ought to have some say."

He sounded pleased with his magnanimity. Tess tried to ignore the prickle of annoyance. *He's not the one to blame for your stupid quarrel with Alec*. She agreed to meet him and hung up.

Nick appeared in the kitchen doorway.

"No school today?" she asked.

"Yeah there is, but I didn't want to leave you like that."

"Like what?"

"You were like right out of it. I mean, even Molly's gabbing didn't wake you. So, I...uh thought I should stick around a bit. Make sure you were okay."

Tess was stunned. In spite of his casual tone, she saw that he'd been genuinely concerned. "Well, thanks, Nick. Thanks a lot. I appreciate having the chance to sleep in. It's been a while," she said, laughing. Too late, she realized how he might interpret that. A reminder of what she'd given up to come to Boulder.

His face turned red and he started to walk away. "Nick," she said, stopping him. "I didn't mean that the way it sounded."

"Sure," he said and moved toward the kitchen door.

"Look, after I shower and grab a coffee, I'll drop you off at school on my way to meet with Mr. Walker."

He nodded and vanished through the doorway. Tess closed her eyes, thinking perhaps she'd just jinxed the whole day. But a shower and cup of hot coffee later, she felt ready to deal with anything. Until Nick mentioned on the drive into Boulder that Molly's birthday was coming up. He seemed annoyed at her ignorance.

"I don't know your birth dates," Tess said. "It's not something that comes up in normal conversation."

"You've been here a whole week—"

"Exactly. How much can I learn in a week?"

Fortunately for her, he didn't answer. Though the expression in his face suggested *not much*. When Tess dropped him off at school and watched him amble inside with little more than a gruff goodbye, she couldn't help but feel that she was losing the battle to win over Nick. Yet why that mattered to her was a puzzle, considering she was most likely going to be an incidental part of his life once she returned to Chicago. She kept her eyes on his back as he slipped through the front door of his school. He looked so downtrodden and despairing. Tess blinked back tears. *I don't think I can go through with this. But what else can I do? Is Mavis right? Can I accommodate two kids into my lifestyle back home?* The answer was of course she could. It just wouldn't be the lifestyle she'd been accustomed to.

She shifted into drive, coasting out to the street. She'd been in Boulder a whole week and other than packing up personal items that belonged to her father and Gabriela, she'd done little else. There was only a week left of her vacation time and she still had to make a decision about the children. So what, she wondered, kept her in this constant state of vacillation? Drifting along from day to day with the hope that something—or someone—would compel her to make the right decision for everyone? Could that someone be Alec Malone? No, she thought, dismissing the idea at once. The man's attractive and could even be charming, but definitely too overbearing.

Tess had to make a short detour because a work crew was repairing traffic lights on the street leading to Jed Walker's office and, realizing she was passing the art gallery, impulsively pulled over to the curb. Kozinski had promised to get the painting to her as soon as it was ready. Why not check now, while she was here?

The gallery was empty of customers and Tess had to call out before Kozinski was aware that someone had come in.

He was obviously startled to see her. Wringing his hands, he kept saying that he'd wished she'd called first.

"Jed told me I could take the painting anytime," she said. It was a small lie, but wasn't she going to get the painting, anyway? "Is it back?"

His eyes answered for him, darting to his left. There, propped against an empty shelving unit, was the painting on wood her father had done so many years ago. Tess walked slowly toward it, almost mesmerized by a surge of memory—a vivid picture of her father standing at his easel, brush in hand and murmuring, "This one's for you, Tessie."

She stared at the framed side, a re-creation of her childhood living room. The rich gold of an autumn sunset burnished the shabby interior of the room, gilding it with a warm ambience it had never really known. A small child, crouching on the sofa in front of a window, was looking out to the street. From another person's perspective, Tess could see how the painting—a blend of light and shadow—would seem banal.

But she remembered sitting on that sofa, gazing wistfully out at a sidewalk teeming with children at play and neighbors chatting on porches. Remembered, too, the tension and strife within the house and how she often longed to be outside, away from the quarrelling.

The reverse side of the painting had been a still life that her father had impulsively painted one rainy afternoon after he'd finished the main portrait. Tess had an instant flash of playing with the items set out for the still life. Her father's initial irritation soon gave way to amusement and before long, they were rolling fruits and vegetables along the floor in a mock bowling game. Until Hannah had interrupted, demanding to know what all the racket was about. Hannah, always on the outside when the three of them were together.

Tess turned away, overcome. She was half-aware of Tomas Kozinski wringing his hands and anxiously repeating that if she waited a day or two he could wrap it properly for her return trip to Chicago. "It's okay," she said, cutting him off. "I'll take it now. I...uh...I can parcel it up properly when I go back to Chicago."

"Will that be soon?"

She frowned, her thoughts still on the painting. "Hmm? Oh, probably." When she picked it up, she noticed the brown paper backing over the framed pine. "There's another painting under that paper," she said.

"Oh, the cleaners covered it up. Best to protect it when it's hanging, you know." He bustled nervously around her as she headed for the door. It wasn't until he held it open for her that she thought of the pieces Walker had taken from the studio.

"Have you had a chance to assess the canvases Jed Walker brought in?"

His brow wrinkled.

"The canvases in my father's studio."

"Oh, those," he said, smiling.

"I gave them to Jed. Hasn't he brought them in yet?"

"Perhaps he hasn't had a chance yet. I'll give him a call."

As she left, he said, "Have a good trip back to Chicago," sounding, she thought, as if she were leaving imminently.

She carefully placed the painting in the back of the Volvo and closed the hatch. When she arrived ten minutes later at Jed Walker's office, his secretary informed her that he'd been summoned away on urgent business. Would she please leave the list of items and he'd call her that evening. Annoyed, Tess handed her the list she'd scribbled down over coffee and left the building.

When she got home, she left the painting in the trunk of the Volvo, deciding to drive the car around to the studio where she would store it. She went inside to check for phone messages first. Molly's school had called to inform her that Molly had been involved in a fight at recess and was very upset. She wanted to go home and could someone pick her up as soon as possible?

Tess grabbed her purse and keys and rushed back out to the car. It was almost eleven and she worried that Molly would think no one was coming for her. Fortunately, the highway into Boulder wasn't busy and twenty minutes later, she pulled up in front of Molly's school. Molly burst into tears the instant Tess walked into the school office, bawling that a classmate had called her an orphan and when she'd denied it, others had joined in chanting the word until Molly started swinging. Good for you, Tess had thought.

But the sight of Molly in such distress made Tess feel helpless. She thought she might burst into sobs herself, right there in the principal's office. On the way out of the school parking lot, Tess suggested they head for McDonald's for lunch. Molly's pinched face broke into a great smile and Tess felt oddly pleased. *I may be hopeless at providing comfort, but at least I can do lunch.*

They shopped afterwards and didn't arrive home until almost five. Molly helped unload the groceries and carry them into the kitchen. Tess didn't notice anything amiss until Molly called from the rear of the house. Her voice sounded urgent. Tess stopped unpacking food and headed down the hall where Molly was standing, Squiggly in her hands, in front of the master bedroom. Her small mouth was shaped into a huge, silent Oh and her eyes were big with fright.

The bedroom curtains had been pulled off their track and hung in a forlorn heap on the floor. Closet doors were wide-open and their contents flung about. The plastic bags of clothing that they had packed up on Friday were untouched, but the chest of drawers had been pulled away from the wall. Tess looked with horror at Molly.

"I'm scared, Tess."

"It's okay, honey. I'm going to call 9-1-1 from the

phone in the kitchen.'' She clutched on to Molly's hand and they walked quickly down the hall. Tess cast a quick but furtive glance in each of the bedrooms and the bathroom as they made for the kitchen. Tess sat Molly in a chair and dialed the number. There was a bit of a hassle with the operator, who didn't consider the call an emergency. But when Tess retorted that the person still might be on the premises, she was told police officers would be right there.

"Do you think someone's hiding?'' Molly asked when she hung up.

"No, no, burglars don't want to get caught, right? They want to leave as soon as possible. I just said that so someone would come right away.''

Molly nodded, but she didn't look convinced.

"I could check and make sure. Would you be okay in here while I do that?''

Molly nodded. "Squiggly will keep me company.''

Tess wanted to stay with her but her impulse to ensure that no one else was in the house was stronger. "I'll be right back,'' she said, dashing from the room and along the hall to the back door.

The door was ajar, one of its window panes smashed in. Tess slowed down. Was someone still outside or in the studio? She hesitated, peering into the empty yard. She waited a few seconds, then stepped out. The studio was at a forty-five-degree angle to the back door, but Tess saw that it had not escaped notice. The hanging planter was lying upside down on the ground next to the studio door while the corner pane of glass in the door had been smashed, allowing someone enough room to insert an arm and unlock the door.

She was tempted to look in the studio but didn't want to leave Molly in the house alone. When she returned to the kitchen, she reassured her that the thieves had gone.

"I'm glad Nick wasn't home when the burglars came," she said.

Tess clasped a hand to her mouth. She'd forgotten all about Nick. He should have been home by then. "You're right," she said to Molly. It had been a stroke of luck that Nick wasn't home, but where the heck was he anyway?

CHAPTER ELEVEN

THE POLICE ARRIVED a little after six. Nick had still not come home and Tess knew she'd have to make a decision about what to do. The problem was, she didn't know any of his friends, nor did she know where Nick kept an address book. If he even had one. She'd never felt so helpless in all her life.

The two officers who came weren't that impressed by what they saw. Minimal damage, they'd said. When Tess was unable to give them a list of stolen items—in fact, when she'd admitted she couldn't be certain if anything had been stolen at all—the police dismissed the break-in as a juvenile prank. Or perhaps, they'd insisted, some juvie had been looking for loose cash or alcohol, rather than the usual electronic equipment. One of the officers found a piece of plywood in the garage and nailed it across the broken window of the door leading into the house.

"You'll want to call the insurance people right away and get those windows fixed," he cautioned.

As they were leaving, a battered pickup roared up the drive, squealed to a halt in a tornado of dust and gravel, and disgorged Nick. The expression in his face as he took in the police cruiser, the officers and Tess, was a mix of confusion and apprehension. Later, Tess realized he'd assumed she'd called the police because he hadn't come right home from school.

The pickup roared off in much the same manner as it had arrived, which allowed a brief glimpse of an older teenager at the wheel. Tess noticed the officers raise their eyebrows at one another.

"What's the matter?" Nick asked, drawing closer. His eyes darted to the police but settled on Tess.

She thought he looked guilty about something and apparently, the police did, too.

"Where've you been, son?" one of them asked.

Nick frowned. "With friends."

"What friends? Other than the guy in the pickup."

Nick's frown deepened. "Kids from school. Why?"

The second officer took over. "Thing is, guy, your house was broken into this afternoon sometime."

Tess saw Nick's eyes widen in disbelief. She saw instantly that he'd known nothing about it. He turned from the police to her.

"I don't think anything was stolen," she said. "Maybe you can look around with me later, to find out for sure."

"Is this not your residence, ma'am? Are you not Gabriela Wheaton?"

Tess felt the color rise into her face. She avoided Nick, turning her head to say, "No, I'm Tess Wheaton. Gabriela and Richard Wheaton—the former owners of the place—are...are dead."

"Oh. So you would be related how?"

"I'm, uh, Nick's sister. Richard Wheaton was my father."

The officers nodded but the puzzled expressions didn't leave their faces.

"So are you this fella's guardian, then?"

"Uh, I suppose you could call me that—for now."

"For now? This is confusing, ma'am. What I need to know is, whom shall we call if we find any stolen property or if we're lucky enough to catch the deadbeat that broke in?"

Now it was her turn for the hot seat, Tess figured. Nick and the police were staring at her with expectant faces. "I'll be here for the next...uh, few days, maybe even a week. But the family lawyer—Jed Walker—is executor of the estate so any information about stolen property should probably be raised with him.''

Their nods were synchronized with growing suspicion in their faces. Something was amiss, their personal radar was warning. But they couldn't quite put a finger on it. Tess might have been more amused had she not sensed Nick's tension.

As if reading her mind, the first officer turned to Nick. ''Can you give us more specific details of your whereabouts today? I assume you weren't at school, otherwise you'd have told us right off.''

Nick cast a quick sidelong glance at Tess, taking one step away from her. ''No,'' he mumbled. ''I wasn't at school. I had a free period, so I left early.''

''Uh-huh. Then maybe you can give us a name and address of someone who can vouch for you?''

''Why? Am I, like, some kinda suspect or something?''

''It happens, fella. In the best of families. Kids feel they're not getting enough allowance—or even attention.''

''I wouldn't break into my own house. That's stupid. Why would I do that?''

''Like I said, there are lots of reasons.''

A heavy silence fell over the four of them. Tess felt she ought to say something, to come to Nick's defense, but found herself focusing on the fact that he'd skipped school again and no one had called. Not even Alec.

After a long moment, the second officer said, ''Well, maybe you can give your...uh, sister some names and she can pass them on to us. Thing is, even if you weren't involved, one of your buddies could have been. This place is mighty tempting, out here off the highway. No close neighbors. A person could take all the time he wanted to have a look around. Maybe even come back.''

Thanks for that, officer. I'm really going to sleep well tonight. Tess rubbed her arms, chilled by the thought.

Nick just stared sullenly at the ground. Finally, the officer reminded Tess to call them with a list of any stolen property and that they, in turn, would get back to her as soon as possible. "Though I hate to say, ma'am, the success rate for this kinda job isn't too good."

As soon as the cruiser was out of sight, Nick wheeled on Tess. "Thanks for all the support—Sis! Great job. Good to have you in the family." He spun on his heel and headed for the front door.

"Wait a sec," she called out. "You don't have the right to speak to me like that. You went back on your word. You promised you'd go to school and then you don't even have the grace to call and tell us where you are or when you'll be home."

"As if that would've made a difference. I don't owe you anything, Tess. Not even promises. 'Cause if adults can break them, so can kids. And like you just said to those cops, like, you don't even know when you're going home. Only that you are. Why don't you just be honest with us and admit that you don't wanna have a brother and sister hanging on your neck like a ball and chain?"

"I've never said that!"

"Yeah, but you never needed to. It was kinda obvious to everyone from the start. Even to Alec, who's, like, the most positive person I know. Even he doesn't believe you'll stay."

The truth in what he said stung. She hadn't been very subtle about her intentions or her feelings. And she had been handing out mixed messages to everyone. Tess closed her eyes. What a screwup. How had she so miserably failed at what she'd thought would be a simple task?

Nick disappeared into the house and when Tess composed herself, she followed. Dinner was eaten in silence. Even Molly was quiet, sensing there'd been trouble with

Nick. As soon as they finished, Nick disappeared without helping to clean up.

"I'm old enough to help, too, Tess," Molly said.

Shamed by Molly's efforts to stay cheerful and suspecting the girl was worried that Tess might just give up and fly back to Chicago, Tess attempted levity by suggesting a board game before bed. Molly's surprised enthusiasm only made Tess feel worse.

Hours later, just before midnight, she went to double-check the back door at the end of the hall and when she found it slightly ajar, an ugly thought took shape in her mind. She strode to Nick's room, knocked sharply and opened his door without waiting for a reply. The room was empty.

ALEC REACHED for the phone but, half-asleep, fumbled the receiver. He groped for it as it swayed pendulum-like between the bed and the table. His groggy senses registered the shrill pitch of a female voice as he kept swinging at the receiver and finally, managed to grasp hold of it.

"What?" he barked into the receiver, realizing the other person hadn't stopped talking—shrieking, more like—the whole time.

"You don't have to shout."

Tess Wheaton. He identified the dulcet but icy tones right away. What now? He rubbed his eyes and looked at the clock radio. Jeez. Midnight. He shot up. "What is it? Has something happened?"

"I just…have you seen Nick? Is he there?"

Oh God. This was not good. "No, he isn't. What's happened? Tell me everything."

She blurted it all out in one long run-on sentence but he quickly synthesized three things. *Break-in. Police. Fight with Nick.* "Have you called any of his friends?"

A loud sigh. "I don't know any of his friends. That's one of the problems. I—I feel so damn helpless."

"Okay. Relax. We should assume that he's run off to spend the night with someone. Any idea when he left?"

"No. He went out the back door and I just discovered he was gone a minute ago. I'm—I'm sorry but you were the only person I could think to call."

Well, at least she hadn't called the police. Or worse, Jed Walker.

"All right. I'm going to get dressed and drive toward your place. I'll go real slow. Maybe I'll see him out on the road somewhere."

"God, he wouldn't be hitchhiking at this time of night, would he?"

"I truly hope not. But unless he's taken the Volvo, his only way to get from there into town is by walking."

"I didn't think to check the garage. I'll go do that now."

She hung up. Alec stared at the disconnected phone then replaced the receiver. Her cool business exterior was unraveling under pressure, he thought. Which may not be a bad thing. Maybe when the outside stuff was completely cast aside, the real Tess Wheaton would be there for all to see and admire. *Maybe.* One could always hope.

He got up to dress and was searching for his car keys when the downstairs buzzer to his second-floor apartment pierced the quiet. He froze, then dashed to the intercom. He knew as soon as he pressed the button whose voice he'd be hearing.

"Alec? It's me, Nick. Can I come up?"

TWENTY-FIVE MINUTES after Tess ran from garage to house, having confirmed that the car was still there, she saw headlights from the front drive sweep across the darkened living room. She reached the front door and had it opened before the Bronco's engine stopped.

"Did you see him?" she asked when Alec stepped out the driver side. She clutched her robe lapels against the base of her throat, as if the night temperature had suddenly dropped ten degrees.

"Yeah, I saw him." He jerked his head to the Bronco. "He's inside. Showed up on my doorstep right after you hung up."

She felt her legs wobble with relief and leaned against the door frame. "Thank God."

"I wouldn't give him the talk tonight, if you know what I mean. He's pretty upset."

"We're all upset," she hissed.

He shrugged his shoulders as if to say, *See what I mean?* Tess bit back her annoyance as soon as she saw Nick climb out of the SUV. He shuffled toward her, barely raising his eyes to watch where he was going. Without a word, he brushed past her and went inside.

"He has a lot on his chest right now, Tess. He needs to talk and most of all, he needs someone to listen. Without judgment."

She felt the little hairs on the back of her neck stand up. *Without judgment.* Why, she was the least judgmental person she knew.

"He told me about the break-in," he was saying, totally unaware that she was still staring at him as if he'd just sprouted another head. She couldn't believe how egocentric the man was. So self-righteous.

"Was anything stolen?"

"I don't know," she mumbled. "Nothing obvious. I mean, the TV-VCR is still here and the two computers. All of Richard's paint things seem to be there, though they were messed up."

"How did they get in?"

"The door windows in the house and the studio were broken."

"Do you want me to stay over tonight?"

"No, no. We'll be fine. The police nailed a board over the door leading into the house."

"Call Walker in the morning and find out if there's still insurance coverage. I imagine there is. Have him give you the name of the company so someone can fix those windows right away." He paused, searching her face. "So what do the police think?"

"Nick didn't tell you?"

"Tell me what?"

Ha. No wonder you're standing here looking so unflappable. "They think some kids did it. High school kids, maybe. Maybe even…Nick."

"He'd never do anything like that."

"I agree. But he may know someone who would. That's what the police were suggesting and he just…just blew up at the idea."

"Because kids are very loyal to their friends. So questioning the value of friends is the same as questioning their judgment in making those friends."

"You sound as though kids never make poor choices in friends."

"I'm not saying that. Just that they're not going to admit it if they do. Certainly not to a parent or a cop. It would be like admitting they made a mistake. And—" he paused a beat "—no one likes to admit that, do they?"

Tess frowned. She had a vague sense the conversation was not exclusively about Nick now. She took a calming breath. "So what's your advice?" she asked, knowing for sure he'd have some.

He did. "Like I said, give him some space. Maybe let him stay home in the morning. But you need to reassure him that everything will be okay."

"How can I do that? I can't guarantee that! No one can."

Alec walked right up to her. He was, she noted with some discomfort, well within arm's reach. "But you can," he said. His voice was low, almost insistent. "You can make a decision right now that will ensure everyone in this house will sleep well tonight."

Except me, she was thinking. She started toward the front door when his hand caught her. "Tess," he whispered. "I'm sorry we had that…whatever it was. I had a feeling on the weekend that we…you and I…had made some kind of connection."

Right, she wanted to quip. *Your lips to mine. End of story.* But she kept quiet, waiting to see where he was going to go with this.

"And I'm not sure exactly how or when, but it all just fell apart before it really even got started."

He gave a woeful grin that almost had Tess extend a hand to him.

"So, I guess what I'm trying to say," he murmured, his warm breath a whisper on her cheeks, "is that, uh, I'm hoping we can try to handle this with kid gloves because I very much want to get back that moment last night. When I…when you…before—"

"Nick saw us."

"Yeah. Jeez. No wonder the kid's confused. Seeing the two of us kissing like that was probably like seeing your friend—"

"Sleeping with your enemy?"

"Huh?" His forehead crinkled. "What's that supposed to mean? That's quite a leap, isn't it? From a kiss to—"

She was in it now, Tess figured. Might as well keep sinking. "Bed? Is that what you were going to say?"

Alec wiped a palm across his brow as if it were high noon, rather than the middle of the night. "Heck no! Not that I…uh, I mean, I'd love to go there but—no, wait. Maybe I shouldn't go there at all, if you know what I mean. I mean—"

Nice to see someone else floundering for a change. "What *do* you mean, Alec?" She inched closer. He was sweating. She was almost on the tips of his shoes. She thought she could hear his heart hammering against his ribs.

Or maybe it was the echo of her own? Never mind. She liked making him sweat. Liked being in control again.

She raised her two hands, cupping his face and lowering it to hers so quickly she heard him gasp. Then she placed her lips on his and pressed him to her.

For a long moment—maybe eternity—he simply stood there, hands at his side. Until something deep inside awoke and he clutched the back of her head, holding it just enough to make sure she didn't pull away any time soon.

Not that she intended to.

TESS WAVED a goodbye that only Molly returned as she and Nick walked down the drive toward the highway. Although Nick was obviously still angry at her, he'd agreed to help her go through the master bedroom and the studio later that day to check for any stolen items. She was about to close the door when she saw a truck turn into the bottom of the drive. It slowed down as it passed Nick and Molly, then proceeded on to the house.

As it drew closer, Tess recognized the neighbor down the road. Stone. But what was his first name? *Larry*. Grateful that she was already dressed, she stepped out to greet him as he climbed out of the truck.

"Good morning, Mr. Stone. How are you?"

He took his Stetson off and smiled. "Please—it's Larry. Thought I'd pop by to see if things are okay here."

"Oh? Well, we're fine thanks."

"Just that when I was going home late yesterday afternoon, I noticed a police cruiser here. I would've called right away, but the wife and I had an engagement in town and I was already late."

She knew he was waiting for her to offer an explanation. "We had a break-in yesterday. When I was in town with Molly."

"No!" The shock in his face brought the whole frightening moment back again.

Tess nodded, suddenly too overcome to speak.

He moved swiftly to her side, wrapping an arm around her shoulders. "You poor thing. You must've been scared out of your wits."

Tess felt herself tear up, but resisted the urge to sob on his shoulder. "It was pretty frightening at first," she said. "The strange thing is that we don't think anything was taken. Nick and I went through the whole place and other than the master bedroom and the studio being messed up a bit, nothing was missing."

He dropped his hand from her shoulder and took a step back, frowning at her. "Maybe your arrival interrupted them or something. You sure you're okay? You look a bit pale."

"I'm fine, seriously." She hesitated.

He insisted on seeing the damage and she walked him around the house to the back door. He inspected it and the broken window in the studio. "These windows can't be left like this. Look, I know a great contractor in Boulder who does a lot of work for me. How about I give him a call and have him come out to fix them?"

"Shouldn't I wait and call the insurance company?"

He pursed his lips in disdain. "Then you'll really wait. If I were you, I'd get them fixed first, then present a bill. I'll make sure the guy gives you a good deal."

"That would be wonderful, Larry."

He smiled. "I'll have him give you a ring later today. And by the way, if you feel nervous about being alone here with the kids, call us. Here," he said, digging into his jeans pocket for a wallet. "Take my card. I know Richard had my phone number in the house somewhere, but just in case you can't find it." He handed Tess a small white business card that read Stone Construction and Development. "You're welcome at our place anytime, night or day. Just give us a call."

"Thanks, Larry. That's very kind of you."

"Hey, neighbors have to be good to one another out here. You never know what can happen." He must have seen something in her face for he quickly added, "I mean, snowstorms in winter or electricity going off. When you live in the country, you depend on neighbors for more than a cup of sugar." He laughed and turned toward his truck. "By the way, Marci's been talking about dropping by one day. Just to let you know we haven't forgotten about you."

Tess smiled and waved as he got back into the truck and drove away. His offer had been friendly and although she doubted she'd ever need to call on him, she appreciated knowing someone nearer than Alec was available. She wandered back into the house and finished tidying up the breakfast dishes. It was only eight-forty-five and the day loomed long and empty ahead of her.

Of course, she reminded herself, there were chores she could tackle. The laundry hamper was growing ominously large and the family room, littered with various articles of clothing, scraps of paper and books and old newspapers cried for attention. But Tess hated housecleaning more than cooking and she rationalized that the place would receive a good clean when it was put up for sale.

It was a bit early to call Mavis, but Tess craved a talk with her, especially after last night's outburst from Nick. *Face it, girl.* It was the subsequent tiff with Alec that had been the actual cause of her restless sleep. She poured herself a coffee and sat down by the phone.

Mavis was shocked about the break-in. "Are you sure there's no danger of that person coming back?" she asked.

Little hairs rose at the back of Tess's neck at this echo of the police officer's very warning.

When she told Mavis about the ensuing incident with Nick, her guardian was blunt. "This can't go on much longer, Tessie."

The childhood nickname indicated Mavis was worried. "What?"

"Don't play with me, lass. You've got to make up your mind about the kiddies. They've been waiting long enough. That's why the lad is so touchy."

"I've only been here little more than a week."

"Doesn't matter," she said. "You get busy with that decision. Those children need to know what's going to happen to them."

Tess massaged her forehead. Mavis's lilt always came out when she was worried or stressed. "I know, Mavis. I just don't know what to do. The more I get to know the kids, the more I worry about who they'll end up with."

"Exactly."

"So what do you think I should do?"

"You know how I feel, but I can't advise you what to do. You have to listen to your heart, not your head."

Tess had to admire Mavis's uncanny ability to bring her to a point in the discussion and then drop her, leaving her to figure things out on her own. It was a strategy the older woman had used when Tess was a teenager and rebelling against curfews and other restrictions. Tess chatted further about more neutral topics like Molly's coming birthday but ended with the promise that she'd make a decision in the next couple of days.

When she hung up, Tess wasn't sure if she felt better after her talk with Mavis or worse. The woman had the knack of reducing complicated issues to simple fact. Tess wished she had the same skills, especially where her feelings toward Alec Malone were concerned. She touched her upper lip. A wonder it wasn't red and swollen this morning, she thought, from all that kissing. Her thoughts began to drift...

The shrill peal of the telephone made her jump. It was the contractor Larry had called about the broken windows. He told Tess he had some free time later in the morning and was planning a visit to the Stone place anyway. Silently grateful to Larry for arranging the repairs so quickly, she hung up. The thought of the studio reminded her that she'd left the painting in the back of the Volvo, now in the garage. She headed out there and carried the painting into the studio, setting it up on one of the easels.

It hadn't been framed when her father had taken it with him, the last time she saw him. It looked as fresh as it had years ago—a result of the cleaning Kozinski had mentioned, she supposed. She decided against leaving it on the easel, in case whoever had broken in did come back, as the police warned. As she removed it to store in a closet, she noticed that part of the paper backing had ripped when she'd pulled it from the car.

It wouldn't hurt, she figured, to have a look at the other painting. She could always wrap it again. She tore at the paper and a long strip came away, revealing not an oil still life, but the coarse grain of wood. The painting was no longer there.

Stunned, Tess ran her fingers along the wood. Someone—and she knew instinctively that it would never have been her father—had cut the board in two, separating the paintings. Tomas Kozinski would have had to know about it, yet he'd not mentioned a word to her when she picked up the painting yesterday. She placed the painting in the closet, locked up the studio and marched into the house to telephone the gallery.

"Mr. Kozinski," she said when his recorded message played. "It's Tess Wheaton. There's a problem with the painting you gave me yesterday. I know there was a still life on the back but it's no longer there. Would you know anything about that? Please call me immediately. I'm also going to be calling Jed Walker, to find out if he knows what happened to the other painting."

As soon as she replaced the receiver, she dialed Walker's number. He sounded only mildly interested, though his tone became more alarmed when she used the words *fraud* and *investigate*.

"I'm sure there's a good explanation for this, Ms. Wheaton. Kozinski is a very reputable art dealer. No way would he be involved in anything bordering on fraud. My bet is that your father either gave permission for the paintings to be split or did it himself."

"He wouldn't," she sputtered, angered by the suggestion. "The paintings had to stay together because they're both connected to me."

"How so?"

"Because…because I was the subject of one and the other was connected to a specific childhood memory."

"Yet you and your father were apparently estranged for years, were you not? And don't forget, the bequest was made as a codicil. Basically an afterthought, Ms. Wheaton."

Tess closed her eyes, pained at the inference in what he said. *An afterthought.* True enough. Perhaps she'd never know what instinct had prompted Richard Wheaton to make that codicil, but he had. And Tess knew he'd never have left her only half of a memory.

"Well, just to reassure you, I'll personally give Kozinski a call to see what I can find out. By the way, the will's in probate and I have a buyer for the house."

"A buyer?"

She must have sounded dumbfounded, for he hesitated briefly. "Yes. The house and contents need to be sold in order for me to tally the full net worth of the estate. Then I can proceed with the trust funds for the children."

"And the children?"

"If you decide against applying for legal guardianship, then Child Protective Services will place them. I know the Sullivans want to keep Molly. As for Nick…" His voice trailed off. "I'm sure Mr. Malone will think of something. At any rate, the children only factor into my job in terms of the trust. When I receive the go-ahead from probate, I'll negotiate the sale of the house."

"Couldn't you put it off for a few days? It's just that I'm not sure yet what I'll be doing. I don't think the kids will be able to handle such a big disruption. They're just settling in now and—"

"I hear what you're saying, but the wheels of business roll on, do they not? Surely you can appreciate that. An interested buyer in today's market cannot be so easily dismissed. In the long run, settling the estate and getting the money from it into a trust is the best we can do for those kiddies. Listen, I've got to go now. There's a call waiting for me. I'll get back to you."

He hung up before she could add another word. Tess held the receiver a moment longer, replaying what he'd just said. His only interest, she realized now, was to rid himself of the Wheaton affairs as soon as possible. Once the estate was sold off and the trust set up, he would no longer have any interest in the children or what became of them. No one would, except for maybe Alec Malone. Who wasn't family.

She tried the art gallery again, but when the answering machine came on again, she hung up. A face-to-face confrontation was exactly what the situation required. After the man came to repair the windows, she would head into Boulder.

THERE WAS A parking space a few yards before the art gallery and Tess angled the Volvo into it. She switched off the engine and had her hand on the door to get out when she saw Jed Walker exit the building, followed by an agitated Tomas Kozinski. He obviously said something that halted Walker in his tracks. The lawyer stepped back and the two huddled in conversation. Whatever they were discussing, they didn't look happy with one another, Tess thought.

After a few minutes, Walker strode toward a car parked farther along the block and drove off while Kozinski

watched from the pavement. The look on the art dealer's
face made Tess shudder. Now wasn't the time to confront
him about the painting. She waited until he went back into
the gallery and sat for a moment longer, trying to make
sense of what she'd witnessed.

They'd obviously been having some kind of disagreement and Tess's sudden idea that the scene might be related
to her discovery about the painting was irresistible. She had
to discuss it with someone and knew the one person who
might be interested was Alec Malone. His office was somewhere in the downtown core. She dug into her purse for
his business card.

CHAPTER TWELVE

ALEC HAD TO restrain himself from catching hold of Tess's hand as it flailed in front of his face. He'd sensed from the sound of her voice when she'd called him at work half an hour before that something had upset her. And although he knew she'd get to the point soon, he wished she'd hurry. Still, it was nice to sit and watch the various expressions play on her face while he recalled last night in every shivering detail.

They'd grabbed for one another as if they were hormone-driven teenagers. He had a feeling she, too, had gone a long time with no loving. Either that or this Doug fella had failed miserably at making Tess Wheaton a happy woman. Not that he himself had been able to satisfy her the way he'd wanted to. Not standing in the driveway, at any rate.

He'd spent the drive home not just aching with unfulfilled desire but also wondering what the heck had happened to unleash such a torrent of passion. What chemical reaction had suddenly exploded between them to carry them from a state of constant disagreement to physical frenzy?

"What?" Tess suddenly asked, catching him in his reverie.

"Hmm?"

"You had a strange look on your face when I said that I decided to tear the paper off the back of the painting."

"I did? Just thinking about last night," he admitted, grinning.

Two round circles of color spotted her cheeks. "Oh. That was…unexpected," she said.

"Damn right."

"I mean, considering how we've been arguing about everything the past few days."

"Not arguing so much as disagreeing."

"More than disagreeing."

"Now we're disagreeing about disagreeing," he pointed out.

She smiled, catching the edge of her lower lip between her teeth. He was beginning to recognize that as her embarrassed look. "True, but last night we agreed on something."

He leaned across the table and grasped hold of the hand clenched at the base of her throat. Another sign of nervousness. "I'll say," he murmured.

She tugged away her hand, ostensibly to reach for her glass of water. "Okay, so back to what I was saying. When I took off the paper, I saw that the painting on the other side was gone."

Unsure of what that signified, he shot her a blank look rather than make it too obvious he hadn't been paying much attention to what she'd been saying.

"My father often painted on wooden boards in those days," she explained. "And he sometimes used both sides to save money. The painting that he left to me was one of those and both sides had something to do with me. One is a portrait when I was five or six. The other side was a still life."

Alec found himself drawn into her story, in spite of his difficulty in focusing thoughts away from last night. He'd never met Richard Wheaton but had read about him. The contrast between the commercially successful painter and the desperate man Tess had known was striking. He could see her logic, that separating the two paintings wasn't something the painter would do. But when he reminded her that the studio fire had destroyed many of Wheaton's works and that maybe he'd needed to raise some hard cash to pay the bills, Alec saw the indignation rising in her eyes. She didn't want to hear that. He backed off. "Tell me why this painting is so important to you?" He saw from the look on her face that his question had startled her.

She took her time answering. "Not just because it represents a time in my life when I was happy. When I thought I'd have a family forever." She dropped her gaze. Finally, she raised her eyes to him. They glistened with tears. "I think he took the painting with him when he left because he wanted to keep some memory of me and the days we spent together while he painted it. And it's important, too, because after he left my mother destroyed the works he'd left behind. So that painting is really all I have left of my father."

Alec didn't know what to say. He knew what he wanted to do—take her into his arms. But she was on the opposite side of the table in a crowded restaurant. Besides, he sensed comfort wasn't what she wanted so much as understanding. So he simply nodded and murmured, "Then you definitely need to straighten out what's happened."

She gave him a grateful smile and was about to say something else when the waitress brought their order.

"I'm glad you like Mexican food," he said, wanting to lighten the moment, "because Juanita's is one of the best in town and I'm hoping we can do this again sometime."

"Uh, sure." She glanced up from the forkful of enchilada poised in front of her mouth.

"That is, if you're still around."

She set the fork down onto her plate. "I need to talk to you about that, Alec."

Uh-oh. Here it comes. You and your big mouth, Malone.

"I spoke to Jed Walker today and he informed me that he had a buyer for the house. He seems to be in a rush to close the sale and when I asked him about the kids and what would happen to them, he was almost dismissive. As if he really couldn't care less."

And why does that surprise you? he wanted to ask, but was quick enough to keep his mouth shut this time.

"I know that probably doesn't come as a surprise to you," she said, reading his mind. "But I was struck by how cool he was about it. All that charm at our first meeting and how he assured me that he wanted my input into what happened to them—all that just vanished. The bottom line was—"

"Money."

She poked at her lunch again. "Yes," she said, sighing. "I can't help but think that not so long ago, I wouldn't have questioned that bottom line."

Alec was certain he was gaping. He couldn't believe she was actually admitting it. She'd come a long way in the ten days or so he'd known her.

"Now," she said, meeting his eyes at last, "I'm more confused than ever. I hate the thought of handing the kids over to just anyone."

He waited for her to make the connections, join the dots to realizing she couldn't leave them at all.

"What should I do?"

Disappointment flooded through him. Not there just yet, he thought. But getting closer. "The decision is up to you, Tess, and it has to be something you can live with."

He saw at once that his response had been an equal disappointment. She ducked her head, picking away at what was supposed to be the best enchilada in town.

"Believe me," he said, his voice low and earnest. "I want to be able to tell you what to do, but I can't. As I said, it's a decision that has to be yours alone."

She nibbled on her food, giving his statement some thought. Then she obviously tucked it away for future reference, because the next thing she said was totally off subject.

"A strange thing that happened, though, was when I drove over to the art gallery to confront Tomas Kozinski about the painting."

It took Alec a second to pick up the thread of thought that led to the non sequitur. "What?"

"I had just parked the car when I saw Jed Walker and Tomas outside the art gallery in deep conversation about something. They looked really ticked off at one another."

"So what happened?"

"Not much. Jed got in his car and drove away. I didn't have the nerve to face Tomas because he looked furious. That's when I called you."

Alec didn't know what to make of the incident. He'd never met Kozinski but figured anyone who had business dealings with Walker had to be suspect, too. With the exception of Richard Wheaton, he amended. Though he couldn't for the life of him work out that business connection.

"I wondered if their argument had anything to do with my painting."

"Perhaps," he said, shrugging. "Seems a stretch, though, don't you think? I mean, isn't their only connection your father? Unless Walker's a customer as well."

"They didn't seem that friendly when Jed took me to the gallery to meet Tomas."

"Maybe they're not friends so much as business acquaintances."

"Perhaps." She had a distant look in her eyes.

"What else is new on the home front?" he asked, wanting to get back to the kids.

"Molly's birthday is on Sunday and I wondered if you would like to come for dinner."

"Sure, great. Is she having a party?"

"Oh, I don't know. I mean, I haven't talked to her about it. Should I?"

Still a ways to go, he was thinking. He smiled. "Most

kids expect or want a party. You could ask—maybe some of her classmates could come.''

The doubt in her face turned to worry. ''I guess. I haven't the faintest idea what to do. I've never put on a kid's party before.''

He had to laugh at the bewilderment in her face. ''Yeah, but haven't you been to any?''

''Not for a very long time,'' she said.

Something in her tone tugged at him. He wished he were sitting on the banquette seat next to her, instead of across the table. He also wished he didn't have to go back to work.

''Look,'' he said, signaling the waitress for the bill. ''Take your time with your lunch. I've got to go. I'll call you tonight, okay?''

The look she gave him made leaving damn near impossible. ''Keep that thought,'' he said, tapping her forehead with the tip of his index finger. ''Until we're alone together again.''

She blushed but said nothing. He walked out, feeling her eyes on him the whole way.

JUST BEFORE TESS turned into the drive leading to the ranch, a car passed from the opposite direction, braked, made a sharp U-turn and drove up behind Tess. By the time she had turned off the Volvo engine and climbed out, the other driver was doing the same. A woman in her early forties walked toward Tess, smiling.

''Hi! I'm Marci Stone.'' She held out her right hand and gave Tess's a firm shake. ''Larry told me about the break-in. That's so horrible! I've been meaning to call and invite you for a drink, but things have been hectic at our place. After what happened yesterday, I bet you could use a drink.'' She uttered a tinkling laugh. ''How about dropping by about fiveish?''

''Sure. That would be great. Thanks, Marci.'' Tess watched the petite blonde get back into her car and drive off. The custom of having a social drink with a neighbor was alien to the workaholic's life Tess had led in Chicago. And after her lunch with Alec, she didn't feel much like making the kind of small talk the occasion would require. On the other hand, Larry Stone had done a wonderful favor for her that morning. She had bought a bottle of wine in town as a thank-you and would take it with her.

When she went inside, she saw that Nick was playing with Molly and her hamster. He'd been almost ignoring his younger sister for the past few days and Tess was relieved to see him giving her some of his time. He looked up as she stood watching them from the family room doorway.

"I've just been invited to the Stones for a drink. Think you two can manage? If you'd rather I stayed here, just say so. It doesn't matter a whole lot to me."

"We'll be fine," he said right away. "Want me to start something for dinner?"

Wonder of wonders, Tess was thinking. Maybe this is his way of apologizing. "I forgot to get something out of the freezer. Any suggestions?"

He thought for a moment. "There may be a pizza in the freezer. Or lasagna."

"Great. Well, whatever you two decide on is okay by me. And if you get hungry before I come back, go ahead without me. Though I doubt that I'll be long."

He nodded, then just as she was about to turn away, said, "I told Molly I'd help her plan her birthday party. Is that okay?"

Oh, are we having a birthday party then? Tess nodded slowly. It appeared that the two men currently in her life— namely Nick and Alec Malone—were one step ahead of her again. "Sure," she said. "You can fill me in on the details when I get back."

Molly jumped up from the family room floor where Squiggly had been trying to master a homemade maze and ran to throw her arms around Tess. "Thanks for letting me have a party, Tess. Mommy always let me have two or three friends with games and videos.''

It was the first time she'd referred to her mother without tears in her eyes and oddly, it made Tess feel weepy. Molly squeezed her again and then ran back to join Nick and Squiggly on the floor. As Tess left the house, she was struck by the full impact of how much the children—at least, Molly—had begun to accept her. How could she possibly leave them with someone else now?

She was still pondering the question when she arrived at the Stones. Their house was also a ranch-style bungalow, but sprawling in the shape of a T. Marci greeted her at the door, martini glass in hand. Tess was surprised that she'd started without her and assumed Larry must be home as well.

''No, he's got some meeting in town tonight. Larry's always busy with something,'' Marci said. ''Come in.''

''I brought this for him,'' Tess said, extending the wine in a decorative gift bag. ''Just a token of appreciation for arranging to get the broken windows fixed at the house.''

''You didn't need to do that, silly. Larry likes to help people.'' Her thickly fringed eyes narrowed. ''I hope the contractor gave you a good deal.''

Tess laughed. ''Oh, yes. I think Larry made sure of that, as well.''

''We'll go out to the patio since you brought a sweater. The evenings are quite cool this high up, no matter how hot the days are,'' Marci said. She took the wine and set it on a table inside the front door. Her high heels trotted along a ceramic-tiled hall with Tess in tow, past a family room and some closed doors to the rear of the house. They exited through the kitchen onto a pretty flagstone patio surrounding a pool. ''We haven't filled it yet,'' she said, ''because we don't want the bother of the expense and work if we move after all.''

''You're moving?''

Marci was pouring Tess a martini from a stainless steel shaker and glanced up sharply at her question. She gave her an ironic smile. "Well, I think so. Though not very far." She handed Tess the frosty cocktail and led her to a grouping of wicker chairs.

"Surely you know?" she asked, taking a seat.

Tess sat down opposite her. "Know what?"

"Maybe I'm not supposed to say anything yet but," she giggled behind her hand, "the cat's out of the bag now, isn't it?"

Tess smiled, completely confused.

"We put in an offer the other day—on the ranch. Richard and Gabriela's," she explained.

Tess wasn't certain if the dizziness she was experiencing was from the martini—not a drink she usually indulged in—or Marci's revelation. Of course, she'd known about a buyer. She simply hadn't considered that it might be Larry Stone.

"You seem surprised."

"Well, uh, I am. Mr. Walker just told me today that there might be a buyer but I assumed it wasn't definite."

"Oh, dear." Marci finished off her drink and got up to pour another. She held up the shaker questioningly.

"No, no thanks. You see, I'm not really certain yet what's going to happen with the kids. I asked Jed to give the matter more time—so I could come up with a plan that would satisfy everyone."

"Then I am sorry, Tess. I shouldn't have said a word. Obviously I've misunderstood the situation. Larry and I have always loved the Wheaton place. There's the studio, which I know Larry would love for a workshop. He makes furniture, did you know that?"

Tess shook her head, focusing on what Marci had just revealed.

"And I weave. Just amateur stuff, you understand. We're not in the same league as Richard and Gabriela were."

A touch of envy there? Tess wondered.

"Plus Larry's always interested in buying property. We may hold on to this place and rent it out for a while, since the market's low for selling right now."

Tess half listened to the other woman babble on about local real estate and all the development in the area. She sneaked a peek at her watch, thinking dinner preparation would be the perfect excuse to leave as soon as possible.

"There are so many tourists coming up here. You wouldn't believe this place in the peak of summer. Especially around Estes Park. Did you get up there yet?"

"Uh, no. I've been to Lyons and a bit past it." She didn't know where exactly the campsite had been located, but vaguely recalled Ken mentioning Estes Park.

"Well, the places south of Estes are unbelievable. It's the gateway to the park—you know, Rocky Mountain National Park?"

Tess gave a faint smile. "Yes, I've heard the name."

"So many people own summer and winter places there. It's really overcrowded now and developers are always looking for new locations." She downed the last of her martini. "I've always wanted a place up there, but Larry says we can't afford it just yet." Marci walked over to the patio table and tilted the martini shaker into her glass. A trickle of liquid came out. She grinned at Tess. "Ooops! Ready for a second? I can make another batch."

Tess jumped to her feet. "No, but thanks anyway, Marci. I've got to get home and get dinner for the kids."

Marci frowned. "Oh, yes. Those poor souls. Unfortunately, Larry and I never had any children." She sighed and looked off into the distance. Then she turned back to Tess. "You must find it a challenge, suddenly being responsible for two children. I mean, someone said you have an important job back in Chicago. Don't you miss it?"

Tess was struck by the question. Until that moment, she hadn't given her job much more than a moment's thought since arriving in Colorado. Of course, she rationalized, she was officially still on vacation. But she wondered if perhaps she was getting too used to being away from the office.

"And I bet those kids—as cute as they are—are a real cramp in your single lifestyle."

"Hmm," Tess murmured. She reached for her purse and followed Marci back through the house and out the front door. The Wheaton ranch was less than a five-minute drive along the highway but it was enough time for Tess to decide not to tell the children about the possible sale of the house to the Stones.

They were setting the table for dinner when Tess walked into the kitchen.

"Just in time," Molly said. "We decided on the lasagna because maybe we'll have pizza for my birthday." She gave Tess an anxious look.

"Oh, well that's a good idea then. So you two have made some plans?"

Molly burbled on about the party throughout the meal. Her excitement was almost matched by Nick's whose offer to organize some games left Tess speechless but pleased. After a dessert of ice cream and berries, Tess announced that she would do the tidying up so Nick could start on his homework. Molly ran off to the family room to watch her favorite television show and Nick, with a fleeting smile for Tess, headed to his room. The smile was exactly the encouragement she needed. Tonight she would have her talk with him.

Once Molly was tucked into bed, Tess walked down the hall to Nick's room. He gave a clear and distinct "Come in," at her soft knock.

"I thought maybe we should come to some kind of agreement. You know," she explained at the question in his face, "about how we can work together so that you can be successful at school and I—I—" Tess stopped, sensing she was floundering badly. She sat down on the edge of the bed.

"The thing is, Nick. I've never dealt with kids before. I was an only child and my only playmates were kids in my class. After my father—I mean, our dad—left, my mother had kind of a nervous breakdown. She'd always been what people called high-strung. Unpredictable with mood swings. I think she might have been manic depressive. Anyway, our household was always in turmoil so I never invited friends over. Never even had a birthday party until I was eleven and was living with Mavis." Tess paused. She was getting off track.

"You and Molly—well, you were right when you said that I considered you two a hindrance. I did. Especially that first weekend. I didn't want to deal with this...this problem that just appeared out of nowhere."

Nick wasn't saying a word, but he kept his eyes on hers. Another good sign, Tess thought.

"But after being here these past few days, the strange thing is that I seem to have taken on another kind of life. When I was at Marci Stone's today, she asked me if I missed my job in Chicago and you know what? I realized I hadn't thought about it at all. Not once. Not even to check my e-mail or phone Carrie." Tess shook her head in disbelief.

"What does that mean?" he asked. "That you like it here?"

She thought about it. "Well yes, I do. But it's not that simple. I have financial obligations, too. Some very serious ones."

"Molly and I are getting money. We can help out."

Tess patted his hand. "I know that, but your money will be in a trust until you're adults. That's the way it should be. That's the way your father wanted it."

"He was your father, too." His eyes narrowed in reproach.

"Yes," Tess said. "My father, too. I have only sketchy memories of him. Maybe you can tell me more—give me a bigger picture."

Nick nodded. "I was wondering if you'd ask," he said. Then he started talking, at first in short disconnected phrases, and as his stories of Richard and Gabriela Wheaton took life, Tess climbed up onto the bed beside him. She leaned back against the wooden headboard and stared at the ceiling while Nick talked for a long time. He stopped for breath, finally, and gasped out, "I miss them so much!" before bursting into tears.

Stunned, Tess wrapped her arms around him. He lowered his head onto her shoulder and sobbed until there were no tears left. Her hands and arms were numb from lack of circulation and her shoulder ached from his body weight, but Tess didn't move a muscle. Eventually, Nick pulled away. He seemed embarrassed and averted his face as he got off the bed.

"Think I'll take a shower," he mumbled, "then hit the sack." After he left, Tess sat a moment longer. Every part of her ached, but the physical soreness was nothing to the pain deep inside. She rose from the bed and moved, zombielike, down the hall to the living room. She was grateful for the protective darkness of the room, needing a quiet place to sit and think. Molly had left the television on and the glow from the family room seeped across the terrace through the French doors in the living room. It was just enough light to catch Gabriela's portrait, so lovingly painted by Tess's father.

Love was everywhere in the house, Tess realized. In every piece of art and in the way the house had been designed, so that all rooms had a connection to the terrace and the outdoors. There was beauty everywhere one looked, from the distant view of the Flatirons to the gardens tucked into every alcove.

She gazed up at the painting of the woman who had

made Richard Wheaton's new life so precious. The woman who made his dreams come true. It was a rare gift to be able to do that for the man you loved and Tess envied her for that. And she knew that she, too, had received a gift. The rediscovery of her father. It was a gift and a chance to change and enrich her life. Tess felt certain about that. Just as she was certain now that being with Molly and Nick was an integral part of holding on to that gift.

THE MORNING was unfolding in a calmer, more relaxed manner these days. The three of them seemed to have developed a routine without Tess having to impose one. She got up with the alarm and woke both kids. Molly got the use of the bathroom first because she was quicker and Nick took a while to get out of bed. Tess started making lunches while Molly set the table and put the cereal boxes or fixings for toast out. She also poured juice and milk. By the time Nick appeared, Molly was usually finished breakfast and busily feeding Squiggly or cleaning his cage. Nick ate quickly, then put all the breakfast dishes into the machine before walking Molly down to the bus.

It had taken several days for this pattern to evolve, but everyone seemed content with it, a fact that Tess noted and was oddly pleased about. She knew this pleasure stemmed from her love of organization, but there was something else, too. A familiarity to the day that was reassuring and comforting. She realized that she no longer had the nervous stomach and jitters that her workday in Chicago began with.

Molly and Nick walked down the drive to wait for their school buses while Tess waved goodbye from the front door. Nick had told her she didn't need to do this, but she suspected their mother had and wanted to continue the practice. Besides, she found herself liking it. After closing the door, she wanted to call Mavis and tell her about the decision she'd made, but sensed that she needed to assess things in the rational light of day. Not that she was afraid of changing her mind, but more that she needed to do some serious thinking about how to raise two children in Chicago.

Still, her most distracting thought of the morning was that Alec hadn't telephoned last night as he had promised. She forced herself to focus on the household tasks of laundry and shopping lists rather than fret over the countless reasons he might have had for not calling. When the doorbell rang midmorning, she was in the laundry room emptying the dryer and she rushed to it, hoping it might be Alec.

Larry Stone was standing on the doorstep. He held his Stetson in his right hand and gestured with it in greeting. "Morning, Tess. Sorry to disturb you so early."

Tess hid her disappointment. "Not at all, Larry. Come in."

He stepped inside, turning to say, "I got home late last night so didn't know until an hour or so ago that you'd dropped by for a drink. Thanks very much for the wine. I love red so you made a good guess."

Tess smiled. "Thank you, Larry, for your help."

"Thought I'd check out the work my man did for you yesterday."

"Would you like some coffee? I can make it while you go out back."

"That would be nice," he said and followed her into the house. He continued on down the hall while Tess began to set up the coffee machine. When he came back, he said, "Well, I'm pleased with the job. I hope you are, too."

"I certainly am!"

"Hold on to the receipts for when you get around to making an insurance claim." He set his hat down on the counter and looked around the kitchen. "Looks like you've got this place in shipshape."

Tess had to smile. She thought the room was a mess

compared to her condo in Chicago, which was spotless. 'Cause you were so seldom in it. "I think you're being polite," she said as she set out mugs, cream and sugar.

"Seriously, things seem to be getting in order and that's great for the kiddies. Does this mean you'll be taking on guardianship of them?"

"Perhaps." She was evasive, unwilling to tell him before she'd even told the children or Alec. "Have a seat, Larry. I must admit," she said, sitting across from him, "that I was surprised that you and Marci were thinking of buying this place."

"Marci told me that she might have upset you, talking about buying the place. But did she mention that we've always loved it? We had a joke between the four of us that whenever Richard and Gabriela decided to move, we'd be all too happy to take the place over."

"I can't imagine their wanting to move," she commented. "The house seems so perfect for them."

He stirred sugar into his coffee and took a long sip. "I agree. In many ways it was, but I had a feeling the last couple of years that Gabriela longed for more. This place is so remote and quiet." He took another sip.

Tess was interested in his version of the family. "Why did you think that?"

He shrugged. "Just certain things she'd say. She was a lot younger than your father, you know." Stone frowned, thinking. "We had just been here at the house for her fortieth birthday the month before the accident." He fell silent.

"I think my father would have been about fifty-eight when he died," Tess murmured. Funny, she'd never thought about his age. Fifty-eight was still so very young, with a lifetime of work ahead.

"Really?" was all he said. Finally, he broke the silence that had fallen over the room. "Look, I don't want to rush things. If I hadn't bumped into Jed Walker at the bank the other day, I wouldn't even have known he was selling the place."

Jed Walker. The name was beginning to conjure the same distaste with her that it did with Alec.

"In fact," Stone was saying, "it wasn't as if I made a serious offer or anything. It was pure impulse on my part." He paused, keeping his eyes fixed on hers. "I can even phone him if you like and tell him I may want to reconsider."

The gesture was a generous one. But knowing the sale of the house might still have to occur, she said, "No, don't do that just yet. As I told Jed, I haven't quite made up my mind. You know, about the kids and everything." Wanting to change the subject away from the guardianship, she asked, "Would you like to see some sketches my father made of a place near Lyons?"

He set his empty coffee mug down. "I would."

Tess rushed to get the folder of drawings that Nick had found. "I forgot to tell Jed that we have them," she said, coming back into the kitchen. She set the folder on the table in front of him. "I suspect Jed will want to have them assessed for the estate. They might be valuable."

She watched him examine them. "Maybe I'll buy them myself," she said.

He glanced up. "If you don't, I will," he announced. Then he laughed. "God, I sound like some crass tycoon, don't I? Coming over here and wanting to buy everything." He looked down at the sketch in his hand. "Just that I know what Richard was getting for his work. Even these pencil drawings would be worth quite a lot."

"We went there on the weekend," Tess said. "Nick took us." She chose not to spell out who the *us* referred to, hoping he would assume she meant the two children. "He seems to think Richard owns the place."

Larry looked up and frowned. "What? The place in these sketches? I doubt it."

"Why?"

He shrugged. "Because Richard was always talking about buying land but he never actually came out and announced that he'd done it."

"Maybe he just never told you."

He thought that over, but dismissed the suggestion with a shake of his head. "Nah, don't think so. Mainly because the two of us were always complaining about the development around Estes. I remember Rich saying once that he'd be tempted to buy some land just so that it couldn't be developed." His eyes focused on hers. "So if he had, he'd have told me."

Tess realized that was probably the case. "Nick may have heard Richard talking about the idea, without knowing it hadn't happened."

"I bet."

The washing machine in the laundry room next to the bathroom suddenly began to vibrate loudly. Tess excused herself and ran to reset the machine. When she returned to the kitchen, Larry was standing beside the table as if to leave. But he was staring at the back of one of the sketches and at Tess's entry, dropped it onto the table.

"Got to go," he said, moving away from the table. "Thanks for the coffee and I promise I'll get back to Walker for you. I can see you'll need more time to think things through. It's a big responsibility," he was saying as she walked with him to the front door, "looking after two youngsters. I have to say," he chuckled lightly, "I don't envy you. It means giving up a lot of the freedom that a young single person like yourself is accustomed to."

Tess merely smiled, noting how he and his wife Marci were on the same track with that. After he left, she cleared the coffee mugs and picked up the sketches to put them away. The one that Larry had been so engrossed in was lying facedown on the others. Tess was about to flip it over when she noticed numbers and letters jotted in pencil in the bottom right corner. She stared at them, wondering if they were what had drawn Stone's interest. Other than the fact that they bore a strong resemblance to a Colorado license plate number, they appeared to be fairly insignificant. She didn't think of them again, until toward the end of her conversation with Alec later that day.

CHAPTER THIRTEEN

ALEC DID HIS BEST to concentrate on what Tess was saying but all he could focus on was the melodious lilt her voice took on when she was excited. He knew now how she sounded when she liked the way he was kissing her but he couldn't help fantasize how those vocal cords might ring when he finally got to make love to her. *Relax, Malone. Calm down. There's most of a workday ahead of you.*

"Are you still there?" she suddenly asked.

"Hmm?" *Some, but not all of me,* he was thinking.

"You're so quiet. I thought you'd be interested that the Stones want to buy this place."

"Well, it is a beautiful house—"

"But they just live down the road in their own beautiful house. Even if it isn't quite equal to this one."

"It was good of the guy to get your windows fixed," he pointed out.

"Yes. He's really a nice man. But there's one thing that seemed odd. Just before he left, I showed him the sketches that Nick found. You know, of the campsite? I had to leave the room for a minute and when I returned, he was staring at the back of one of them. After he left, I noticed a set of numbers and letters. I went out to check the Volvo and for sure these numbers are from a Colorado license plate."

Alec's head was spinning. Had she always been this talkative, he wondered? While he had a chance, he got to the reason for his call. "Tess, listen. The reason I didn't phone last night was because Karen needed me to come out and help Ken with a shipment of stuff he'd ordered. By the time I got home, it was kinda late so I didn't bother. But Karen has invited the kids for the weekend and—''

''She has?''

''Yeah, she really likes them and apparently last weekend Nick had offered to help Ken with the late spring planting, which is what Ken plans to do this weekend.''

''But what about Molly's birthday?''

''It's on Sunday, isn't it? We can make sure everyone's back by then.''

''Well sure, I'll mention it to them. I guess they'll want to go. What about me?'' She gave a little laugh.

This was the best part. ''I thought you'd like to come over to my place Friday night for dinner and…and, uh, well maybe we can get together for the weekend.''

There was a long silence that had him sweating until she uttered another laugh—more of a giggle really—and said, her voice all throaty, ''That sounds very…nice.''

Nice. Personally, he thought he could do better than that. ''Okay, great. So will you be able to drive them out to the ranch yourself after school on Friday? Think you can remember the way?''

''Oh, yes, and Nick can help. He's good with directions.''

He is? It wasn't a trait Alec had particularly noticed in the boy but he liked the fact that Tess had. It showed promise, he thought. Before he rang off, she asked, ''Listen, I know this is crazy but can you do me a favor?''

''Yeesss.'' He wasn't sure what he was getting into, but the prospect of Friday night loomed.

''Is there any way you could find out who the owner is of that license plate? You know, on the sketch?''

''Maybe, but why?''

''I'm curious. I wonder why my father jotted it there, just on the back of a sketch. I mean, would an artist mark up his work like that?''

Jeez. "I'm not an artist, Tess," he said, feeling a tad impatient with all the license talk. "I couldn't say. But I do have a buddy in the Denver police. Maybe he can find out the owner. That okay?"

"That's wonderful," she gushed. "Oh, and one more thing."

Uh-oh. Friday night better be fantastic. "Yes?"

"Larry also mentioned that he doubted very much that my father owned the land where we went camping. Is there any way—?"

"To find out who does?" he interrupted. "Yeah. Like calling the Denver Land Registry. There must be a local office here in Boulder." He sighed, sensing where this was going. "You want me to—?"

"Oh, yes!"

Before he hung up, she gave him the license plate from the sketch.

AFTER TESS REPLACED the receiver, she ate a quick lunch and decided to drive into Boulder to confront Tomas Kozinski about the painting.

He didn't look well. In fact, he looked downright unhappy to see her standing in the middle of the art gallery. Tess noted his hollow cheeks and dark-circled eyes. Either business was bad, or he had a guilty conscience. She was betting on the latter, though wasn't sure where her suspicions were leading her just yet. She simply believed, in spite of all of Kozinski's protestations to the contrary, that her father would never cut apart a painting. Especially that particular painting. For the second time, she tried to explain it to the art dealer.

"But he did!" Kozinski repeated, forking his long thin fingers through his spiked blond hair, then dragging them down the sides of his unshaven cheeks.

The effect, along with his haggard face, was scary. Tess shifted into power-play mode. "Look, Mr. Kozinski, the fact is that the painting—in its entirety—was left to me. Since part of it is missing, I can only conclude that some kind of fraud has occurred."

He shook his head vigorously. "Someone was interested in buying the still life side. This was right after the fire and Richard was desperate for money until the insurance company paid up."

"Then who bought it?" she asked, "because I want to find that person and buy it back if I can."

"I can't tell you who bought it. That kind of information is confidential. My clients are wealthy. They're also very paranoid about people—especially government people—finding out how they're spending their money. Your father gave his consent."

Tess pursed her lips. She didn't believe him, but knew that unless she pursued the matter through the civil courts, it wasn't likely she'd get the truth from him. Still, she wasn't about to let him sense her lack of confidence.

"Fine then. You'll be hearing from my lawyer."

"Mr. Walker's already talked to me about this," he said, his voice pitching in anger.

"Great. But Mr. Walker isn't *my* lawyer," she said. The look in his face was worth the trip, she was thinking, as she marched out the door. Even if she'd learned nothing. While she was on a roll, she decided to visit Jed Walker.

She hadn't phoned for an appointment, Walker's secretary solemnly informed her fifteen minutes later, so Tess could either wait or schedule an appointment for the next day.

"I'll wait, then I won't have to come back into town," she said and plopped down in one of the leather chairs in the tiny reception area. Tess was thumbing through her third magazine when Walker's office door opened. A handsome, brown-haired man in an expensive suit stood in the doorway. In spite of his relatively stocky frame, his bearing was confident. He glanced quickly around the reception, his dark-brown eyes sweeping over Tess, before turning back to shake hands with Jed Walker.

The man said something that Tess didn't catch, but what did attract her attention was the expression in Walker's face when he noticed her ensconced in one of his chairs. *Strike Two. Someone else who isn't happy to see me today.* She stood up as the man brushed past her on his way out.

"Tess, I wasn't expecting to see you today," Walker said.

"I decided to drop in on Tomas Kozinski and then thought maybe I should see you. It won't take long, if you're busy."

He loosened the tie at his throat and waved a hand in obvious resignation. "No, no. I can spare five or ten minutes." He asked his secretary to put any incoming calls on hold for the next ten minutes and preceded Tess into his office.

She took a seat in front of his desk while he hurriedly swept up documents and a large piece of paper that looked like some kind of a map. These he stashed on top of a tall filing cabinet directly behind his desk. Then he turned round and asked, "What can I do for you?" He managed a smile.

Tess couldn't help but think, as she took in his chiseled features, cool blue eyes and styled blond hair that a month ago she'd have been attracted to a man like Jed Walker. Of course, he was practically a clone of many of the well-groomed men working in Chicago's financial district, like the man who'd left his office minutes ago. The comparison took her right to Douglas Reed and how hollow their relationship had been. That it had never ignited a spark inside, much less released the kind of passion she'd felt with Alec Malone the other night.

"You wanted to see me?" he prompted.

"It's about my meeting with Tomas Kozinski."

"Yes?"

"I wanted to find out what had happened to the painting."

"And what did Kozinski have to say?"

"I thought you called him about it. What explanation did he give you?"

Walker's expression implied she was belaboring a point. "That Richard had given permission for the piece to be separated because there was a buyer who wanted the still life but couldn't afford the price of both."

"That's what I can't believe. My father would never do that."

"Unless you can prove otherwise, I don't think you'll have much success pursuing this matter in the legal system, Ms. Wheaton. My advice is to take the piece you've got and drop the matter."

Which obviously was what *he* wanted to do, she thought, noticing that he had dropped her first name as well. This wasn't going well, but she sensed that she wasn't going to get any further with the painting issue right then. She wasn't finished with it, but he didn't have to know that. Perhaps she'd have to carry out her threat to Kozinski after all, and look for another lawyer. For now, Jed Walker—as imperfect as the man was shaping up to be—was all she had.

"There is one other business matter to clarify," she said. "About my father's estate. Nick took us—"

"*Us?*"

Tess was annoyed at the surge of heat at his question. Was it any of his business? "Well, Alec Malone and me."

Walker gave a thoughtful nod.

Tess continued. "We went camping to a site outside Lyons, off Highway 36. Nick said his family went there quite often and he thinks Richard owned it." She stopped, watching his face for any sign of recognition. "Do you know anything about it? Is it listed in the estate inventory?"

"As a matter of fact, I have no knowledge of any land—

other than the ranch—that Richard and Gabriela owned. Now, is there anything else?''

So scratch that idea, Tess thought. ''The main reason I came to see you,'' she said, changing the subject, ''was that I've decided to apply to be the legal guardian for Nick and Molly.''

If he was surprised, he hid it well. Scarcely a flicker of an eyelid. Tess had expected some sign of pleasure—she was, after all, relieving him of the task of the children's welfare. Though she wondered if he'd ever considered himself responsible for them at all, given his willingness to pass them over to foster care.

''Have you given this serious thought?''

''I hardly think someone in my position would take on such a responsibility without doing just that.''

A faint smile came and went. ''Of course, I don't mean to patronize. Just that you seemed so uncertain only a couple of days ago. I'm curious as to what made you change your mind.''

''Getting to know the children better and—'' she paused slightly, wanting him to take note ''—realizing that they needed someone to advocate for them. To ensure that their full legal rights and benefits now and in the future would be a priority.''

''I hope you're not suggesting that I would act otherwise on their behalf, as executor of their parents' will?''

Tess chose her words carefully. She still needed the man's assistance. ''I'd never suggest that. Just that I know how busy you are and I also know that in a situation like this there really can't be a substitute for family. Can there?'' she asked, flashing her sweetest smile.

''No, of course not. I imagine it'll be a simple matter, considering you are next of kin and there is no other applicant for their guardianship at this time. Very well, I'll find out what I can and get back to you.'' He rose from his chair, indicating the meeting was over.

Tess stood up, too, saying, "Thank you."

She moved toward the door, but halted when he added, "You may want to give the guardianship more thought. As well, I'd like an answer on the house sale as soon as possible, but I'm willing to give you a couple more days." He joined her at the door, standing close enough for a strong whiff of his cologne to fall over her. He lowered his voice and said, "I don't think I need to remind you that, as sole executor of the will, I'm giving you this extra time as a courtesy."

There was nothing in his eyes or face that held the slightest hint of a threat, but Tess felt one all the same. She shivered inwardly at the idea that Nick and Molly's welfare might have rested with the man. "I appreciate that very much, Mr. Walker."

Her response resurrected his charm. "Please, whatever happened to Jed?" He extended a hand and when she placed hers in it, placed his other hand on top.

She had an uncomfortable sense of being trapped, though the smile on his face was warm and reassuring. She also knew there was no way she was going to repeat his name. "Thanks again," she said, extricating her hand.

Tess reached for the doorknob behind her and spun around as she opened it. By the time she got to the elevator, the trembling in her arms and legs had eased, leaving behind the echo of something he had said. Something that she hoped wasn't significant.

There is no other applicant for their guardianship at this time. At this time?

FRIDAY ROLLED AROUND eventually, though Tess had to admit she thought it never would. The big decision she had to make that day was how much extra vacation time she'd need. Her two weeks in Boulder were already up and as far as her secretary was concerned, Tess was due back in the office Monday morning. The strange thing was, she no longer felt a strong urge to get back to work. The merger, her clients, even her colleagues—all had been slowly replaced by her life in Boulder. The more she thought about it, the more she realized how busy her days there had been. She decided to telephone Carrie right away, before yet another crisis demanded her attention.

"Another week, then?" Carrie asked.

"Unless you think that'll be a problem. I know I've got the time."

"I'll pass it by your boss. How're the kids doing?"

"Great!" Tess felt herself warm up inside and filled in Carrie on the latest, including Molly's planned birthday party.

"Jeez, I can't picture you doing all that stuff," she said.

A twinge of annoyance surfaced at that. "You'd be surprised at what I can do. Anyway, I'm managing just fine."

"That's great, Tess. If there's a problem with the extra week, I'll get back to you. Otherwise, enjoy!"

"Okay. By the way, how're things in the office? The merger went through okay, I know, but any fallout about it yet?"

"Nope. You may not want to believe this, Tess, but absolutely nothing has changed or happened here since you left. Same old–same old, as the expression goes." There was a pause, then, "Will you be bringing back the kids with you?"

The question of the week, Tess was thinking. "I'll keep you posted on that."

Another pause. "They're nice kids. You'd be great for them. And they'd…"

"What?"

"Nothing. Just, I hope everything works out. Let me know when you're coming home."

After Tess hung up, she went over Carrie's words. She had a feeling what Carrie had intended to say was *they'd be good for you.* Carrie was right. That's why she'd made the decision she had. But after her visit to Walker, Tess decided not to mention the guardianship to the children until she learned more about how difficult or easy her application would be. They'd been through enough and there was no point in raising their hopes until it was all worked out.

The children—especially Molly—were excited about spending the weekend at the ranch. Nick seemed more than a little concerned about what Tess would be doing. Did he suspect she would be getting together with Alec, she wondered?

They reached the Malone ranch just before five and because she wasn't due at Alec's until seven, Tess accepted Karen's invitation for coffee. The children went upstairs to unpack while Tess followed Karen into the kitchen, where delicious aromas were wafting from the stove.

"My famous chicken-and-rice casserole," Karen said at Tess's appreciative sounds. "Nothing special, but it's good. I thought I'd send a container back with you." She caught Tess's eye and grinned. "Alec told me he was cooking dinner for you tonight, but knowing him, dinner could likely be served sometime tomorrow morning." Then she clapped a hand to her mouth. "Gee, I hope that didn't sound the way I thought it did. I meant that he tends to overdo things and gets caught up in all these elaborate preparations so his meals end up on plates much later."

Tess could think of nothing to say, so smiled.

Her silence had little effect on Karen. "You know," she said, pouring water into the coffeemaker, "I've noticed a change in Alec over the past couple of weeks. Ken says it's all my imagination, but I don't think men are very intuitive about these things. Do you?" She looked across the room at Tess.

Tess gave a half shrug and murmured, "Perhaps."

"I mean," Karen continued, "he's lost some of that

tightness around his jaw. I call it his clenched-teeth look. Ever notice it?''

Tess thought she had, but gave an evasive "Hmmm."

"And those little lines around his eyes? They seemed to just sprout after he got back and Sherry took off. Not that I think he was madly in love with her. But no one had ever dropped him before and he was feeling very vulnerable after his stint in Kosovo.''

"Why did she leave him?"

Karen sat down next to Tess. "I think she was looking forward to being the wife of a career military man. Alec had just been promoted and he was getting a lot of offers— even one from Washington—when he returned to the States. When he decided to resign and took the job with Child Protective Services, Sherry had a fit. No way was she going to be the wife of a lowly social worker in Boulder, Colorado.''

Tess sensed the bitterness in Karen's voice came from her protective loyalty to her brother. She wondered what it would be like to have that sibling bond but realized almost at once that she was developing something similar, with Nick and Molly. It was a satisfying feeling.

There was a brief silence while the coffee was poured. Then Karen said, "I don't suppose you're thinking of staying on in Boulder for a while longer?''

Tess took a moment to respond, uncertain of the subtext in Karen's question. She didn't have to reply, because the other woman blurted, "Alec would kill me if he heard me pumping you for info like that. I...uh just think you might be the reason for his new interest in life.'' She gave an embarrassed laugh. "'Course, I could be way off base. It's just a feeling I have. It would be great if you hung around a bit longer—got to know the place and...and—''

"Alec." Tess smiled.

"Yes, poor man. He needs a life so badly."

Don't we all, Tess thought. Fortunately, she was saved

from further exploration of her future plans by the arrival
of Ken, through the back door leading into the kitchen. He
greeted Tess warmly, saying how happy he was that Nick
had offered to come and help that weekend.

"He's a strong boy, with a lot of potential," he said.
"Seems to know instinctively what to do, which is a far
cry from some of the young help I've had."

Tess felt pleased, as if she personally had had something
to do with Nick's character.

"He was telling me how much you all enjoyed the camping last weekend."

That *did* surprise Tess. But the comment reminded her
of something. "Nick thinks the land where we camped belongs to his father. Would you happen to know anything
about land ownership in this area? Alec said the site isn't
far from the Malone property."

Ken thought, then said, "I've got a map somewhere. Be
right back."

"More coffee?" Karen asked.

"No, thanks. As soon as Ken shows me the map, I'll
have to get going."

"Okay. I've put some of the casserole in this aluminum
pan. If Alec has dinner all ready, you guys can always eat
it tomorrow or he can freeze it. I'm going to see how the
kids are doing."

Tess thanked her, touched by her thoughtfulness. When
Ken returned, she noticed that the map he was unrolling on
the kitchen table was a similar type and size to the one Jed
Walker had had on his desk that afternoon. Ken set the
empty coffee mugs, sugar jar and milk jug on the four
corners of the map.

"Okay," he said. "Here's our place," he pointed with
a thick, callused finger, "and this area northwest of us all
the way to the highway leading to Estes is privately owned.
This bit here," he circled a section adjacent to the Malone
land, "was up for sale about two years ago. Karen and I

wanted to buy it but we'd just found out I had MS so we were afraid to dig into our savings. Someone did buy it, I heard, but it was all hush-hush. Some kind of numbered account or such. People were expecting the land to be developed right away, but it hasn't been yet.''

He studied the map, then looked at Tess, peering over his shoulder. ''The campsite I think you're referring to, the site Nick thinks his parents owned, is right here.'' He enclosed that area with a square. ''Looking at this map now, I bet the reason that middle section hasn't been developed is because there's no main road access to it. And it would cost a fortune to build a road. But this part,'' he said, jabbing at the square he'd drawn on the map, ''could be worth a lot.''

''I'm not sure I get what you mean.''

''The land between my place and the campsite is all on its own. No road access and therefore, no good for development unless—''

''That person also owned the campsite area.''

''Exactly. Or our land.'' He stared thoughtfully at the map, then at Tess. ''Well, very interesting. So we need to find out who owns the middle section and confirm if the Wheatons own the camping spot.''

''I think Alec is looking into that,'' she said.

''Is he?'' His expression grew even more pensive. Finally, he rolled up the map and said, ''Good. Let me know what you find out.'' He started to leave the kitchen when he thought of something else. ''If I were you, Tess, I wouldn't mention any of this to Jed Walker. Karen told me he's the executor for the Wheaton estate. Has he said anything about the Wheatons owning that land?''

''He said he didn't know anything about it.''

Ken's laugh was more of a bark. ''Keep in mind that when the bank forecloses on us, Walker will own our ranch. Personally, I don't trust the guy. But I don't want to prejudice you against him,'' he said.

No problem there, she was thinking.

"I mean, don't feel you have to tell him everything just 'cause he's the family lawyer and all."

Tess mulled over Ken's warning all the way back into town but by the time she found the area where Alec lived, near the University of Colorado campus, her thoughts were definitely elsewhere.

"So, WHAT do you think?"

"I thought *I* was supposed to ask that question."

Tess caught his grin and smiled back. "I meant about the land thing."

"And I meant about my place. Like it?"

She gave the room another 360 degrees and came back to his smile.

"It's very nice. Very…" she searched for the right word.

"Not preppy. Please don't say preppy."

"Relax. Definitely not preppy. Rather…um…spartan, I think."

"That's what Karen's always saying—liven it up. Here, where's your wineglass?"

Tess held up her empty glass. "Will we be eating soon?" she asked. "If not, then maybe I'll wait for seconds."

He paused, wine bottle poised midair. "Uh, sure."

She couldn't resist glancing to her left where the kitchen counter was visible through the doorway. When she'd arrived half an hour ago, Alec had been chopping vegetables. Their colorful, unchopped remnants still littered the counter.

"Maybe the casserole tonight, after all," he quickly said, noticing where her eyes had drifted.

When she laughed, he set the wine bottle down and held out his hand to her. Tess reached out hers, not certain what he was doing. But when he gently tugged her to her feet, she had a pretty good idea. The casserole, she was thinking, would have to wait, too.

His smile turned serious, his eyes intent. His fingers ran along the back of her hand and up her bare arm. Tess shivered.

"Cold?" he whispered, drawing her closer.

"No," she said, her answer brushing against his ear as he lowered his head. His mouth found the nape of her neck and she trembled again. This time, from the explosion of heat that soared upward. She clung to him, pressing as much of her body against him as possible. When his mouth caressed a line from the base of her throat, up her neck and onto her mouth, Tess was certain that every nerve cell in her body was afire.

But his lips abruptly broke free and he pulled his head back to look down at her. "I've a feeling this may not be a good idea right now," he said, his voice low and husky. "At least, until we've resolved certain things. You know, about the children."

Tess felt the adrenaline surge from his kiss go into a tailspin. She knew what he was referring to, but the nerve centers in her body weren't listening to reason. And how could she blurt out the decision she'd made when she hadn't told the kids yet? She moved away from him, averting her face. Exposing her disappointment would be too humiliating.

His hand reached out for her arm, but she gently brushed it aside. "You're absolutely right, Alec," she said. Her voice, unsteady, gained strength as she went on. "And now that we've had appetizers," she laughed, wanting him to believe how lightly she was taking his rejection, "shall we dig into that amazing casserole your sister made?"

DINNER WASN'T the romantic experience Tess had anticipated, in spite of the candles and Alec's attempts at lightheartedness. His humorous accounts of events at work fell flat and after their small talk about the meal and the virtuous attributes of Alec's sister, they took their coffee and dessert to the sofa area.

"Look," Alec said. "I had hoped you'd be spending the night but I realize now how presumptuous that was. I'm sorry. I've been aware of an attraction between us for the past week—certainly since the camping trip. But I've let my feelings for you get ahead of what's best for the kids. It won't be good for them if we…well, complicate things right now by starting up a relationship." He forked his fingers through his hair. "Do you know what I mean?"

Tess nodded. The obvious misery in his face tugged at her, despite the letdown she'd been feeling through dinner. He was right, of course, and she, too, had allowed the strong physical attraction to take over. For that was exactly the problem, she realized. It had been such a long time that any man had stirred her as he had when he touched her that she'd lost all sense of her priorities.

"I do," she said briskly. "And I should be leaving soon." She set her half-eaten piece of cheesecake on the coffee table.

"I can drive you back."

"What would be the point? Then you or I would be without a car tomorrow. I'll be fine, don't worry."

He looked unsure. "I don't like the thought of your driving home alone at this time of night."

"It's only nine o'clock," she said, laughing. Nine o'clock on a Friday night with no kids to worry about. And now, no man to worry about either. Ah, well.

"I'll call you in the morning. Maybe we could get together for breakfast or something."

Tess was tempted to quip if that was the case, then why was she leaving? But no. He'd made his feelings clear. "Perhaps," she murmured. She walked over to the chair where she'd left her jacket and purse earlier and headed for the door.

"Oh, before I forget," Alec said. "My friend on the

police force called me about that license plate. It's registered to a Mark Kaiser in Denver. Don't know yet who the
guy is or what he does, but my buddy said he'd check it
out for me. Is that any help to you?''

"Thanks, Alec. I honestly don't know what it means but
at least there's a name attached to the mystery. The why
of it will come out later, no doubt." She hesitated, half
hoping he'd find an excuse to delay her. Or change his
mind about her staying. But he didn't. He simply bent down
to give her a brotherly peck on the cheek. "Bye," she said
without turning around and closed the door behind her.

CHAPTER FOURTEEN

ALEC BLINKED and rolled over. He had sensed a warm huddle next to him but the instant he turned over, he saw the other side of the bed was indeed empty. He had been dreaming after all. Moistening his dry lips, he craned his head to the clock radio behind him. Almost ten. He couldn't recall when he'd last slept in so late, but then, he had been awake most of the night. Replaying the whole unhappy scene from the second he foolishly had pulled back, overcome by guilt. He'd seen the regret and embarrassment in her face immediately and wished he could take the moment back, time travel to the kiss that revealed she wanted him as much as he wanted her.

But then he'd had a flash of Molly's small pale face, her eyes big with worry. Worry about losing her only family and having to move away from Nick. Maybe even away from Boulder. Nah. He still got the shivers thinking about it. He couldn't do that to her or to Nick. Couldn't jeopardize their future simply because he wanted to bed their sister. And the thing was, he reminded himself as he dragged his body out of bed and headed for the shower, if the sizzle between him and Tess meant anything at all then last night's disappointment would be a mere glitch. A difficult but temporary pause in what could be a real love story. At least, he hoped that would be how events would turn out.

Refreshed from the shower, he headed into the galley kitchen and put on the coffee machine. Ten-thirty. Maybe too early to call her. He grabbed a muffin from the freezer, nuked it in the microwave and carried it with a mug of coffee to the sofa. It wasn't the breakfast in bed he'd anticipated yesterday afternoon, when he was still living in fantasyland. He clicked on the television and watched it on mute while he skimmed the morning paper. The news had just started and he wasn't paying much attention until a vaguely familiar face loomed on the screen. Alec clicked the mute button as the news anchor's voice boomed into the room.

"Mr. Kozinski, owner of the Rocky Mountain Art Gallery, was found early this morning by his longtime companion, Brent Holloway. Mr. Kozinski, a well-known and respected dealer and agent in Colorado, was thirty-nine years old. Police are not releasing details of the murder, other than to say that robbery is a possible motive."

There was another flash of Kozinski's photograph and then the anchor went on to the next news item. Alec turned off the television and hastily thumbed through the paper until he remembered that the murder had just been discovered that morning. Too late to make that edition of the paper.

The face on the TV screen came back to him then. The night he'd driven by Jed Walker's office and had seen him arguing with another man on the sidewalk. The other man had been Tomas Kozinski, owner of the art gallery that handled Richard Wheaton's work. The very man Tess had been talking about the last couple of days. The one she suspected of separating the painting she'd inherited.

Alec rushed to the phone and called her. She picked up just before the voice mail came on. "Sorry to wake you, Tess," he blurted. "But I've just seen something on the morning news. That guy, the gallery owner Kozinski?"

He could hear her clearing her throat. "Yes?" she finally answered.

"Well, he's been murdered."

Silence. Then, "Omigod. When? How?"

"Don't know when but someone found his body early this morning. The police suspect robbery but aren't releasing many details yet."

Her breathing sounded labored, as if he'd caught her after a run. "Are you okay?" he asked. "Want me to come out there?"

"Uh, no. But I feel I should do something. I mean, I knew this man. And maybe…maybe the painting had something to do with it."

"How so?"

"Doesn't it seem a coincidence to you that practically the day after I confronted Kozinski about the painting and threatened to go to police about it, he ends up being killed?"

"Whoa! You threatened him?" He didn't like the sound of that. "Then wouldn't that have made it more likely that *you'd* have been the murder victim, rather than Kozinski?"

From the tone in her voice, she didn't like the sound of that, either. "Good heavens! That's a crazy suggestion."

"But given that Kozinski did commit some kind of fraud with the painting, wouldn't he have had a motive to bump you off, rather than have you go public with it and basically ruin his reputation and business?"

A nervous laugh escaped her. "You must be an Agatha Christie fan." A pause. "Maybe I should phone Jed Walker to see if he knows anything."

Alec's hand clenched down on the receiver. He couldn't follow her logic there. "Why?"

"Because he knows—knew—Kozinski, too."

"And?"

"I don't know." She sighed. "I just can't shake the idea that his murder has something to do with the painting."

"Where is the painting now?"

"In the studio. I got it from the gallery the day our house was burgled." Another pause.

Was she putting it all together? Alec wondered. Because he certainly was. "So where was the painting at the time of the break-in?"

"I'd left it in the trunk of the car. That was the day I had to pick up Molly early from school and I was in a rush to get her. We went to town for the rest of the day and when we got back home, the house had been broken into."

"But the painting wasn't there," he repeated. "And if nothing was taken, maybe the painting was what the thief was looking for."

"But why?"

"Did you know at the time that it had been separated?"

"No, not till later. After the break-in."

"Then that could be the reason right there. Kozinski might have broken into the house because he wanted to get the painting back before you realized it had been split in two."

She didn't speak for a long moment.

"You still there?" he asked.

"Yes. Just trying to figure out what all this means."

"I think it's obvious, don't you? You say your father would never have given permission to split the painting. Kozinski doesn't want you to find out and ruin his business—career, whatever—so right after you leave, he follows you home. Waits until he sees the car leave again and, thinking you've taken the painting into the studio, breaks in to get it back."

"And he probably knew where my father kept the key to the studio—in the planter box. But I had taken it out so he had to break the window instead. When he didn't find it there, he broke into the house and searched the master bedroom."

"Then something—maybe a passing car—frightened him and he left."

"But if he only came for the painting, he figured out that it wasn't there."

"Right. And did some random ransacking to make it look like a real burglary."

Neither spoke for a moment, digesting what they'd worked out. Finally Tess said, "But why was he killed?"

Alec had considered that question already and he didn't like the answer he'd arrived at. "Because he wasn't working alone."

There was a drawn-out sigh from the other end of the line. "God," she whispered. "And some person out there knows I still have it."

Alec closed his eyes. He didn't want to go there. "Look," he said, wanting to reassure her, "the fraud thing no longer matters because Kozinski is dead. You can't prove—or disprove—his part in it or even if there *was* fraud. So you don't need to worry about anyone coming back for the painting."

"True, but maybe I should go to the police anyway."

He blew out a mouthful of air. He wished she were there so he could wrap his arms around her and forget Kozinski. "Or maybe you should give it some more time before you go to the police. Wait and see what comes out in the news later today."

"Perhaps," she murmured.

She sounded doubtful. "How about getting together for lunch?" he asked, wanting to get back to what remained of the weekend.

"I've got to buy stuff for Molly's party."

Expectation at seeing her again vanished. Alec tried to keep the disappointment out of his voice. "Right," he said. "I'd forgotten. What time tomorrow?"

"Uh, how about two? I'll pick them up in the morning. Molly wants pizza so we can make it a late lunch kind of thing."

"Great." He felt the energy of the conversation fizzle away and didn't know how to revive it. Seeing her, having her next to him would help. But apparently that wasn't going to happen now. When she said goodbye, he hung up and stood by the phone for a long time. Until the walls of his single bedroom apartment began closing in.

ON THE DRIVE into town, Tess tried to persuade herself that their murder theory was a bit farfetched. The logic was compelling, but a nagging voice inside whispered maybe she had been watching too many British mysteries on PBS. The reality was that likely Kozinski's death had been the result of a robbery at the gallery and the timing purely coincidental.

Although she had told Alec she should call Jed Walker, she remembered today was Saturday and it was unlikely he'd be at his office. She didn't know where he lived, but thought if she phoned, he'd get back to her. She passed a bakery café and pulled over to the curb. There was a phone booth outside the place and she called Walker. As she'd expected, she had to leave a message. She heard her voice wobble slightly when she said that no doubt he'd heard about Tomas Kozinski's murder. Rather than repeat her theory about the painting as a motive, she simply asked him to call her at home.

She grabbed a coffee inside the café, hoping to inject some energy into her veins, and finished it at a table. What were her options for the day? Shopping for Molly's party was a must, but could be postponed until later. Alec might still be at home and she was tempted to drop in, but dismissed the notion almost at once. No point in deliberately setting up a replay of last night. Perhaps she would drive by the art gallery to see what was going on. Having made a decision, she got up and left the café.

An hour later, as she sat on a hard bench in the small and unpleasant waiting room of a Boulder City Police station and miserably watched the minutes tick by on the large wall clock, Tess wondered what she could have been thinking. And why, she asked herself for the hundredth time, hadn't she kept on driving when she passed the art gallery and saw police officers going about their business within the cordoned-off area? Why hadn't she minded her *own* business and driven on to the shopping mall?

A door opened down the hall and a heavyset man in a rumpled suit walked toward her. His middle-aged face was lined with fatigue and transmitted an expression of, *What crackpot do I have to interview now?* Or so Tess thought as he bore down on her.

"Tess Wheaton?" he asked.

She stood up, having an instant flashback to a childhood classroom and an impatient teacher. "Yes."

"I'm Lieutenant Slegers, Homicide. I understand you've been speaking to officers about the Kozinski case?"

"Uh, yes. Though I really don't know too much about it."

His forehead wrinkled as if he'd just detected a bad smell. Or perhaps, Tess thought, he's realized his valuable time is about to be wasted.

He sighed. "Well, come with me anyway and we'll talk." He stood aside as she entered a tiny office down the hall. "Coffee?" he asked.

"Uh, no thanks. I've had one too many today as it is."

His bland eyes fixed on hers. "Oh? Why is that?"

Then Tess realized her misgivings about talking to the police were about to prove true. The interview was going to be a disaster.

THE FIRST THING he did was to call the Wheaton place. As he'd expected, all he got was the answering service. So Alec crossed off the remote possibility that Tess had stayed home. He decided to call his sister to make sure she hadn't gone out to pick up the kids a day early. When Karen asked if there was a problem, he had to lie.

"Tess is doing some shopping for Molly's party," he

said. "She can't remember when she agreed to pick up the kids tomorrow."

"I'm sure she said around ten. Why? Does she want to change the time?"

"No, no. If she does, she'll let you know." He hung up before his sister's mental radar picked up a suspicious signal. Four years older, she'd always had the knack of squeezing the truth out of him when they were kids.

Option number two was Jed Walker. Alec headed out to the Bronco, hoping she hadn't gone there. It was all he could do to be civil to the lawyer. And now, after Ken and Karen had just received a final warning that the end of May was two weeks away, Alec figured he was as likely to punch the guy as he was to speak to him.

No way could they raise the money by then. Alec was all set to sell the Bronco and he had some savings from the military. Hell, he even offered to see if he could use his future pension as collateral but Karen and Ken had refused. They were still pitting their hopes on some elderly aunt of Ken's in Colorado Springs or even on Walker changing his mind. *As if.*

So scratch checking out Walker's office. The guy likely wouldn't be around on a Saturday anyway. That left the art gallery. Alec scrawled a note for Tess, on the off chance she might come back there, and taped it to the door on his way out.

The gallery area was still crawling with cops and assorted other homicide investigator types. There were a couple of local TV station vans parked outside the yellow crime tape and as Alec scanned the area for a parking space, he noticed a woman with a microphone interviewing a man in a suit, probably a detective. The area was also teeming with Saturday shoppers and curious bystanders gawking from the sidewalk. By the time Alec found a place—illegal, but he hoped the parking meter guys were staying clear of the confusion—and jogged back to the front of the gallery, the TV reporter was just wrapping up her interview.

He hung around in the background, feeling a bit like one of those dorky people who mug for cameras filming live in the streets. When the journalist turned off her mike and started conferring with her cameraman, Alec made his move. The detective wasn't thrilled at being interrupted again from his investigation and gave Alec a you've-got-thirty-seconds kind of nod. As soon as Alec started describing Tess, he caught a glint of recognition in the man's eyes.

He found out that the detective had been the person Tess had come to when she'd arrived on the scene earlier in the afternoon. She'd been advised to go immediately to the precinct handling the case and Alec might find her there. Fifteen minutes later, he did.

"IT'S NOT JUST that I've wasted the better part of a day, but after going round in circles with the same questions and answers for hours, they made me feel I was wasting their time, too. And I thought I was doing them a favor!" Tess ranted all the way out to the parking lot.

When she reached her car, she realized that except for his initial greeting, Alec hadn't said a word. She hesitated beside the Volvo, keys in hand, searching for a face-saving way to tell him he'd been right all along. But true to form, he saved her the trouble.

"Look at it this way," he said, his eyes fixed on an unseen object beyond the top of her head, "one—you weren't arrested as a key suspect," his eyes flicked down to hers and she thought she saw the start of a smile, "and two—I bet you learned something from them about the investigation. Correct?"

She dismissed his first point because she'd never thought she might be—the idea was ludicrous. "You're right about the second one," she said. "That lieutenant said he would have his men look for a bill of sale or receipt for the painting that Tomas separated.''

Alec nodded.

''And,'' she went on, ''he said they would also look for the canvases I gave to Jed Walker last week for Kozinski to assess. Apparently they weren't on the list of stolen items that the police have so far put together.''

''Oh? Who was helping them with that? Walker?''

''Of course not. He doesn't have any connection with the gallery except through my father. Kozinski's companion and another man who works in the gallery got together this morning. The list isn't complete yet. Lieutenant Slegers said it might take a couple of days.''

''Did you find out how Kozinski was killed?''

''The detective didn't tell me but I overheard someone giving him a report, just outside his door. I think he was hit on the head with something. When his partner realized this morning that Tomas hadn't gone home last night, he went to the gallery and found his body.''

''And what did this detective—Slegers?—have to say about your theory? The painting and all.''

''He literally dismissed the issue, saying I would need concrete evidence of fraud. He also said the contents of the will were the responsibility of the executor and the lawyer who drew it up.''

''Did you tell him that was Walker?''

''Yes, but once again he wasn't surprised or concerned. I guess Walker is fairly well-known in Boulder. The detective also said people usually murder for three reasons—for gain, revenge or fear of some kind of exposure. I…uh…I was thinking about what you'd said on the phone. You know—that if Kozinski feared being exposed, he'd have murdered me.''

''Likewise, you could have murdered him out of revenge for splitting the painting.''

Tess gave him a sharp look and saw his grin. ''Very

funny," she drawled. She jiggled the car keys and looked at her watch. "It's almost three and I still haven't bought Molly a present or any of the supplies for the party."

"I'll help if you like. Follow me to my place and we'll both go in the Bronco." When she thanked him, he added, "There is a string or two attached to the offer."

Tess narrowed her eyes. "Such as?"

"You have dinner with me after and maybe we can go back to my place for coffee."

After a moment's thought, she said, "Dinner sounds wonderful. Not sure about the coffee...just yet."

His grin spread across his face. "Okay. Great. Let's get rolling, then."

"COFFEE?" the waitress asked.

Tess tried not to catch Alec's eye as the young woman began to clear their dishes.

"Uh, Tess? Coffee?" he echoed.

She looked up and across the table and saw him wink. "No, thanks," she said to the waitress, but as soon as she left, Tess added, "Not here, anyway."

Alec's grin broadened and he signaled for the bill. It was as if he couldn't get out of the restaurant fast enough. But he obviously chose to play along with Tess, saying on their way out to the parking lot, "You have to come back to my place to pick up your car. Might as well pop up for—"

"Coffee."

"Exactly."

She kept him to his word, almost relishing his transparent efforts at actually brewing coffee neither really wanted. There was a moment when their hands touched briefly as they reached for the mugs he'd filled and Tess had felt a tingle from the brief contact. She sat across from him in the living room, not trusting herself to share the sofa, remembering all too well what had almost transpired last night.

"Want me to come out a bit early tomorrow, to help set up for the party?"

"If you like," she said, her tone as casual as she could manage. "Nick's offered to help so I think we can manage."

A flicker of disappointment swept across his face. He blew on his hot drink, keeping his eyes fixed on Tess. "About last night—" he began.

Tess waved a hand. "It's okay. I understand."

"I don't know if you do. Not even sure if I do, to be truthful." He set the mug of coffee down and came over to her chair.

Tess looked nervously up at him. He took her mug from her and placed it on the coffee table. Then he clasped her hand and gently pulled her to her feet. His hands clutched her shoulders and she had no choice but to meet his gaze straight on.

"I want you to know how hard it was for me to stop." His fingers tightened their hold of her. "When I'm with you, all I think about is touching you. Inhaling that perfume or soap or whatever it is. That intoxicating fragrance that's as much a part of you as your silky skin and green eyes. I was aware of your amazing physical presence from the moment we first met but all that stuff about the kids and your coming here complicated things for a while. Since you've been in Boulder these last few days, I've seen a side of you I never knew existed." He grinned. "I bet you never knew it did, either."

Tess laughed, feeling the heat of a blush rise in her face.

"You've handled one obstacle after another and haven't complained or cried for help."

Tess kept quiet, but thought of her phone calls to Mavis.

"And now that I know you so much better—know what a magnificent person you are—I want this electricity between us to mean something more than just going to bed for a night. I want to know that there'll be many more nights together. That we'll really be a couple in every sense of the word. Do you understand now?''

She couldn't speak for the lump in her throat. When he leaned down to kiss each eyelid, the tip of her nose and finally, her lips, Tess wrapped her arms around him. He held her close against him as if he were afraid to let go, his mouth tracing all the features of her face. Then he raised his head away from hers and hugged her close for a long moment, until Tess gently removed herself from his arms.

''I really should go,'' she whispered, ''before one of us persuades the other to forget all of our noble intentions.''

His laugh was deep and husky. ''Yeah.'' He dropped his arms, but held on to her hand. ''Big day tomorrow.''

Tess caught her lower lip between her teeth. ''For me, too,'' she said. ''The first birthday party I've ever thrown.''

His smile was tender. ''But hopefully, not your last.''

She nodded. ''Hopefully.'' Then she left before she could change her mind about staying.

CHAPTER FIFTEEN

MOLLY CLUTCHED Squiggly with one hand as she waved goodbye to the last of five friends who had attended her birthday party.

"Can I show Squiggly my presents now?"

"Sure, sweetie. Go ahead."

Molly hesitated and said, "That's what my daddy used to call me."

"Oh." Tess closed the front door and looked down at Molly's face, flushed from the party. "Do you mind if I call you that, too, sometimes?"

"Oh, no, I don't mind. You're my sister, so you can call me whatever you like."

Tess watched her skip along the hall to her bedroom. *My sister.* What struck her was how easily the phrase had slipped out. Yet the word still sounded so foreign. Other people had sisters and brothers, but never Tess Wheaton.

She was thinking about that when she walked into the kitchen and found Alec cleaning up with Nick. Not only was she now a sister, but she'd also thrown her first birthday party. Both experiences were exhausting and exhilarating in their own way.

"I've poured you a glass of wine," Alec said, pointing to the table. "Why don't you put your feet up in the family room while we finish up here? I'm sure no one will want a big dinner after such a late lunch. And there's a heck of a lot of leftover pizza."

Tess eyed the pizza boxes on the counter and groaned.

"Those little girls didn't have the kind of appetites I thought they would."

"No," Alec agreed. "Though if you'd been hosting Nick's baseball team, you'd have run out so…"

"I'll get it right eventually," she said. "And I'll just sit here and watch you two work." She sat down in one of the kitchen chairs and watched Nick put clean dishes away from the dishwasher. He had been wonderful with Molly's friends and had voluntarily assumed the burden of entertaining them during lulls in the party. She had a feeling he'd done that before, and thought again how tragic it would have been for the two to be separated. Watching his thin, serious face as he went about his task, she was overwhelmed with an emotion she couldn't at first identify. Not love maybe, but something very close.

The rush of affection moved her to an impulsive decision. "Nick," she said. Both Nick and Alec turned her way, caught perhaps by the tone in her voice. "I was going to wait until I knew everything was arranged, but perhaps I should tell you and Molly now."

Nick stiffened, his eyes instantly wary. But he didn't say a word.

"I spoke to Mr. Walker the other day," she began, noting Alec tense up at the name. "I told him that I wanted to apply to be your and Molly's guardian."

It took a moment for that to register and when it did, relief washed over Nick. He seemed to almost inflate. He gave a small shudder, his face crumpling with emotion, and flung his arms around Alec's waist, burying his face in his chest.

Before Tess had time to feel sorry for herself at being left out, Nick wheeled around and rushed to her side. His breathing was labored and he was on the verge of tears. He gave her an awkward hug. "Thank you so much, Tess," he gasped. "You won't regret it. I'll always be good for you so you won't be sorry. Can I tell Molly?"

Numbed by his response, she nodded. When he dashed from the room, Tess looked at Alec and said, "I thought he would be happy, but he seems almost upset."

Alec came to her and held out a hand, pulling her up into his arms. "He *is* happy. And scared and overwrought. Every emotion he's been feeling for the six weeks that his parents have been dead are rising to the surface. Don't worry if he seems anxious to please you over the next few days. It's a natural reaction. He'll be worried that you'll change your mind."

Tess buried her face in the crook of Alec's arm. "I won't change my mind."

Alec smoothed back her hair from her face, tilting her chin upward so her face could see his. "That's very important, Tess. I can't tell how happy I am that you made that decision, but please don't even consider changing your mind now."

That got to her. "How can you have so little faith in me? Especially after last night?"

Alec stopped her with a kiss. A long kiss that was interrupted by Molly's screams from her room. "I didn't mean that the way it came out," he blurted. "Let me explain."

She saw the urgency in his face and her annoyance vanished. Could she ever be angry with him again, she wondered? Especially after what he'd told her yesterday?

Molly snowballed into the room and flung her arms around Tess and Alec, oblivious to the fact that they were embracing. But Nick noticed, as soon as he followed Molly into the room. His eyes darted from Tess to Alec and back to Tess. The guarded look in his face came back. Tess had the distinct feeling that, although she'd made a significant gain with Nick, the battle wasn't yet over.

Molly bounced around the kitchen, then ran off to tell Squiggly. Nick loitered in the doorway. Waiting, Tess wondered, to see if she and Alec would resume their kiss? Then

Alec dropped his hands from her shoulders and said, "Guess I'd better go." As he approached Nick, he gave him a light tap on his upper arm.

"So when are the play-offs?"

Tess looked from one to the other, puzzled.

"Didn't Nick tell you his baseball team is in the finals for the Boulder County Cup?"

"No," she murmured. It was clear that Nick had chosen to selectively exclude her from parts of his life and she wasn't certain what that signified.

Alec didn't give the matter serious weight. He said, "That's Nick. He likes to keep things close to his chest, as the saying goes. Right, fella?"

Nick shrugged, his face impassive. But not his eyes, Tess noted. They were on full alert, boring in on her as if he were some sideshow psychic trying to read her mind.

A silence ripe with thought filled the room. Finally, Alec shifted farther into the doorway until Nick had to step aside. "So," Alec asked, "when is the game?"

"Wednesday night," he muttered.

"Time?"

"Six."

"Okay. I'll be there. How about you, Tess?"

Tess was still trying to sort out why Nick had never talked about his baseball games. "Uh, of course. If Nick wants me to come."

Nick looked down at his feet and gave another shrug. "If you want," was all he said before he shuffled out of the room.

Alec hesitated another minute and said, "Walk me to my car."

The sun had already dropped behind the mountains and the air was heavy with the crisp dampness of dusk. As their feet crunched across the gravel drive, Tess was aware again how utterly quiet the countryside could be. They might very well be the only people left on earth.

At the driver side of the Bronco, Alec took her into his arms. He ducked his face into the hair at the back of her neck and she heard him inhale deeply.

"You smell so good," he whispered. "Flowery and soapy and most of all, sexy."

Tess felt the tiny hairs on her arms prickle. She moved closer into his embrace, so that her body fit perfectly into his. She tightened her grip around his back, pulling him closer. Then realized Molly or Nick might come outside.

"Alec! Not here." She loosened her hold on him and drew back her head from the hollow of his neck and shoulder.

He closed his eyes for an instant, then let his hands fall to his side as he stepped back from her. He rubbed a hand over his face and Tess saw that he seemed to be struggling to compose himself.

"You're right," he said, huskily. "Time to face up to the fact that the weekend is over and tomorrow it's back to business as usual."

"Well, it doesn't have to be all business all the time," she murmured, wanting to hold on to some of the weekend magic.

He managed a faint smile. "You really didn't know about the baseball?"

Tess wrapped her arms around herself, feeling the night's chill. "No, he hasn't said a word. He's been late coming home a couple of times but always had some excuse. If he'd told me he had practices, I'd have driven him home. He just left me out of the whole equation."

"Because he wasn't sure how long you'd be in the picture. Know what I mean? What's the point in having you cheer from the sidelines if he doesn't even know if you'll be around for all the games?" He paused, adding, "At least, I think that might have been his take on things."

"But when I told him about the guardianship, he didn't seem as excited as Molly."

"You saw his immediate reaction. That was pretty emotional."

"Yes, but when he came back with Molly he was so distant again."

"That's because he'd seen us in an intimate manner and now he's wondering what we might have been doing all weekend."

"Ohhh. You think so? Oh, God."

Alec laughed. "What do you expect? He's a teenager. He's both fascinated and repelled by the fact of adults being intimate. Plus," he hesitated, "he's probably assessing the situation and trying to figure out what it all means. Especially for him and for Molly."

Tess could relate to that. *What did it all mean, anyway?* She studied Alec's face but read nothing in it. He was staring into the night, lost in thought himself. She waited for him to go on, to add something about what the weekend had meant for him personally. But he didn't say a word.

She shivered. "It's getting cold. I should go back in and help Molly get ready for bed. She's pretty hyper tonight and I think it may take two or three stories before she calms down."

She started to move away but he placed a hand on her forearm. "Thanks so much for doing this, Tess," he said.

"Doing what?"

"Taking on the guardianship. It's a big responsibility for you, but basically," he paused a beat, "it's a lifesaver for those kids."

Tess frowned. Something in his words rang false. As if he thought she'd made the decision to please him. "I'm not doing it as a favor to them," she said. "It's because I...I've grown very fond of them over the past two weeks. When I started to think about leaving them here, I realized I simply couldn't."

"Look, I'm sorry that I implied you might change your mind—back inside. It's just that I wasn't sure if you were aware that having the kids wasn't going to be simply about feeding and clothing them. You know Nick—he's going to continue to be a challenge, even now after he knows he and Molly will be together. Other issues will crop up. He's only thirteen and he lost his parents suddenly and tragically." Alec paced as he talked, coming to a standstill at the front of the Bronco. "I know something about it—post-traumatic syndrome. That's what made my life unravel when I came back from Kosovo."

Tess looked at him, but his eyes were fixed on some distant point in the darkness. "Karen told you about my flying for NATO. I was just starting my career when the Gulf War started. I was young, brash and pumped up. Afterward, my military career seemed too slow. I took some NATO missions for the experience and action." He stopped talking for a long moment. When he continued, his voice was low and somber. "Kosovo was so very different. I mean, the cause felt right to me. But there were too many mistakes—too many civilian casualties. Not to mention the atrocities I saw on the ground. When my tour finished, I couldn't psyche myself up for flying anymore. I just wanted to settle into my hometown and grow some roots. Have a family." He paused again. "And to spend the rest of my life just hanging out with reasonably normal and sane people."

After a long silence, Tess said, "You chose the right profession then. Because you're wonderful at your job."

"Yeah," he said. "I think I'm pretty good at it, too. It's not glamorous, but it's damn rewarding most of the time."

She wanted to fill the lull with movement—to reach out for him and touch him. But he stayed apart, keeping a distance between them that confused her. Instead, she babbled. "Hopefully the kids will adjust to me and to a new environment. Nick will find new friends in Chicago and maybe—"

"*Chicago?*"

"Yes. I'm sure Molly will adapt quicker but Nick—"

"You're taking them back to Chicago? To *live?*"

The incredulity in his voice startled her. "I'll have to. Everything I have is there. My condo. My job. Mavis." She waited for him to say something. Then she added, "The kids can make a new life there but…but there's nothing here for me."

As soon as she uttered the words, she wanted to take them back. Their awful implication roared in the still night, like some monster let loose. Tess tried to put together the words to clarify what she'd really meant. But she also knew everything hinged on Alec. Was he going to give her a signal that there was something in Boulder for her after all?

He didn't speak for a long time. "Nothing," he repeated at last. He made the word sound almost obscene.

"I didn't mean that the way it sounded," she began.

But he was already on the move, wrenching the driver side door open. It slammed behind him and just before he turned over the engine, he stuck his head through the open window and said, "It's probably a good thing you've discovered that now, Tess."

Then he was gone, reversing at full speed down the drive to where it widened, made a three-point turn and headed for the highway.

Tess didn't dare go back inside. Not just because of the threat of tears that were welling up already. But because she wanted to wait for the nausea rolling up from the pit of her stomach to settle.

MOLLY WAS the only lively one during breakfast, Tess noted. Nick slurped at his cereal, picked up his backpack and was halfway out the door behind Molly when Tess stopped him. "Do you have a practice today after school?"

"Yeah," he mumbled without turning around.

"I'll pick you up then. What time?"

There was a slight hesitation before he mumbled again. "Six o'clock."

"I'll be waiting in the school parking lot."

The door slammed behind him. Not a happy camper, Tess thought. Obviously yesterday's news hadn't made a big difference. Tess sighed and massaged her forehead with her fingertips. She couldn't seem to get anything right. She thought back to what Alec had said last night. About being aware of the huge responsibility and how the hard times might continue. Then she thought about handling all of that on her own. Doubt began to churn around inside her.

MIDAFTERNOON the telephone rang. Tess had been packing books in the master bedroom and froze at the sound. Was it Alec? She walked over to the bedside and the extension.

"Miss Wheaton?"

An unfamiliar baritone told her immediately that it wasn't Alec Malone. Disappointed, she muttered a faint, "Yes."

"Lieutenant Slegers here. Just calling to report that my people failed to come up with any bill of sale or receipt regarding a Richard Wheaton painting sold in the past three months. There were plenty before that, but you seemed to think this sale was a recent one. Am I correct in assuming that?"

"Uh, yes."

She was focusing on his comment about no sales in the last three months and wondering at the reason when he added, "Also, we found no sign of any canvases by Richard Wheaton. Kozinski's assistant at the gallery as well as his companion went through everything very carefully all weekend. Neither of them has any recollection of any Wheaton canvases coming in. Holloway—he's Kozinski's mate—insists Kozinski would have mentioned them. Apparently they'd be worth quite a lot of money."

"But I gave them to Jed Walker so he could have them assessed for the estate," she said.

"Well then, guess you'd better check with Walker. Obviously, he never got the paintings to the gallery." His voice was brusque, anxious to get off the phone.

Tess didn't bother clarifying that Jed Walker claimed he'd passed them on to Kozinski. The whole business was getting too complicated. She thanked him for his help but before hanging up, impulsively asked, "Have you found out anything more about the murder?"

"Not much that I'm free to tell you, ma'am, at this point. Autopsy report does indicate death due to blunt trauma of the head and as you already know, there is evidence of robbery. Some items were taken, as well as cash Kozinski kept in his desk. If you think of anything more to add to our investigation, feel free to call," he said.

As in, don't call us, we'll call you. Tess replaced the receiver and thought about the canvases. What had Jed Walker done with them? She considered phoning him right away, but then decided she wanted to see his face when she told him the police had found no record of them.

HIS FACE was impassive. Nary a flicker in it, Tess noted. Not even a flinch or tensing in the jaw. But his annoyance at being interrupted yet again by Tess Wheaton was obvious in his voice when he reluctantly greeted her.

"A telephone call would have sufficed," he reiterated as she sat opposite him in his inner office. "You needn't have gone to all this trouble."

"I was expecting you to return my call. Didn't you get my message?"

"Not until this morning and it's been a busy day."

"Well, I had to come to town anyway," she said. "What do you think has happened to the canvases?"

He raised his shoulders and shook his head. "As I told

you, I handed them over to Kozinski. He said the appraisal would take a few days.''

''They couldn't just disappear! His partner—Holloway— claims Tomas never even mentioned them.''

Another dismissive shrug. Tess felt like lunging across the desk and grabbing him by his neatly knotted tie.

''My only thought,'' he quickly went on, ''and I've no proof, is that Kozinski decided to pull some kind of scam. Maybe he had a buyer for the canvases and sold them under the table, avoiding both Internal Revenue and paying the estate its share.''

''But how could he expect to do that, knowing that you would be waiting for the appraisal?''

Walker let out a frustrated sigh. ''I don't know. As I said, it's only a suggestion.'' He pursed his lips. ''He might even have staged the robbery with someone and then…I don't know…something went wrong. Maybe they quarreled and Tomas was killed as a result.''

''Did you suggest that to the police?''

He flashed her a patronizing smile. ''Tess, one doesn't pass on wildly speculative ideas to the police.''

Not unless one's name is Tess Wheaton.

''But I did tell police,'' he went on, ''that I had given the canvases to Kozinski.''

''When? I just spoke to them after lunch.''

''Then they called me after that, to check for themselves I suppose. About an hour ago.'' Reminded of time, he looked at his watch. ''I do have another appointment,'' he said, standing to see her out.

Knowing she would get no further, she followed him to the door. He opened it and added, ''By the way, I'll have the papers for guardianship ready the day after tomorrow. There's no problem, as we anticipated.''

Strangely, Tess felt relieved, as if there might have been a threat of some kind.

"And I assume you'll be returning to Chicago with the children?"

She noticed he was one of the few people to automatically assume that, though she wasn't certain if that was a good sign or not. "Yes," she said. "Probably."

"Then if you don't mind, I'll proceed with negotiating a sale price for the ranch. The sooner the better, don't you think? So that the trust fund can be established?"

Tess stepped into the outer office where Walker's secretary was conferring with someone on the telephone. "Yes, of course," she said. She had a vague sense of being rushed—out the door, through the sale of the ranch and back to Chicago as soon as possible.

She paused, irritated by his apparent brush-off. "When I'm legally their guardian, I'll be able to oversee the trust on their behalf. Isn't that correct?"

He thought that over, then said, "Yes."

Tess left, with the distinct impression that the *yes* had been very reluctantly pronounced. She noted it was past four. There was time to kill before Nick's practice finished. She had a crazy impulse to drive by Alec's office to see if he was available for a drink and scarcely ten minutes later, was pulling into a free space just yards before the building where he worked. Now that she was here, she was eager to see him and to explain her blunder last night. She was partway out the door when she saw Alec exit the building. Tess stretched her arm to wave to him, but his attention was taken by the petite blonde at his side.

They were chatting in a way that stayed Tess's hand midwave. Alec stopped to say something that obviously pleased the woman who laughed, patting him on the arm. The unexpected familiarity struck Tess along with the sobering reminder that, although she'd shared some of Alec's weekend, she really had not shared much else in his life.

CHAPTER SIXTEEN

TESS DEDUCED that her early arrival at Nick's practice yesterday had had something to do with his warmer manner, though she suspected the real reason was her talk with him later. The vanished painting had been on her mind and, on the drive home, when he'd startled her by asking what she was thinking, she'd told him about it.

He remembered the work and said his father had refused to sell it, though Nick thought he'd had many offers over the years. When they arrived at the ranch, she took him into the studio and they had silently studied the painting together for a long moment. Nick said that the reason he recalled the still life so well was because, as a young boy, he had asked his father why the fruits and vegetables were lying around the outside of the bowl, rather than placed inside it.

"I don't remember his exact words," he told Tess, "but I do know that Dad said he'd been playing a game with them and that was the way he decided to paint it. Instead of the usual way."

Tess fell silent then, thinking back to that rainy afternoon so many years ago.

He had agreed with her that Richard Wheaton would never have consented to the paintings being separated. "Like I said, he always used to say he would never sell it in a million years."

Tess couldn't explain why, but she was glad that she and Nick had found some common agreement. So when she awoke the next morning, she was feeling optimistic. Until Molly asked, "Will you sleep in Mommy and Daddy's room now, Tess?"

Two pairs of eyes focused on her. She hadn't planned to tell the children like this, but felt she had no other choice. "Actually," she said, "I won't have to. I've spoken to Mr. Walker and he's going to try to sell the ranch."

Nick's jaw dropped and Molly's eyes grew big. But neither spoke.

"I...uh, I thought it would be best if we all went back to Chicago."

"To *live?*" Molly gasped.

"Of course, sweetie. Would you like that?"

Molly frowned. "I'm not sure. Maybe. Can Squiggly come?"

"Certainly. And all the toys and books you want to bring, too."

Nick scraped his chair along the floor as he leaped to his feet. The chair toppled over behind him, but he was oblivious to all but Tess. The anger in his face was frightening.

"When were we supposed to find this out? Like, two days before we moved or something?" He backed away from the table toward the door. "I'm not going. I don't care if you put me in a group home or whatever. I'll live on the street, but I'm not going to live in Chicago." He ran from the kitchen.

Tess and Molly stared at one another, listening to his feet pounding along the hall, then his bedroom door slamming. What seemed like hours later, they heard the front door open and close.

"Is Nick still going to go to school today?" Molly asked.

Distracted by the chaos she had unwittingly released, Tess murmured, "I hope so."

"Well, he didn't wait for me. Who's walking me down to the road?"

Tess looked at the little girl's plaintive face. "I will, Molly."

When they reached the end of the drive that joined the ranch to Highway 36, there was no sign of Nick.

"Did his bus come already?" Molly asked. "Cause usually his bus comes after mine—that's why he waits with me."

Tess sighed. She stepped out onto the shoulder of the highway and, shielding her eyes from the sun, looked for Nick. If he was walking into town—which is what she suspected—he was already out of sight. Molly's bus arrived and Tess helped her climb aboard, waving goodbye half-heartedly while wondering what to do about Nick.

When Nick's bus arrived on time less than five minutes after Molly's, Tess asked the driver if Nick had gotten on at the previous stop. The negative answer confirmed what she knew she had to do. Go looking for Nick.

She hurried into the house to dress, pulling up jeans under her nightie T-shirt. The mornings were still cool so she tugged on a pair of socks, slipped into loafers and picked up her cotton windbreaker. Reaching for her purse and car keys on a hook by the front door, she was in the car and on her way to Boulder in a scant five minutes.

By the time she arrived at Nick's school, the bell had rung and students were strolling inside. She waited in the parking lot a few minutes, guessing that if she rushed in to find him sitting at his desk in homeroom, he'd be embarrassed. Not to mention, ticked off. She knew that attendance was taken during the first twenty minutes and drummed her fingertips on the steering wheel while she put in the time.

What also troubled her was the fact that, if Nick wasn't at school, she might have to see Alec. She simply wasn't up for that. All night long she'd replayed the scene outside the house a hundred different ways and in each one, she came out looking a lot better than she had in the original.

If only. Those two small words had tormented her until daybreak. Tess peered at the dashboard clock. Time.

She hurried across the parking lot and entered the school by a side door. Lost, she stopped the first two girls she encountered and asked for directions to the office. They'd looked at one another and tittered before pointing the way. The halls were teeming with adolescent bodies in all forms of dress and, Tess couldn't help noticing, undress.

The office was busy, too, with students and parents clustered about waiting to speak to someone and others dropping off slips of paper that Tess saw were attendance sheets. She had to suppress an impulse to riffle through them and rocked back and forth on her heels until she caught someone's attention. Surprisingly, that didn't take long. One of the secretaries—a young woman who looked as if she'd recently graduated from high school herself—timidly approached the counter and asked Tess if she could help her.

"Yes," Tess announced, impatience rising into her voice. "I want to find out if Nick Wheaton is at school today."

The woman's eyes swept up over Tess but she didn't say anything. Tess felt her irritability factor surge.

"Nick Wheaton," she repeated as if she hadn't been heard.

A slight frown marred the young forehead. "Are you his...uh, mother?"

"No," snapped Tess. "I'm his sister. Could you please check? I'm in a hurry."

While the secretary picked up the attendance slips to thumb through them, Tess noticed a few surreptitious glances seemed to be aimed her way. Perhaps she ought to have taken the time to brush her hair or put on some lipstick. Fortunately, she was saved the worry of mentally assessing her appearance by the secretary returning to say that Nick was not in school.

On her way out, Tess craned her head around to ask the woman to call her at home the instant he arrived. If he arrived. Then she jogged out to the parking lot and drove toward the center of town and Alec Malone's office, a place she was hoping Nick would go if he wanted to talk to someone. What would she do once she was back in Chicago, if Nick were to take off like this? Alec Malone would be a heck of a long way away.

Tess shoved the question aside. *Finding Nick was the objective here. Not organizing your life six months from now.* Fortunately she found a parking space close to the building where Boulder County Child Protective Services was located.

She walked through an empty reception area into a maze of cubicles, scanning the room for Alec's tall, husky form and reddish-brown head.

"Can I help you?"

Tess stopped to peer down at a young woman sitting behind a desk to her right. The woman had a bemused expression on her face. Perhaps because people were supposed to check in with reception rather than wander aimlessly about inside.

"I'm looking for Alec Malone," she said.

That arched a single, plucked eyebrow. "Are you a client of his?"

"Well, my brother is. Nick Wheaton."

She nodded. "Alec's office is at the very back. Take the center row and you can't miss it. I'll call and tell him—?"

"Tess Wheaton," she said, already moving toward what could be a center row. Several heads raised to follow her. Some appeared to be faintly amused. Tess was just beginning to wonder if she had accidentally wandered into the inner sanctum of a top-secret organization. How out of place did she look, she asked herself?

Then she spotted a familiar face and all of her anxiety about confronting Alec Malone so soon after her stupid remark last night simply evaporated. His grin was cautious and a bit lopsided, but she was so relieved to see it that she had to steel herself from rushing at him and throwing herself into his arms.

"Tess?" he asked, his eyes sweeping over her from top to bottom and back again. He steered her into his office, closing the door behind him. His forehead wrinkled in a hesitant frown, as if he were unsure how to respond to her unexpected presence. "What is it?"

"It's Nick," she said. All of her pent-up anxiety gushed out of her and she couldn't have stopped herself from babbling if she'd wanted to. "I told the kids we'd be moving to Chicago and he just flipped out. I mean, Molly was okay with it once I said Squiggly could come too—and all of her stuff, you know—but Nick just raced out of the house without even thinking about walking Molly to her bus. So I had to do that and when Nick's bus came and he wasn't there, I got in the car and went to his school. But he wasn't there, either, and to be honest, Alec, I'm sorry to bother you at work like this but you were the only person I could think of to turn to." She had to stop then, for air.

Alec had been nodding his head throughout and when she paused, he asked, "You went to his school just now? Like that?"

Confused by this obviously irrelevant question, Tess just nodded.

Then she followed his gaze, now resting somewhere on her midsection. Her windbreaker was unzipped and gaping open to reveal her T-shirt nightie, complete with its fluffy oversized pink bunny and the logo Sleepytime Bunny scrawled in pink beneath it. The bunny was grinning and flashing a mischievous wink as it munched on a carrot.

Tess closed her eyes and lowered her head on to her fist.

"YOU WANT A LARGE, or regular?" Alec asked, leaning over her at the coffee shop outside his building.

She was definitely preoccupied, he thought, as she seemed to be pondering his question longer than necessary. At least he hadn't had to convince her to zip up her windbreaker, in spite of the warming day. And he'd managed to find a battered comb in a desk drawer that she'd used to tame some of the sleepy tangles in her hair.

Speaking of sleepy. He couldn't hide a grin even now, placing their coffee orders, as he once again pictured her whirling down the middle of the fifth floor, the shocking pink Sleepytime Bunny hopping up and down as she went. Once she'd calmed down, she'd tried to explain that the nightshirt had been a joke present from a friend at work and was very comfortable. So cozy, she'd forgotten she'd been wearing it when she'd rushed out of the house.

By then Alec's head was spinning and his suggestion of coffee—outside, away from the mild curiosity of his co-workers—was readily accepted. He left instructions in case Nick showed up.

Alec was worried about the kid. He realized the gains Tess had made with him, but knew Nick was still fragile. Molly, on the other hand, was appearing to be managing quite well. Except for the initial disruptions in sleep and some mild regressive behavior, she had responded warmly to Tess. Her confidence had soared and would continue to do so, now that she knew for certain that she and Nick would not be placed in foster care.

But adolescents were tougher in many ways. Nick was old enough to know that adults could be deceptive and self-interested. He was smart enough to figure out that, if Tess had initial doubts about taking him and Molly, those doubts could easily return. And he probably knew that looking after two kids—one of them a teenager—was going to offer challenges Tess had never experienced.

Alec set the coffee down and took the chair next to Tess. "Okay, so how about you call home to see if he has turned up there after all and I call the school? He may simply have gone somewhere to cool off before starting classes. I gave him that advice a few weeks ago.''

Tess was stirring her coffee and raised her head to ask, ''You did?''

He hoped she'd understand. ''I told him it was better to be a bit late for school than to show up all hot and bothered and ready to explode.''

She thought that over and nodded. He was relieved. At least their strategy planning wasn't going to begin with yet another quarrel. Alec sipped on his hot coffee and tried not to stare at her. She looked pale and genuinely distraught. Probably kicking herself, he thought, over how she might have handled the situation differently. Or perhaps—and he didn't seriously want to consider this one—having second thoughts about taking the kids.

He had to choose his words carefully. From what he could see of her current mental state, she might respond by flaring up or worse, by dissolving into tears. He was hoping for something between both extremes. The problem was, he didn't have a very good track record so far in communicating with Tess Wheaton. It seemed to him that just as their relationship was beginning to show some promise, he—or she—would say or react to something in a completely irrational manner. Or maybe, the problem had more to do with what *wasn't* said, than what was.

''I'll call the house, maybe he went back there. Drat, I left my cell phone at the house.''

Alec shrugged. Personally, he disliked cell phones and refused to own one. Though he accepted that someone like Karen should have one, in case an emergency turned up and she wasn't at the ranch. ''Here,'' he said, handing her a quarter. ''There's a pay phone right outside.''

He watched her go through the motions, but he got the feeling she was thinking it would be a waste of time. She doubted Nick had gone back home, and he did, too. Still, it was one option that had to be ruled out. When she came back, confirming no one was home, he went to call the school. His eyes remained fixed on her as he placed the call. Something in the slump of her shoulders and the way she fixated blankly on her coffee made him want to rush back inside and sweep her into his arms. Make her feel that everything was going to be just fine.

He knew it would be, too. Nick would turn up as usual and be remorseful, as usual. Until the next time. Alec waited for the connection to come through, wondering what would happen if the next time occurred in Chicago. A secretary finally picked up and informed him that yes, Nick Wheaton had arrived late but was now in class. *Thank God.* Alec hung up and headed back to Tess.

When he gave her the good news, her relief was so sweet he wanted to reach out for her. It was all he could do not to stroke the soft silk of her cheek and brush back the fluff of curl at her ear. Then draw her close and kiss that ear tenderly, whisper in it all the things they could do if they just made a detour back to his apartment. But he had work and she had other things on her mind. Besides, he was almost afraid to touch her, in case she interpreted it as another ploy of his to persuade her to stay in Boulder.

"Look," he said, downing the rest of his coffee and risking another disagreement. "You may not want advice from me—God knows, I seem to hear myself giving it all the time and you must be sick and tired of it." Encouraged by her wan smile, he plunged on. "But when Nick comes home, you need to let him know that what he did was unacceptable. But you also need to tell him that, in the end, he made it better by making the right decision to go on to school."

"I know. You're right. And he has the big game tomorrow," she said. "I don't want him to feel...I don't know," she hesitated. "Cornered. That's the word. I don't want him to drop out of the game if he's feeling hurt and threatened."

She'd made amazing progress, Alec noted, to come up

with that. And of course, she was perfectly on target. If Nick felt cornered, he'd punish them both by refusing to play in the final game. Illogical, but typical of the adolescent mind-set.

"Another thing you should know," Alec said, "that might explain his behavior this morning. I was talking to Karen last night after I got home and she told me that Ken had asked Nick if he was interested in a summer job. Of course, the job is contingent on their keeping the ranch. Ken made that very clear, but Nick was really excited about the possibility."

Her face registered surprise and something else he couldn't determine. She thought for a long moment before fixing her green eyes on his. "Thanks, Alec. For…for listening and helping me. Even after…you know…what I said last night. I don't know why that came out, but I just—"

"It's okay," Alec interrupted. Now wasn't the time or place to settle what he knew had to be settled between them.

"And I drove by your office yesterday to apologize but then I saw you with…well, an attractive woman and…"

Alec had to think. Then it dawned on him. "You mean Linda, my boss?" He smiled and patted her hand. "I think Nick's having a practice again tonight, so if you turned up for that to give him a lift home, he'd probably be grateful." Alec laughed. "Even if he doesn't show it."

She smiled and got up to leave. "I guess I'll see you at the game then—tomorrow night?"

"Six o'clock," he said. "I'll be there. Maybe we can all go for a late dinner after—whether to celebrate a victory or not."

"That would be nice," she said and left.

Alec headed back to the office, aware that the full day ahead of him was going to be monopolized by thoughts of Tess Wheaton.

THERE WERE A FEW messages awaiting Tess when she arrived back at the ranch, but the first thing she did was to change, adding underwear this time and an ordinary T-shirt. Then she listened to the saved messages. The first was her own to see if Nick was there. Then Nick's school, confirming his arrival. The next was a slurred message from Marci Stone, asking her to drop round and collect a birthday gift for Molly. The last one was, surprisingly, from Alec.

"Hi, Tess, trust you got back okay. Listen, I just had another call from my buddy with the state police. The one I called about that license number? Apparently, the owner, Mark Kaiser, works for an international development company with an office in Denver. That's all I could find out. Have you had a chance to check with the land registry? I haven't, but if you want me to, call me at work or home. I may get a chance to do that tomorrow. Otherwise, see you at the game tomorrow night and…uh…well, I'm looking forward to that. Take care."

Tess deleted the messages. She didn't know what to make of Alec's information, either. Without context, it had little meaning on its own.

After lunch, Tess decided to collect Molly's birthday gift from Marci Stone. She decided to drive to the Stones', rather than walk and risk being late for Molly's bus. When she pulled up to the house, the only vehicle she saw was Larry's pickup. He answered the door and seemed surprised to see her.

"Marci went to Denver," he said. "When did she call you?"

"I don't know. Sometime this morning."

"Well, that's Marci. Impulsive as always. She knew she had an appointment in Denver. Come on in. I think I saw Molly's present in our room."

Tess followed him inside. There were some empty cardboard boxes lying in the hall.

"Getting ready to start packing," Larry said. "Jed

Walker called me late yesterday to say that you all were heading back to Chicago. I'm real happy to say that he took my offer on the Wheaton place.''

Tess felt her jaw drop.

"He told you, didn't he?" Larry's face filled with concern. "God, I trust this is what you wanted. I mean, he said you were definitely leaving the area—"

"It's okay, Larry. I'm just surprised that…you know, it's all happening so quickly."

He nodded, but his frown deepened. "You're sure?"

When she reassured him, he smiled and patted her on the shoulder. "Walker may be in a hurry with this, but Marci and I aren't. Believe me," he said, jerking his head toward the boxes. "Take your time with the move. And whatever things you don't want to take with you—or physically can't—well, we can help you sell them."

And guess who would be the buyer? Tess knew he was trying to be helpful, though found his gesture a tad self-serving. She waited in the hall while he went farther into the house. She could see the French doors at the end and the patio beyond. When she'd been there before, the doors along the hall had been closed. As she paced back and forth, she noticed one of the rooms was a wood-paneled study obviously decorated with the country sportsman in mind, complete with a mounted elk's head and a big-horned sheep's.

Mesmerized and repelled at the same time, Tess stepped into the room for a closer look. But what captured her attention—freezing, in fact every nerve cell in her body—was the framed still life hanging on the wall opposite the animal heads.

A still life of fruits and vegetables, lying haphazardly around the base of a polished wooden bowl. The still life Richard Wheaton had painted on the back of her own portrait.

IT DIDN'T TAKE LONG for the whole story to burst out. Larry had guessed something was wrong when he found her in the den. His concern had compensated somewhat for her shock and Tess agreed to a cold drink in the kitchen while he gave his account of the story.

"It must have been mid-March. We were about to celebrate our twentieth wedding anniversary and were having lunch in town. I'd only been to the art gallery once before—to one of Richard's exhibits a few years ago. Anyway, Marci wanted to have a look and we were in the area. The owner—can't recall his name—you know, the one they just found dead?"

"Tomas Kozinski."

"Yeah, that's it. We introduced ourselves, said we were neighbors of the Wheatons and he asked if we'd like to have a look at a painting he'd received from Richard for cleaning. As soon as Marci saw it, she fell in love with the still life side. I offered to buy it, but Kozinski said he doubted Richard would sell because it had a special meaning for him." Larry paused, taking a sip of beer. "Course at the time, I thought it was a portrait of Molly. I mean, it looked like Molly."

His gaze fell on Tess, as if comparing the original model. She ran a fingertip along the edge of her iced tea, anxious for him to get on with it.

"I know I'm an insistent guy, especially when it comes to getting something I want." He gave a self-deprecating little laugh. "At any rate, Marci was so taken with the still life that I asked Kozinski if he'd call Richard and see if he might change his mind. We told him we'd wait while he made the call. He came back a few minutes later and said that Richard didn't want to sell the portrait but if Kozinski was able, he could separate the two paintings and sell us the still life."

Tess looked over at Larry. "Kozinski said my father gave him *permission* to cut the board in half?"

"That's what Kozinski said. Hell," he swore, laughing

again, "I didn't know such a thing was possible but Kozinski insisted he could find someone to do it. He told us to come back in a week or so. We did and we got the painting."

Tess didn't know what stunned her more. The fact that Stone's story corroborated Kozinski's so perfectly or that her father might have consented to the act after all. But she knew there was very little she could do about the painting now. Overwhelmed by the thought, she also knew she wanted to leave as soon as possible.

She looked at her watch and said, "You know, Molly's bus is arriving soon. I've got to go." She grabbed the gift bag at her elbow and stood up.

Larry stood, too, but his face was serious as he said, "I can see this has really upset you. I don't know what to say. Obviously both paintings were intended for you. I don't understand why Richard let it happen, unless he was thinking he'd probably never see you again."

"Perhaps," Tess murmured as she moved toward the hall. She didn't feel like analyzing her father's motives with Larry Stone.

He was close on her heels, rambling on about how Marci might be persuaded to give up the painting. That made Tess pause at the front door. "What do you mean?"

Larry gave a helpless shrug. "Marci likes a lot of things. I mean, I could probably offer to substitute the painting with a new pair of diamond earrings or something."

His grin suggested the ploy had worked in the past. "Hell, why don't I just give it to you right now? If she's ticked off, well, I'll come sheepishly back for it."

Tess was speechless. She watched him wheel around, march to the den and return with the still life.

"Here," he said, holding it out to her. "Take it."

"But it's yours. You paid for it."

"I'll get my money back from the gallery. After what

you've told me, I'm sure it won't be a problem.'' He frowned at Tess. ''I mean, the guy could have been scamming us both, right? Maybe he didn't call Richard at all. Maybe he just thought he'd get away with it and make a bit for himself on the side.''

Tess shook her head. ''I've thought of that, too. But surely my father would have found out.''

''Maybe. But then, two weeks later, your father was dead.''

There was nothing Tess could add to that. She stared up into Larry's face and then at the painting. His offer sounded sincere. The smile on his face certainly was. When she held out her hands, he passed over the painting.

''Enjoy,'' he said softly.

''Thank you so much, Larry. This is so kind of you.''

''Not at all. It's going back to where it belongs. That's all.'' He followed her outside and helped her set the painting in the back of the Volvo. When he closed the hatch, he held out a hand.

Tess placed hers in his and smiled. ''If you ever get to Chicago—''

''I'd love to,'' he said, his weathered face crinkling in a big smile.

Tess got behind the steering wheel and just before turning over the engine, thought of Alec's message. Perhaps Larry might know something.

''Do you remember when you came over to the house last week and I showed you those sketches we found?''

He looked puzzled.

''Of the campsite where Nick said the family often went on weekends.''

''Oh, right. Why?''

''I noticed that you were looking at some numbers on the back of one of the sketches.''

A frown replaced the confusion. ''Oh? I don't recall.''

By now Tess wished she hadn't raised the matter. He

obviously didn't have a clue what she was talking about. "It's okay. Just that I thought the numbers on the back of one of the sketches looked like a Colorado license plate and I was right."

"Really?"

"Apparently it's a plate registered to someone from Denver. A man by the name of Mark Kaiser. Does that ring a bell for you?"

He pursed his lips and thought long. "Nope. Can't say it does. Does it mean something to you?"

Tess shook her head. "Not really. I just couldn't understand why my father had jotted them down on the back of a sketch."

"Can't help you there, either. As I said, it's not a name I recognize. Unless the guy was a friend of your father's."

"Then why would he copy down the license plate? It doesn't make sense."

Larry moved closer to her opened window. "No, it doesn't. But there's no way of finding out the reason now, is there?"

The expression in his eyes was a mix of kindness and pity. Tess knew he was right. "No," she murmured. She turned over the engine, said a quick goodbye and reminded him to thank Marci for the gift. As she headed down the drive to the highway, she glanced in the rearview mirror to see Larry standing, arms crossed, watching her leave.

CHAPTER SEVENTEEN

TESS SHOWED NICK the painting after dinner. She and Molly had picked up Nick after his practice. He'd looked surprised when she'd told him they'd watched most of the practice itself, but he also looked pleased. On the way home, he quietly apologized for the morning's escapade and Tess simply said that she had been worried. When she suggested that they would all discuss the move to Chicago after the big game was over, he had muttered a barely audible sure. But Tess was satisfied with that.

"It's very different, isn't it? Even for Dad," he said, staring at the still life on its easel in the studio. "A lot of stuff was destroyed in the fire." Nick wandered around the studio, occasionally picking up something, examining it and then setting it back down.

Tess watched him, wondering if he was memorizing things before he'd have to leave for good. "All of it?"

"Most. And Mom's, too. I think Dad had some pieces at the art gallery, but they all got sold right after."

"Probably for a lot more money."

He looked across the room at her, his face set in thought. "Yeah. I overheard him say something like that to Mom. He sounded almost bitter about it."

"So then he eventually got back to work. I saw at least six paintings at the gallery when I visited there last week. And then there were the unframed ones here."

"Oh, yeah?" Nick resumed his wandering. He picked up a small clay pot and held it aloft. "See this? I made this when I was about Molly's age. Mom helped me, of course. But, like, I did most of the work.'' He let out a loud sigh. ''It was fun.''

''You miss them,'' Tess said softly.

''Yeah, well…that's life.'' He shoved his hands into his jeans pockets, but kept on the move.

''Tell me about the day they died,'' she said, on impulse. ''No one's really told me about it. How it happened and everything.''

She saw him frown, as if he didn't like where she was leading him. His face was flushed and she thought he might cry. ''Look, never mind. I shouldn't have asked,'' she quickly said.

''No, no. It's okay. Alec said I should talk about it whenever it felt okay.'' He scanned the inside of the studio, then looked at Tess. ''This feels okay, though. Know what I mean?''

She nodded, afraid to speak.

''It was a Friday. March 28. I was spending the weekend at a friend's place and Molly had a sleepover that night with some friend in her class. That morning, before I headed for the bus, Dad got a phone call. He took it in the kitchen at first, but then he told Mom he'd get the extension in their room. When he was telling her that, I remember thinking he had this strange expression on his face. Like someone had died or something.'' Nick paused, his memory taking him back to that day. ''Anyway, I went out to the bus. Molly was running ahead of me and then I remembered I'd forgotten my lunch. I went back inside and Mom and Dad were both in the kitchen again. They were talking in these real low voices. Almost hushed, kinda. Know what I mean?''

Tess gave a vague nod, picturing the scene.

''I asked them what was wrong and Mom said nothing, go to school. But Dad mumbled something about being stabbed in the back and I said, like, *what?* Then Mom said to never mind, everything would work out and to have a good weekend. See, I was going to my friend's right after school so I wouldn't see them till I came home on Sunday.''

He stopped then and coughed. His voice grew hoarse as he went on. ''All these last few weeks, I've been wishing so much that I'd said something nice to them before I left. Like, I didn't even wish them a good weekend or anything. I just grabbed my lunch, waved and walked out the door.'' He sniffled, wiping his nose on the back of his hand. ''That was the last time I ever saw them.''

Tess moved swiftly across the room, wrapping her arms tightly around him. She rocked him gently back and forth until his trembling ceased. Then she kissed him lightly on the forehead and whispered, ''Let's go back to the house.''

She lay awake most of the night, thinking about all of them. Molly, with her tiny pixie face and toothless grin. Nick, who could almost be a poster boy for the troubled teen, but who doted on his little sister and had found the resourcefulness and courage to set out on a journey to find Tess. Then there was Alec. Tess shied away from his image, knowing she could spend an entire sleepless night on Alec Malone himself. Finally, she played over and over again one of Nick's comments—the one about Richard being stabbed in the back.

It wasn't a casual expression, she thought, but one a person used on learning about a betrayal. So who, she wondered, had betrayed Richard Wheaton? The first name that came to mind was Tomas Kozinski.

AFTER LUNCH the next day, Tess decided not to wait any longer. Molly had been invited to a friend's for dinner after school and had preferred to go there, rather than see the game. So Tess didn't have to worry about being home at a certain time and could go right to Nick's game after her errand in Boulder.

When she got into the Volvo, she gave herself a quick once-over in the rearview mirror. She had taken extra effort to look as good as possible. Not simply for any friends of Nick's who might have seen her at school yesterday, but mainly for Alec. She had decided in the night that if she was only going to be able to see Alec Malone for the next week or so—before their move to Chicago—then she'd better make the most of her time.

It took her a while to find the registry office in downtown Boulder. After a couple of false leads, she eventually located it and was dismayed to find a lineup of more than a dozen people ahead of her. She took a number and sat down, wishing she'd brought a paperback novel with her. Almost an hour after her arrival, her number was called.

She had obtained the information about the campsite location that morning from Ken. He'd sounded surprised on the telephone, not just to hear her voice but at her request. He'd also asked her to copy down the ordinates and lot numbers for the other property between the Malone ranch and the campsite.

"I'm curious to find out who owns that piece, too," he'd said.

She'd jotted those numbers down as well but by the time her turn came, she realized that she might incite a minor riot if she took up more of the clerk's time than was justified. There were at least another fifteen people behind her and closing hour loomed. So she decided to have the clerk obtain the documents only for what she suspected was the land owned by her father.

The frazzled clerk returned some ten minutes later with a thick file folder. "Property in question," he mumbled, "is owned by one Jed Walker."

Tess stared openmouthed long enough for the clerk to think she had a hearing problem. He repeated the name.

"Is there a bill of sale or something?" Tess asked. "I thought my father owned that property."

The man shuffled through some papers, pulling out a thin document. "Here it is, if you want to have a look." He shoved the paper across the counter toward Tess.

Aware of fidgeting behind her, Tess skimmed the document and all of its mind-numbing legalese. Somewhere toward the end of it, she saw two signatures. One belonged to Jed Walker, as buyer. The other, was Richard Wheaton's. The vendor. The last thing she noticed—and this she had to read twice—was the date. *March 28. The day of the accident.*

The low rumble of voices behind her brought Tess back to present time. "Can I get a photocopy of this?" she asked the man.

"Yes, but I have to fill out a requisition for you, then you take it downstairs to the main desk and wait. When the file gets down there, someone will copy the document for you. There's a fee," he added, as if that might deter her.

"Please fill out the requisition then," she asked, ignoring the complaining behind. When he finished, she grabbed it and rushed out the door.

The whole process took a lot longer than Tess had anticipated. Half an hour into her pacing around yet another small waiting area clustered by yet another group of restless customers, she realized how the wheels of government worked in that particular office. Rather than send down her file right away, the clerk likely had placed it in a growing pile of files which would eventually work their way downstairs to the photocopy and main reception area.

Just when she thought she might chew the end of her fingers off midknuckle, Tess's number was called. As she approached the counter, she saw that her fears had proven true. Bundles of files sat like dominoes along the counter behind the clerks. She tried not to hum and haw while her paper was being copied and luckily had the correct amount of money so she wouldn't have to wait for the payment person to make change. Finally, she plucked the photocopy from the clerk and wove her way through the lineup out onto the sidewalk. She peered at her watch. It was almost four-thirty but not quite closing time, she guessed, for lawyers.

She had to circle the block twice before finding a good place. Not that she couldn't have walked, but she thought if she was pushed to punching Jed Walker in the nose— for example—she'd be able to make a hasty escape.

It just might come to that, she told herself on the drive over. Because he had lied to her, pretending to know nothing about the land at all. Because obviously he, too, was pulling some kind of scam, otherwise why wouldn't he simply have fessed up? Said, *Yeah, you know that sounds vaguely like a bit of land I bought from your father on the day he died.*

Not bloody likely, she thought, hastily backing the Volvo into a parking space right in front of Walker's building. It lurched to a halt and she turned off the engine. She reached for her purse and the brown envelope containing the photocopy when the SUV directly in front of her caught her eye. Not the vehicle, so much as its license plate. The number swam in a blur until her mind swiftly came up with the answer. The license number from the sketch. The one belonging to some Mark Kaiser from Denver.

Tess opened her door and stuck one foot onto the road. The other was about to follow when the owner of the SUV made an abrupt appearance at its hood. He hit a remote door opener and walked purposefully to the driver side.

Mark Kaiser? If so, then Tess had seen him before. Only days ago, in Jed Walker's office. The executive type who'd shaken hands with Walker on his way out the door.

Tess withdrew her foot, closed her door and turned over her engine just as the SUV in front of her fired up. She changed her mind. She'd visit Jed Walker later. Maybe even tomorrow. Right now, she wanted to find out who Mark Kaiser was, where he was going and why he was in

Boulder. The dashboard clock registered four-forty-five. She figured she had plenty of time.

He wasn't in a hurry, which was a good thing because even downtown Boulder had its own miniequivalent to a big city rush hour. The other good thing was that he was driving a shiny all-white SUV, which made following him a bit easier. Tess didn't have the faintest idea what she would do or say to him when he reached his destination. She hoped she would have time to come up with a plausible explanation. At least, one that would keep him from immediately calling the police on his cell phone.

When the SUV made a left turn onto Twenty-Eighth Street—otherwise known as Highway 36—a prickle of apprehension crept up Tess's spine. But she stuck with him, all the way to the edge of Boulder where the street became the highway and there was no longer any doubt in her mind that both of them were heading out of town.

Her eyes flicked to the dashboard clock. Five. Well, maybe she'd follow him just to the point where she'd still be able to turn around and make the game. Even if Tess was a bit late, Alec would save her a seat. Decision time came less than twenty minutes later, as she and the SUV passed the Wheaton ranch. She looked at the clock, as if it might do a time reversal and make the decision for her. Continue on or return to Boulder?

She clenched her jaw and decided to give the SUV another ten minutes. Where the heck was he going, anyway? The Stones' place had no vehicles parked outside. Perhaps Marci was still in Denver, or they were both out for dinner in Boulder. When she saw the sign announcing the approach to Lyons, Tess knew she was definitely going to be late for the game.

How long did a baseball game take, she wondered? She'd never been to one in real life and television had corrupted all sense of time for the game with its incessant commercials and info breaks. If she made it before the end, that was the most important thing. Wasn't it?

Tess shook her head, as if freeing it from the crazy thoughts bombarding her concentration. Lyons came and went. So did the turnoff to the Malone ranch. She glanced longingly at it, wishing she were dropping by on an impromptu visit instead of following some stranger into the middle of nowhere. When the SUV slowed down just before the cutoff to the campsite—*the Wheaton campsite*— Tess took her foot off the accelerator. She pumped the brake, knowing she'd have to give the SUV enough space so Mark Kaiser—whoever he was—wouldn't freak out about her following him all the way from Boulder.

As she had dreaded, the SUV made the turn. She coasted by, driving onto the shoulder and braking the Volvo a few yards beyond. She stared at the clock, willing it not to change. But it did. Five-forty-five. Okay. She'd definitely be late. Nothing anyone would really make note of—except maybe for Alec, and he might be persuaded to focus on other things. Like her welcoming kiss.

Tess shifted the Volvo into reverse and slowly backed along the shoulder to the turn. Then she cranked the wheel and headed along the dirt trail. She thought about casually pulling in behind the SUV, because she knew it could only drive as far as the crest of the sandstone cliff overlooking the lake. But then she wondered what her first words could be. *Hi, I'm Tess Wheaton. I noticed you were in the area and blah blah blah.*

No. The fact that Mark Kaiser was coming out to see land owned by her father and fraudulently taken by Jed Walker had to be part of some business deal. The kind of business deal people wanted to keep secret. Otherwise, she'd know about it. Walker would have informed her. And where did Alec say Kaiser worked? Some kind of development company. Developing exactly what, she wondered?

She took her foot off the accelerator again and let the

Volvo coast a bit farther before turning off the engine. She figured she was at least fifty yards from where they'd parked on the camping weekend. She hesitated a minute before getting out of the car, asking herself if she'd done the right thing. Too late now, she decided, and got out. The SUV was parked up ahead near the stand of fir trees. It was empty. It was also sitting next to another SUV. A dark maroon one that Tess didn't recognize.

As Tess neared the crest, she could see two figures standing side by side down at the lake. One of them was pointing east while the other seemed to be consulting a map. She couldn't identify either man and knew she had no choice but to get closer. She picked her way carefully down the rocky path, not wanting to alert them. Mainly because she hadn't yet come up with a good excuse for her presence. When she was almost at the end of the path and on the valley floor, she stopped to ease the jitters that were making her legs feel like rubber.

One of the men had his back to her but the other was, as she'd expected, Mark Kaiser. He was looking through a pair of binoculars and saying something to the second man, who was jotting notes on a clipboard, the map now rolled up under one arm. Something in his stance made her pause. She squinted, wishing she had her own binoculars. Then the second man removed the baseball cap he was wearing and his light hair glinted in the remnants of the setting sun. He turned, his profile registering all too clearly with Tess.

Jed Walker. Of course. Why hadn't she guessed? He was officially the landowner and this Kaiser—*a possible buyer?* She watched them for a few more seconds before deciding that now she wouldn't bother confronting Kaiser. Now she would return to the car, arrive late at Nick's game and then discuss everything she had learned that day with the one adult in Boulder she knew for sure she could trust. Alec Malone.

Tess dug her heel into the sand to turn herself around, but met with some resistance. The human kind.

CHAPTER EIGHTEEN

FIVE MINUTES before the game was due to start, Alec resigned himself to the fact that Tess was going to be late. He corrected himself. Was already late. He hoped she'd make it before the end of the first inning and that Nick wouldn't notice. His windbreaker was balled up beside him on the bleacher, reserving a place for her. A place that was shrinking rapidly as more and more latecomers arrived. He'd had to use those damning words, "It's saved" more times than he could count and every time he received a glare or a grumble.

Frankly, he hadn't expected the outdoor stadium to be so packed for a junior high game. But it was the final, the last game of the season and an unusually balmy evening for mid-May. Alec craned his neck to look for Nick, whose team dugout was right beneath him. *There.* He spotted the top of his head at the end of the bench. Looked like Nick might not get to play in the first inning anyway.

The game started and Alec tried his best to concentrate on it, but found himself constantly checking his watch and then staring down at the empty place beside him. If thoughts counted, she'd be there in a flash. He'd be squeezed against her warm body and gazing like some lovesick dope into eyes that sparkled in a mix of greens and blues. She'd probably keep those eyes fixed on the game below and run the tip of her tongue along her lower lip before tucking the edge of the lip under her teeth. He'd watched her do that a lot during the past two weeks, whenever she was thinking serious things.

A cheer from the crowd forced his mind down to the field. The first inning was wrapping up and she still hadn't arrived. Alec stood up to scan the bleachers below and the knots of people filing out to get snacks or talk to friends. It was so noisy he'd never be able to get her attention by shouting. He waited until the crowd began heading back up into the bleachers. Then he began to consider the ugly thought that, if Tess wasn't coming, something must have happened. Either to her or to Molly. He knew she wouldn't miss the game.

He vacillated a few minutes longer, then grabbed his windbreaker and trotted down the steps. Maybe Nick knew something. He had to stoop when he reached the back of the dugout and scrambled along the mesh fencing separating the team from the spectators. He quickly located Nick in the middle of the bench.

"Nick!" he called and stuck his fingers through the wire mesh to rub the back of the boy's head.

Nick jumped, turning around at the same time. His startled face relaxed when he saw Alec. "Hey! You scared me!"

Alec didn't want to alarm the kid so he managed a weak smile. "Look, did Tess say if she had anything planned this afternoon?"

Nick shook his head. "No. Why?"

Nothing to do but get on with it. "Just that she's not here yet."

"Maybe she had car trouble or something. Or maybe she just forgot." Nick looked back to the field.

Alec tapped him on the head again. "No, buddy, she wouldn't do that. Would she?"

"I don't know. Like, I've only known her a couple of weeks."

"But you know enough about her already, don't you? To know that she would be here if she could?"

"Yeah. Look, I'm gonna be up soon...."

"Okay, just thought I'd check with you first." Alec considered pretending to go back into the stands, but knew he couldn't. "Nick, the thing is, I'm getting a bit worried. I mean—" he held up a hand at the alarm in Nick's face "—I'm sure it's something simple like car trouble, as you said. But would you mind if I missed the rest of the game and went looking for her?"

"I guess not. You don't need to worry about Molly. She's at a friend's place for dinner."

"Okay, that's one problem out of the way. Look, just in case neither of us is here when the game finishes, can you get a lift home with someone?"

"No problem," he mumbled.

But Alec saw the disappointment in his face. "We'll have our celebration later tonight or tomorrow. But it'll happen. Okay?"

"Sure."

He didn't appear any happier. "What is it?" Alec asked.

"Just that...you know...I don't want anything to be bad. You know. With Tess."

Alec blew out a mouthful of air. "Me, neither. And you know what, I don't think there will be anything awful. Tess is a pretty determined woman. And she can handle tough things."

Nick nodded. "Yeah. I think she can, too."

Alec tousled the boy's hair, wished him good luck and strode out of the stands in search of a pay phone. Wishing, for the first time in his life, that he had a cell phone. His first call was to the house in case, for some reason, she'd gone back home after all. No answer. He hung up, stumped. The only people he could call on for advice were Karen and Ken. They were a long way from Boulder, but might have a suggestion he could follow up on before he started driving around looking for Tess and her car.

"Yeah," Ken said at Alec's opening question about having heard or seen Tess.

Alec's heart rate soared. "Yeah, what? She's there?"

"No, but she called me this morning. Why? What's up? I thought you guys were at Nick's game."

"I am but Tess hasn't shown up yet."

There was a short silence. "She said she was going," Ken said.

"I need to know why she called you. It may have something to do with where she is."

"She said she planned to go to the land office downtown to find out if her father did own that piece of land off the road to Estes. You know, where you went camping. I thought you were going to check it out for her."

"I didn't get around to it," Alec said, somewhat lamely.

"Well, I gave her the ordinates and lot numbers and so on. My guess is that she went there sometime after. It'll be closed now, so…"

Yeah, Alec thought. So that's a dead end. "Maybe she contacted Walker about it, after getting the information from the land registry."

"Could be." There was another silence, then Ken broke it. "Good luck then. If I were you, I'd maybe think of calling the police if she doesn't turn up soon."

Alec hung up and dashed to the Bronco. He was outside Walker's office building in less than ten minutes. The night security officer bluntly told him everyone had gone home and no, he couldn't give him Walker's home phone number.

"Can you at least tell me when Walker left for the day? It's just that my…my wife had an appointment with him and she hasn't come home. I don't want to go to the police just yet, but…"

The security guard's eyes widened, but he didn't offer

much more except to say Walker had left the building shortly before five and hadn't returned. At Alec's expression, the guard relented somewhat, adding, "He was talking to another man in the lobby here just before he took the elevator down to the underground parking. If that means anything."

"Do you know who the other man was?"

"A client, maybe. Not someone who works in the building. I know all of them," he boasted.

"You're sure of the time? Before five?"

"Yup. I'd just come on duty and was talking to the day guy while he packed up."

"Then I guess you didn't hear any of their conversation?"

"Wasn't paying attention. I think the client said something about 'meet you there' as he went out the door."

Meet you there. Could be anywhere. A bar. A restaurant. God. Alec wiped his face with his hand. Had to think. *Where?*

He turned away from the reception desk and started for the door. The guard stopped him partway.

"Hey, I don't know if this is any help."

Alec spun around.

"Just that, it was kinda unusual. Mr. Walker wasn't wearing his normal work clothes. You know—suit, tie. He wore jeans and a jacket, something like yours. And one of them baseball caps. For a sec, I didn't even recognize him 'cause he's always dressed for business. Know what I mean?"

Alec nodded, trying to make some sense of the information.

"And he was carrying this big roll of paper under his arm." The guard screwed up his face. "The other weird thing was, he had a pair of binoculars over his shoulder." He thought for another minute, then shrugged. "That's all I can tell you."

Pieces of the puzzle started to slot together. Alec thanked him and ran for the door. He was out of Boulder and on Highway 36 in record time. Outside the city limits, beyond the mushroomed spread of malls and strip plazas, the highway veered into the inky black void of country and mountains. Alec flicked on his high beams and put his foot to the floor. He passed the Wheaton ranch and cast a quick glance. No vehicle in the drive and, other than the exterior light, the house was in darkness.

He had to slow down on his approach to Estes. Now wasn't the time to be stopped for speeding. And he doubted he'd convince a state trooper of any emergency. He could almost picture the hooded disbelief in the trooper's eyes at Alec's raving about lawyers and land developers. Maybe fraud. *Maybe even murder.* The sudden image of Tomas Kozinski almost made Alec swerve off the road.

As the Malone ranch appeared ahead, outside Estes, Alec shifted gears and made the turn. Someone needed to know where he was going. Besides, he wanted Karen's cell phone.

Tess saw the boot first, shoved at right angles to her own foot. Her head shot up to Larry Stone's friendly face.

"Larry!" she cried, relieved. "You startled me." Then she continued, "What are you doing here?"

He crossed his arms. His smile became indulgent. "I was about to ask you the same thing. Imagine that."

Something in his tone wasn't right. Tess glanced back to the lake where the two other men were still talking.

"Shall we join them?" he suggested, grasping hold of her elbow and gently turning her around. "Were you planning on meeting someone here, Tess?" he asked as they picked their way down the rest of the stony path to the lake.

"No," she blurted. "At least," she scrambled to correct her mistake, "not just yet. But soon."

"Great. But I'm curious about why you decided to drive all the way out here."

Tess forced herself to think before speaking. She didn't know yet what was going on and what—if any—Larry Stone's role was in it. "Remember how I asked you the other day, about this piece of property? You claimed not to know who owned it."

"*Claimed?* That sounds like lawyer talk to me." He chuckled. "Good thing Jed is here to sort things out for you." The wind picked up his voice and caught the attention of the other two men, who began to slowly walk their way.

As they drew nearer, Tess could see the furled brow and narrowing in Jed's eyes that signaled serious displeasure. He said something to Mark Kaiser and proceeded ahead of him to where Tess was standing tight against Larry, his hand clamped on her elbow.

"Tess? Some problem at home?"

His nonchalance almost made her quip, *No, why? Should I have made an appointment?* "I was visiting the Malones," she said, catching a sharp glance between Walker and Stone. "Then I thought I'd just come up here—to see the sunset."

"I think you missed it," Walker said, nodding his head behind her, to the west.

Tess looked from him to Mark Kaiser, who had now joined them. "Are you Mark Kaiser?"

He nodded. "Have we met?"

"Outside Jed's office."

"Ahh. Another client?"

"Not exactly. I—"

"Must be going, didn't you say?" Walker interrupted.

"Yes, of course," Tess agreed, eager to get out of there. "I was just about to head back to town. Nick's big game tonight," she babbled as she took a step backward, easing out of Larry's grasp.

"And I'll be going, too," put in Kaiser. He turned to Jed and said, "What time do you want to meet in the morning?"

Without taking his eyes off Tess, Walker replied, "Nine sharp."

Kaiser stepped around them and began to climb the path up to the top of the cliff. Tess started to follow when Walker's voice cut the silence. "One minute, Tess."

She didn't turn around, but kept her eyes fixed on the path, taking another step away from Jed and Larry Stone. Until an arm grabbed the sleeve of her sweatshirt, yanking her to a halt.

"I think there's a bit more to say before you leave." Stone pulled Tess back with one meaty hand while the other dug into his jacket, retrieving a light-brown envelope that was disturbingly familiar. "Found this in her car. Think you should take a look at it."

Jed took his time extracting the thin piece of paper from the envelope. Time that crawled for Tess. Time that she used to once more question her impulse to follow Kaiser out here. But it didn't take Jed long to identify the document. He shoved it back into the envelope, which he tucked into his own jacket pocket.

"So, what do you think about this?" he asked, patting the pocket.

"You lied to me."

He gave a dismissive shrug. "How did you know I'd be out here?"

"I didn't. I went to your building and…" she stopped, sensing she'd said too much already.

"Saw Kaiser leave? Then followed him?" He made a clucking sound. "Now who's a liar? I have to hand it to you, Tess, you've a lot more gumption than I figured."

He shifted his attention to Stone. "What do you think?"

"She knows about Kaiser and now she knows about this. That's maybe a bit too much knowledge."

"Yes, I think you're right." Walker craned his head back toward the mountain peaks. "It'll be completely dark soon. I think we'd better continue this discussion from up top." He started up the path.

Larry wrapped his arm around Tess. "Come, Tess," he said indulgently, as if she were a child.

And without any choice, she stumbled meekly alongside him. When they reached the top, she saw at once that the white Explorer—Mark Kaiser's—was gone. Her stomach churned. She looked from left to right, then back to the other SUV and her own Volvo, a few yards away.

When her gaze fell on Larry Stone, he answered her unspoken question. "My truck's parked at the turnoff. I was leaving Estes when I saw the Volvo drive by and, just as you followed Kaiser, I trailed you." He snorted a laugh.

"We'll talk inside mine," Jed decided, opening the rear door of the maroon SUV. "Get in, Tess."

Tess yanked her arm from Stone's grasp and clambered inside. To her relief, Stone and Jed got into the front. Jed clicked on the overhead light and studied Tess for a long time. "Too much knowledge," he was murmuring.

"I actually don't know anything," she said. "Except that you bought the land from my father and lied to me. That's what I don't understand. Why didn't you just tell me the truth?"

As soon as she saw the look pass between Walker and Stone, Tess had a hunch she knew what his answer would be.

It was Stone who spoke. "Because he forged Richard's signature and he can't have anyone examining that piece of paper too closely. Can you, Walker?"

Jed's expression fell just a bit short of accusing Stone of being a moron.

"I knew my father would never have sold that land!"

"Just like you were so certain he'd never separate those two paintings," Jed sneered.

Tess waited for the hammering in her chest to ease up. She moistened her lips and said, "He didn't."

"No," Jed agreed. There was a glint in his eye, as if he were enjoying the talk. "But Kozinski was all too willing to split them and sell the still life, wasn't he, Larry?"

"Apparently," Larry cracked. He paused a beat and then murmured, "Another accident?"

There was a rush of sound in Tess's ears. She stiffened, trying to hear over the pounding that had suddenly resumed deep inside.

Walker nodded. "Not the same, though. It's convenient for us that her car is already here. Maybe driving along the path in the dark, she misjudged the distance to the edge of the cliff."

Stupidly, Tess wondered for a split second who they were talking about until she put it altogether with horrifying clarity. "You had something to do with the car accident. My father…" She couldn't go on.

"Your father had no vision when it came to business," Larry snarled. "We had it all sewn up. Walker was going to foreclose on the Malone land, I had the piece in the middle and we thought we'd convinced Richard to join in, with this part. He could have made at least a million on the deal. Maybe more."

"What's the point in going over it?" Jed asked. "Anyway, now we split it two ways, instead of three."

He sounded tired, Tess thought. As if he simply wanted to get things over with and go back to town. *But without her.* "You were forming some kind of group," she said. "To sell off—"

"A hell of a big chunk of land. Yeah. Kaiser is a scout for an international conglomerate. They build resorts, casinos—you name it—all over the world. Most of the choice land around here belongs to the National Park Services. There's little room for expansion around Estes or to the west. But Kaiser says this section is perfect for what his company has in mind.'' Larry stopped to catch his breath. His face was red and he was sweating, in spite of the cool night air.

''My father would never have gone through with a deal like that.''

Walker smirked at her outburst. ''You sound like you actually knew the man, Tess. I mean, come on. He walked out on you years ago. You don't know him any better than you know Larry...or me.''

His gibe stung.

''Richard had a serious cash flow problem after the fire,'' Larry went on. ''That's what motivated him to consider the deal in the beginning. But I guess after he got talking it over with Gabriela, they decided not to join us. Which made things damn difficult for us. I mean, we'd already got the ball rolling.''

''Did you set the fire at the studio?''

Stone shook his head. ''No way. That was Kozinski, the crazy bastard. Months before any of this came up. He had some wild idea that the fire would drive up sales and business had been poor at the gallery. He knew where your father kept a key to the studio and when they all went away for a weekend, he tinkered with the wiring in Gabriela's kiln. Then the jerk hung around to see if it would catch. That's how I knew he'd done it. I was coming home late that night, saw the flames and also saw Kozinski leaving. It gave me something to hold over him. That's how I persuaded him to cut that blasted painting in half.''

''What about those other canvases in the studio?'' She looked at Jed. ''You were going to sell them behind Kozinski's back, weren't you?''

He grinned. ''I have buyers for them.''

''Is that what you were arguing about with Kozinski? In front of the gallery, the other day? I was coming to see him.''

"See, ever since you've arrived in Boulder, you've seen just a bit too much."

"And were you the one who broke into our house?"

Walker smirked, as if the act were beneath him. "Kozinski again. He was determined to take back the painting you inherited. He knew for sure you'd discover the truth and go to the police. But he never found it. Then after your visit to him, after you did learn the truth, he completely lost it. Threatened to go to the police himself and confess."

"So why not let him? You didn't have anything to do with separating it, did you?"

"Of course not. I didn't give a damn about the painting. But we couldn't afford to have police start making a lot of inquiries. Not when the land deal was so near to closing."

"And the estate?" she went on, her anger taking control, giving her confidence. "Were you going to cheat Nick and Molly, too?"

Jed scowled. "No, I wouldn't do that."

As if he had to draw a line somewhere, Tess thought.

"The trust is all kosher, believe me."

"But you *would* stoop to murder," she said.

Silence fell heavily inside the SUV. "I think I'll leave you to it, then," Walker said, looking across the seat at Stone.

"Why me?"

"Why not? You've already got some experience in the craft, so to speak. Call me later tonight."

Stone didn't argue, just opened his side of the SUV and climbed out. Tess flinched when her own door was wrenched open. She clung to the back of the front seat.

"You won't get away with this. People are expecting me. They'll go looking for me."

Stone chuckled. "Maybe, but they won't know where to look, will they? And by the time someone notices your car down there by the lake…"

He didn't need to spell out the word *futility* for her. He

used both hands to pull her loose and lift her out of the rear seat. He was a big man, and her kicking and flailing fists had little effect on him. Stone kicked the door shut and dragged her off to the side while Walker turned over the engine. When he had turned the SUV around, he rolled down the window to quip, "Nice meeting you, Miss Wheaton. Too bad we couldn't have struck up a different kind of relationship." Then he laughed and drove the car into the darkness ahead.

When its taillights disappeared, Larry bent his head down to Tess, his breath sour on her face. "Sorry about this, Tess. But there's way too much at stake and you can imagine how expensive it is to maintain someone like Marci."

"Poor Marci," she gasped. "Or does she know what kind of man you are?"

"She doesn't know about any of this—and she never will." He began to drag her toward the Volvo, using a flashlight he had pulled from his pocket to light the way.

Tess let herself go slack, her eyes desperately trying to penetrate the dimness cast by the flashlight, hoping in vain for a glimpse of a branch or rock. Anything to reach out for. He grunted with her dead body weight and yelled something but she didn't hear in the gust of wind that had picked up once the sun fell behind the mountain peaks.

When they reached the Volvo, he loosened his grip to open the door. Tess made her move, flinging out an arm and sending the flashlight clattering into the dark. But before she could run, Stone's hand came back and struck her on the side of the head. Dizzy with pain, Tess staggered against the rear side of the car. The door was open, spilling light onto Stone as if he were an actor on a stage.

He raised his hand again and took one step toward her. His last one.

A figure lunged from the shadows, grabbed Stone by the collar of his jacket, spun him around and landed a punch forceful enough for Tess to register the sickening crunch of bone. She pressed into the car door, expecting to see Jed Walker move into the spotlight.

"Tess?"

Her relief almost made her throw up. She held out her arms and let Alec clutch her to him. They stood, locked together, for a long time. The wind whistled through the conifers and scattered dust up around them but all Tess could hear was the steady beat of Alec's heart against her ear.

When she could speak, she asked, "Nick?"

"Later," he murmured, tucking her head back under her chin. "Right now, just hold on."

And she did, a few minutes longer. Until she couldn't keep any of it inside anymore. She started to talk, but he placed a fingertip to her mouth. "It's all finished, Tess. When I saw Stone's pickup at the turnoff, I knew my hunch was right. Then Walker left and I knew you were here alone with Stone." He made a soft shushing noise in her ear. "Everything will be okay."

He smoothed her hair back from her face, his fingers running along the edge of her chin and raising her head just enough for his mouth to find hers. She let his kiss flow through her, easing the tremors of the last hour. Soothing her qualms about Stone, prone on the ground. Reassuring her that now, at last, everything *would* be all right.

And then she heard above the wind and Alec's soft breathing, a shrill ring. He pulled back, frowned for a second and flashed a sheepish grin.

"See? That's exactly why I hate cell phones," he muttered, digging into his windbreaker pocket.

CHAPTER NINETEEN

"I CAN'T BELIEVE how so much can change in forty-eight hours."

Tess leaned back into the crook of Alec's arm. She tossed a small handful of tamari roasted almonds into her mouth and crunched contentedly. Alec made some kind of murmuring response as he continued to nuzzle the base of her neck.

"Pardon?"

He raised his head. "I said, don't chew so loudly, you're hampering my concentration."

She laughed. It was a rich, throaty laugh that brought his face up level to hers. His breath puffed against her, carrying with it the bouquet of the Merlot they'd shared at dinner. "I'm ready for dessert. How about you?" he whispered in her ear, running the tip of his tongue along her lobe until she shivered and gently pushed him away.

"We had dessert," she teased. "At the restaurant."

"Not me," he said. "I was saving mine for later."

Tess decided to stop playing coy. "Maybe you were, but I've had mine and so have the kids." She jerked her head in the vague direction of the family room where the television was blaring.

He made a low grumbling noise and sagged back into the plumped cushions of the living room sofa. They had taken Nick and Molly out for the promised celebratory dinner and called Mavis in Chicago to fill her in on recent events. Now, Tess sensed Alec was hoping to defer the thorny topic they still hadn't discussed.

She glanced at him out of the corner of her eye, taking in the lines that seemed to have been etched into his face since Wednesday night. Some of his stress had been alleviated by the bank's willingness to reexamine the loan held by Walker. They'd agreed to a time extension, allowing Ken and Karen to pursue other loan options.

Still, Tess knew she ought to relieve Alec of the worry that was still on his mind. The move to Chicago. But she had agreed to Nick and Molly's request for a family talk first.

Family. She couldn't ever recall using the term except in reference to other people. As a teenager, whenever she'd been asked about her family, she'd shrugged and sullenly replied, "Well, there's Mavis, my guardian." A sure conversation stopper.

"Before the show finishes that the kids are watching," she said, "I wanted to tell you what I found out from Lieutenant Slegers."

Alec shifted on the sofa, facing her. "When did he call?"

"As we were walking out the door to meet you at the restaurant."

"And?"

"Apparently Jed Walker wants to cut some kind of deal with the District Attorney."

He gave a derisive snort. "Of course. He's a lawyer, isn't he? The nerve of that son of a—"

"Yes, well I agree totally with you on that. But the thing is, there's not a lot to pin on him. Larry Stone confessed to setting up the accident that killed Dad and Gabriela." She had to stop for a moment, replaying the scene that had been in her head since Slegers had described it for her.

First there had been the early-morning phone call on the twenty-eighth from Mark Kaiser in Denver, asking if the meeting that afternoon could be changed to Saturday as he was going to be delayed. Kaiser didn't know that Richard was no longer part of the deal. Richard, confused and suspicious, contacted Walker who was out of the office. But his secretary said that Walker was meeting with Kaiser later that afternoon. At the lake site. Richard had guessed right away that Walker was somehow trying to pull a fast one on him.

Slegers had implied that at that point, Richard should have contacted police. Instead, he and Gabriela had driven out to the property to confront Walker and Stone. There was a vicious argument. Richard and Gabriela drove away, threatening to go directly to the police. It was late March and snow flurries made driving treacherous.

Tess closed her eyes, thinking of how it had ended. Larry Stone and his truck, forcing Richard and Gabriela off the road.

"Walker's just as responsible as Stone," Alec was saying. "And what about Kozinski? Who killed him?"

"They're running DNA tests. Both Walker and Stone are denying it but it had to be one of them. Although Slegers did say there might be another suspect. Brent Holloway."

Alec straightened on the sofa. "What? Like a lover's quarrel or something?"

Tess nodded. "I suppose. And guess what? Walker confessed to forging the bill of sale so the land problem is all settled."

"Great. And I can recommend a good lawyer in town to go over the trust that Walker set up for the kids, to ensure it's all above board."

Tess nodded. Everything was unfolding perfectly. There was just one more piece of business. "Listen, I need to tell you something. I called my office today and had a long talk first with Carrie, my secretary, and then with my boss."

Something flickered in Alec's face. He didn't want to hear this now, Tess figured. He picked up her hand and brought it to his lips. "Can we get serious later?" he murmured, intent on her fingers.

Tess laughed and pulled her hand away. "You're impossible, Malone. You've got to listen to me. I—"

Alec raised a forefinger to his lips, shushing her. "I think their show is over. Any second, they'll—"

Nick and Molly swarmed into the room. "It's time," Molly announced solemnly, standing in front of Tess and Alec.

"Yeah. Remember?" Nick was staring at Tess. "You said we'd have our family talk right after dinner."

"She *did?*"

Tess almost lost it at the incredulity in Alec's face.

"Yeah. About the move to Chicago. Molly and I kinda talked about it already and—"

"You said I could tell," Molly whined.

"Jeez," muttered Nick. "So do it!"

"We voted to stay here in Boulder."

Tess felt Alec's eyes on her but didn't look his way. "Is there more?" she asked Molly.

Molly frowned. "Not from me. I don't think so. Is there more, Nick?"

"No, not from *you,*" he said patiently, exercising what Tess considered remarkable restraint. "From *me.* It's about the family thing."

Tess saw Alec make a move to stand up. "I should leave," he was saying. "Let you guys have your family talk."

"Why?" asked Nick. "Aren't you part of this now?" His face broke into a bewildered frown. "Have I been getting that wrong? I mean, I thought you and Tess…"

Tess felt the heat rush into her face.

"Alec, we want you to be part of our new family. With Tess. And she wants it, too," Molly piped up.

Tess looked at her in disbelief.

"Right, Tess?" Molly asked.

"Well, uh, yes but you know…" How could she just come out with it? *Yes, I've already given my employer notice and I'm willing to look for work in Boulder—there is a first-rate university here where I might get a teaching job—but I've been waiting for a specific sign from a certain someone.*

Nick took charge. He turned to Alec, standing beside the sofa. "Alec, we want to know. Do you or do you not love Tess?"

Tess covered her face with her hands, stifling laughter. She didn't dare look at Alec.

There was the briefest of pauses that had Tess a bit concerned. Then Alec said, in a clear and deep voice, "Of course I do. Doesn't she know that?"

Tess uncovered one eye to see Nick raise his shoulders as if to say, *Maybe you should ask her.*

"Do you, Tess?" Molly was bending over to whisper between Tess's fingers.

Tess dropped her hands from her face and burst into laughter. "I think I need to hear it. You know? From Alec."

As if Alec had missed the entire conversation, Molly raised her head and said to him, "Well, Alec. I think she wants to hear you say it yourself."

By now, even Nick was unable to control his laughter. Alec was beginning to figure out the whole scene had been a setup. He got down on one knee in front of Tess, placed his right hand over his heart and said, "I love you, Tess Wheaton. Will you marry me?" He squinted at Nick and Molly, as if noticing them for the first time. "And will you let these two wretched children and I start a family with you?"

Nick moaned. "Oh, God, I don't believe it."

When Tess dissolved into laughter, opening her arms

wide and cried, "Yes, yes, yes!" Nick, Molly and Alec
piled onto her.

Suffocating but deliriously happy, Tess knew just at that
moment what family felt like.

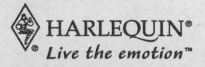

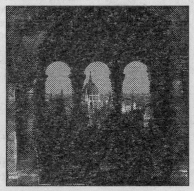
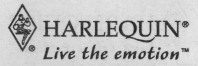